DICKENS: NOVELIST IN THE MARKET-PLACE

DICKENS: NOVELIST IN THE MARKET-PLACE

James M. Brown

First published 1982 by
THE MACMILLAN PRESS LTD
London and Basingstoke
Companies and representatives
throughout the world

ISBN 0 333 30083 1

Printed in Hong Kong

FOR MY PARENTS

Contents

Part One

Some Sociological Approaches to Dickens's Novels

1 The Inadequacy of the Documentary Method

From Taine to the present day critics have argued that literature reflects society in holding up a mirror to the age, thus revealing the surface details of contemporary social life. To the modern reader the nineteenth-century English novel offers a mine of documentary evidence about everyday social affairs, and it is no surprise that social historians have fastened on the novels of Dickens, Eliot, Thackeray and Trollope in search of raw material from which can be refined insights into the ways in which social forces operated on individuals, groups and classes, influencing life-styles and values, ways of thinking and patterns of behaviour. These literary illustrations of social forces at work have more recently attracted sociologists of literature whose research has been concerned with checking and commenting on the accuracy of these social reports, some of which, like Dickens's description of workhouse conditions in the early chapters of *Oliver Twist*, have been reinforced by taking on a mythic identity.

What is happening here is that literature is being treated as documentary reportage, and regarded as if it were no different from journalism. This is clear from the jacket notes of the 1960 paperback edition of Humphrey House's book *The Dickens World* (first published in 1941), an influential work which pointed the direction for much of modern Dickens criticism. The jacket notes assert:

Dickens's works are so filled with actual experience of the world in which he lived that they can be used as documents — perhaps the most vital documents — for the understanding of nineteenth-century social history in Great Britain. This is the use Humphrey House has made, not only of the novels, but of the minor works and the journals, *Household Words* and *All the Year Round*. He has made Dickens and his period illustrate each other. He has, in fact, treated Dickens more as a journalist than as a creative artist.

While some of the results of this type of criticism have been interesting and worthwhile, there are unfortunate, indeed fatal, implications for a developing sociology of literature in treating a novel and an article in a journal as one and the same. There is an essential difference between, for example, a chapter in *Little Dorrit*, the literary meaning of which is to be discovered in its relation to the artistic whole of which it is a functional part, and an article in *Household Words*, which is no more and no less than a self-contained journalistic project. This book argues that treating literature as a documentary report is a simplistic and inadequate approach, which denies the specifically literary characteristics of literature.

It also ignores the complexity of the way in which social forces and values are reflected within great literature. Regarding the novelist as a passive chronicler of existing social facts both explains away literature and ignores the creative and critical aspects of the novelist's role. The relation between the novel and society in Dickens's mature work is not simple or passive, as is implied in many reflection theories of the documentary type. It is a complex relationship in which the novelist's critical vision of social reality is mediated through both literary conventions and his affiliation to class values.

An example of class ideology as a mediating factor is Dickens's artistic treatment of trade unions in *Hard Times* (1854). Dickens's artistic commitment to class values is complex and problematic (and will be considered in detail in Chapter 3). For the moment it is enough to remark that *Hard Times* reflects a middle-class distrust of and antipathy towards trade unions in a manner which reduces the treatment of this theme from social realism to class propaganda, thus rendering it useless as an accurate sociological/historical document. The degree of authority and influence enjoyed by Slackbridge, the ranting despotic union leader, gives a false and unrepresentative image of mid-Victorian trade union practice and policy at a time when union leaders such as Robert Applegarth and George Odger preached a hard-headed creed of responsibility and moderation. Of Slackbridge Shaw remarked, 'All this is pure middle-class ignorance. It is much as if a tramp were to write a description of millionaires smoking large cigars in church, with their wives in low necked dresses and diamonds.' Indeed the whole treatment of the union theme in the novel (e.g. the punishment meted out to Stephen Blackpool by his fellow-workers) reinforces the hostile contemporary middle-class view of trade unions as undemocratic organisations which eliminated the individuality of the workers and imposed a crude tyranny and coercive authority on the minority view within their ranks.

It is equally misleading for the documentary critics to ignore the mediating influence of literary conventions and tradition. (House acknowledges the importance of these in the closing pages of his book, but their influence on the nature of his analysis is small.) Throughout his career Dickens deferred to the conventions and taboos imposed on him by the tastes of a predominantly middle-class reading public. At a time when reading aloud in the family home was still an extremely popular custom, avoidance of indelicate language and unsavoury topics (virtually everything connected with sex) was held to be necessary in order to 'protect the Young Person'. Although his satire on Podsnappery, and less obviously the Mrs General passages of *Little Dorrit*, reveal a resentment of this limitation and imposition on the novelist, Dickens always adhered to the code – from the moment when he reassures readers, in his Preface to *Oliver Twist* (added to the third edition, 1841) that he had decided to portray the very dregs of life, with the significant addition 'so long as their speech did not offend the ear'. Not just in a censorship of language but in selection and treatment of subject-matter all was written in accordance with middle-class propriety and delicacy, with the surprising exception of Meagles's apparently explicit accusation that Miss Wade had drawn Tattycoram into a lesbian relationship. That the operation of literary conventions could be a mechanism producing a flawing distortion and emasculation in the novels' reflection of social reality is clear from examination of Dickens's artistic treatment of the theme of prostitution.

Prostitution was an important social fact in Mid-Victorian England, recognised as 'The Great Social Evil'. By 1850 there were 8,000 prostitutes known to the police in London alone, though a more accurate figure for mid-Victorian London would appear to be 80,000. Though in *Sketches by Boz* Dickens writes of prostitution as 'a last dreadful resource' of poverty, and in his Christmas story *The Chimes* (1844) depicts Lillian being driven to prostitution by poverty and hunger, prostitution is almost always presented in the novels as the result of seduction and abandonment. Of course, not all prostitutes were the abandoned creatures of the orthodox view, economic necessity taking many women on to the streets, their wages being insufficient to avoid extreme poverty, even starvation, without the added income provided by casual prostitution. Among other social factors involved in the alarming increase of prostitution in the mid-Victorian period W. E. Houghton[1] names the growth of

industrial cities, which provided a cover of secrecy, the maintenance
of large armed forces, and the social ambition which required the
postponement of marriage until a young man could afford to live like
a gentleman. None of these figure in Dickens's novelistic treatment of
the theme, which characteristically presents prostitutes as romantic
studies of the tragic plight of the fallen woman. Nancy (*Oliver Twist*),
Alice (*Dombey and Son*) and Martha and Emily (*David Copperfield*),
are all self-lacerating and consumed with guilt. For example, here is
Martha:

> 'Oh, the river!' she cried passionately. 'Oh, the river!' . . . 'I know
> it's like me!' she exclaimed. 'I know that I belong to it. I know that
> it's the natural company of such as I am! It comes from country
> places, where there was once no harm in it — and it creeps through
> the dismal streets, defiled and miserable — and it goes away, like
> my life, to a great sea, that is always troubled — and I feel that I
> must go with it! . . . I can't keep away from it. I can't forget it.
> It haunts me day and night. It's the only thing in all the world
> that I am fit for and that's fit for me. Oh, the dreadful river! . . .
> What shall I ever do!' she said, fighting thus with her despair.
> 'How can I go on as I am, a living disgrace to everyone I come near.'
> Suddenly she turned to my companion. 'Stamp upon me, kill
> me!' (*David Copperfield*, Penguin edition, 1966, pp. 749–51).[2]

All this within a few pages, and there is more to follow.

That this is inadequate as a means of describing and understanding
prostitution as a social phenomenon was clear to many of Dickens's
contemporaries. A leading article in *The Times*, 25 February 1858,
declared:

> The great bulk of the London prostitutes are not Magdalens either
> in esse or posse, nor specimens of humanity in agony, nor Clarissa
> Harlowes. They are not — the bulk of them — cowering under
> gateways, nor preparing to throw themselves from Waterloo
> Bridge, but are comfortably practising their trade, either as the
> entire or partial means of their subsistence. To attribute to them the
> sentimental delicacies of a heroine of romance would be equally
> preposterous. They have no remorse or misgivings about the
> nature of their pursuit; on the contrary, they consider the calling an
> advantageous one, and they look upon their success in it with
> satisfaction.

It is not as if Dickens was ignorant of the topic, his charity work with Miss Coutts bringing him into direct contact with (admittedly reclaimed) prostitutes. Yet in trying to communicate the prostitute's social situation in a way which would not outrage public morals Dickens only falls into the dual trap of bad art (cf. Martha's speech above), and inaccurate social representation (realism having lapsed into sentimental wishful thinking).

Of course, he avoids the full sexual implications of the prostitute's role in his novels. Humphrey House makes the point of *Oliver Twist*,

> Nancy's job would certainly have been to use her sex as much as possible with boys like Charley Bates and the Dodger; and the whole atmosphere in which Oliver lived in London would have been drenched in sex; but Dickens does not even obscurely hint at such a thing.[3]

Dickens's 'treatment' (i.e. censorship) of the language spoken by his novels' prostitutes involves him in impossible characterisation. George Gissing commented pertinently (in 1898) on the unreality of Alice Marlow, the fallen woman in *Dombey and Son*:

> It is doubtful whether one could pick out a single sentence, a single phrase, such as the real Alice Marlow could conceivably have used. Her passion is vehement; no impossible thing. The words in which she utters it would be appropriate to the most stagey of wronged heroines – be that who it may. A figure less life-like will not be found in any novel ever written. Yet Dickens doubtless intended it as legitimate idealisation; a sort of type of the doleful multitude of betrayed women. He meant it for imagination exalting common fact. But the fact is not exalted; it has simply vanished.

For our purposes 'social fact' could be substituted for Gissing's 'common fact'. Contemporary literary conventions dictated that certain social facts, taken raw or undiluted, were not acceptable literary food for the Victorian middle-class reading public. They had to be treated, exalted, in some way 'cleansed', and made respectable. Yet in the process the social fact itself might vanish. Certainly this is the case with Dickens's treatment of prostitution throughout his novels – of no use whatever to the social historian as a document or analysis of an important mid-Victorian social fact.

However, it would be wrong to regard Dickens's artistic delicacy as *wholly* imposed on him against his will, for, in a manner which brings together the mediating factors of class values and novelistic conventions, many of Dickens's private views and conscious artistic principles were consistent with the most conservative elements of middle-class taste and propriety. Witness his attack on 'The Carpenter's Shop', a painting by Millais, an attempt to paint a religious subject in accordance with the creed of Pre-Raphaelite realism. The unsentimentalised scene, the details of which had not received the conventional artistic 'treatment', revolted Dickens. In *Old Lamps for New Ones* (1850) he attacked the naked realism of the painting as indecent, not to say irreverent, in a hysterical tone which we recognise as that of outraged bourgeois morality.

> You behold the interior of a carpenter's shop. In the foreground of that carpenter's shop is a hideous, wry-necked, blubbering, red-headed boy, in a bed-gown; who appears to have received a poke in the hand, from the stick of another boy with whom he has been playing in an adjacent gutter, and to be holding it up for the contemplation of a kneeling woman, so horrible in her ugliness, that . . . she would stand out from the rest of the company as a Monster, in the vilest cabaret in France, or the lowest gin-shop in England. . . . Wherever it is possible to express ugliness of feature, limb, or attitude, you have it expressed. Such men as the carpenters might be undressed in any hospital where dirty drunkards, in a high state of varicose veins, are received. Their very toes have walked out of Saint Giles's.

This is not to argue that the dominant voice of Dickens's novels is the value stance of middle-class morality — the crucial role of middle-class values within the structure of Dickens's novels will be considered in Chapter 3. However, what is interesting is that, though there were unquestionably times when the tastes of the reading public prevented Dickens from reproducing all the details of a social fact, there were also occasions when Dickens would artistically have had no wish to reveal all, probably sharing the squeamishness of his readers.

The crucial issue here (and it is of great importance to the sociology of the novel) is that critics who ignore the mediating factors of literary conventions and the novelist's loyalty to class values and treat literature merely as documentary reportage are denying the literary nature of literature. There is a crucial difference between a passage in a novel and, for example, an episode in Mayhew's *London Labour and the London Poor*. A chapter in *Bleak House* can be a realistic description of the contemporary scene and at the same time, without ever rendering this realistic meaning redundant, it can carry a figurative or representative significance of generalising importance to the world of the novel. This means that the *literary meaning* of a passage in a novel can only be ascertained by considering the artistic function of the passage within the total imaginative structure of which it is a contributory part. And it is precisely the figurative, representative or emblematic dimensions of an episode in a novel (i.e. its literary dimensions) which are ignored by the critics who treat literature as documentary reportage.

Ignoring the literary characteristics of literature is fatal to a sociology of literature,[4] and especially damaging to any attempt to consider the novels of Dickens, whose characteristic method 'is at the same time realistic and figurative'.[5] Indeed, the representative or emblematic suggestiveness of the details which make up the world of the novels is crucial to an appreciation of the social insights contained in the mature work. These are not articulated explicitly, by authorial intrusion into the narrative or through a literary spokesman or mouthpiece, and the shortest route to the way in which society is seen in the later novels is by means of a study of recurring patterns of imagery, and a discussion of Dickens's artistic use of emblematic locales or episodes – in short, by an examination of how Dickens utilises specifically literary techniques and devices as the chief means of commenting on the social life of his society.

As an example of how the documentary method fails to elucidate the literary meaning of episodes in the novels, consider the Circumlocution Office satire in *Little Dorrit*. Dickens would defend the surface accuracy of the details in his novels to his critics – as when he defended the realistic validity of the incident of Krook's spontaneous combustion against G. H. Lewes's criticism – and there is no doubt that he was concerned about the issue of civil service reform, especially in the aftermath of the tragically inept administration which characterised the Crimean War. However, the Circumlocution Office passages do *not* form a self-contained essay on the need for administrative reform which can be uprooted from the rest of the novel and considered in a way similar to a journalistic essay. To concentrate, as the documentary approach would, on whether the novel's criticism of the civil service was accurate is to obscure the literary interest of the Circumlocution Office passages and underestimate their imaginative weight in the novel.

The Circumlocution Office operates within *Little Dorrit* as both the novel's chief representative social institution, and a microcosmic model of a total society (which connects it to the other literary means of expressing the general social condition in the novel – the prison motif, and the market imagery, etc.). It is only in relation to the Marshalsea, Mrs General's surfaces of High Society, Pancks's mechanical official life, etc., that the full significance of the Circumlocution Office for the social world of *Little Dorrit* and the full contribution of the Circumlocution Office passages to what the novel tells us about industrial society can be understood.

The relations of the individual suitor with the Circumlocution Office are representative of the essential relations between the individual and what the novel presents as the indifferent machinery of the Victorian social system – and it is in this that the weight of the Circumlocution Office passages lies. We are told that 'the Circumlocution Office went on mechanically every day' and within this hostile mechanism ('numbers of people were lost in the Circumlocution Office'), the individual suitor (e.g. Meagles, Doyce, Clennam) journeys in a confused movement between indifferent and impersonal officials until his will is exhausted, and he resigns himself to his lot. The Circumlocution Office, like Chancery in *Bleak House*, is an alien force in itself, a thing with its own life, external to the individuals who have created it – hence, an appropriate symbol for the essential condition of mid-Victorian England, presented in *Little Dorrit* as a hostile and alienating social environment. Thus, in treating the Circumlocution Office passages as a social document, an essay arguing a case for civil service reform, critics are at best asking only one of the relevant questions and at worst asking the wrong one.

Indeed the Circumlocution Office satire could be quite prejudiced and mistaken in its analysis of the contemporary civil service (i.e. a useless or misleading historical document) and yet still fulfil its literary function as emblematic institution and social microcosm in an artistically successful fashion. That is, the details of the Circumlocution Office passages might be mistaken but these passages might make a powerful contribution to a way of seeing industrial society in the novel which is essentially true. Regarding literature as a social document does not take account of this possibility.

Similarly the documentary method could be applied to Chancery in *Bleak House* (for example: 'In fact, I am sure that it would be possible to produce an edition of *Bleak House*, in which all Dickens's statements could be verified by the statements of the witnesses who gave evidence before the Chancery Commission, which reported in 1826'),[6] without elucidating the meaning or significance of Chancery within the novel's structure. Within their respective novels both Chancery and the Circumlocution Office are 'the starting point capable of becoming the central point',[7] and it is this specifically literary nature of the presentation of social facts in Dickens's novels which prevents the documentary method from being the most satisfactory analytical approach for the sociologist of literature.

It is worth considering in more detail some of the critical implications for a sociology of literature of reading descriptions in a novel as symbols or emblems. To argue that elements in a Dickens novel have a generalised significance or weight of implication is not to argue that the novels are symbolic structures which can *only* be approached through symbolic analysis, or that the *sole* justification for an element's existence within the novel is its emblematic function. At their most successful Dickens's symbols and emblems are given a sensuously described concrete reality in the world of the novel and 'do not make the fundamental mistake of appearing to owe their presence to their symbolic function'.[8] There is no need to choose between realistic or figurative interpretations. In Dickens's mature work realism and symbolism are complementary principles.

However, recently there have been objections to the use of symbolism as an appropriate analytical tool for considering Dickens's novels. This is largely because some critics have utilised symbolic interpretations to impose a false unity and coherence on the complex, and often inconsistent structures of the novels. Their analysis has concentrated on the 'symbols' at the expense of other elements within the structures to make claims for an organisational and artistic unity which can only be justified if large areas of the novels are ignored. Far from ignoring or sweeping under the carpet inconsistencies in the novels' attitude to social issues the readings in Part Two of this book argue that the characteristic flavour of the mature work derives from the tension between unresolved contradictions within the novels' structures.

Other objections to readings which emphasise the emblematic function of episodes can be summed up in John Carey's impatience with those who ignore the poetic force of descriptions testifying to the power and fertility of Dickens's imagination, to stress their figurative role. For example, admitting that in *Bleak House* the floodwaters which cover Chesney Wold in Chapter 2 are brought into significant association with Sir Leicester Dedlock's oft-repeated warning about the bursting open of 'the floodgates of society', Carey argues:

> The Lincolnshire floods and the breaking bridge now look sociological for a moment. But they have been too firmly established in the novel in their own right to be replaced by an interpretation, least of all one supplied by Sir Leicester. The 'symbolism' is best forgotten.[9]

Carey's remarks imply a curious view of how a novel is organised. The 'interpretation' is not Sir Leicester's but a connection made by the novelist, and this connection contributes to the novel's way of seeing society. To argue that it is best forgotten is to argue that a novel's attempt to illuminate the nature of the social world, to tell us something about our society and the direction in which it is going is unimportant compared to the quality of the language.

Carey's remarks also imply that if we stress the symbolic significance of an episode its concrete identity in the novel becomes redundant and shrinks to be 'replaced' by its figurative role. This is not so. The two identities – realistic and emblematic – coexist in a complementary fashion. Indeed the figurative suggestiveness of an episode can never be separated from the poetic density of the language used in its description, for, as we shall see, the novels' symbols *need* a rich particularity of detail and a vividly realised identity in the naturalistic scenery of their novel, if they are to satisfactorily sustain their intended emblematic suggestiveness.

To prevent the reader labouring under false expectations of the type of material which will be set before him it is probably helpful to summarise the aims of the book. This study is not primarily concerned with Dickens's use of language but considers his mature novels as an imaginative attempt to understand, explain and illustrate the way industrial society works, the future direction it is likely to take, and the effects of an industrial environment on the everyday lives and social relations of all members of society. This book will *not* present detailed social/historical evidence to demonstrate the validity of set-pieces of social criticism, or the accuracy of the novels' descriptions of the surface of everyday social life. It will *not* treat the novels as journalism, concerned with exposing specific social issues. It *will* regard the novels as uniquely literary works, total imaginative structures, concerned with presenting the nature of industrial society in terms of a general vision of the essential nature of social life. At all times the novels will be considered in their own right and will be kept separate from Dickens's own journalism, letters and speeches. These will not be used to provide 'background' information, or to help elucidate 'difficult' passages, or to justify critical arguments which cannot be supported from the text. In Lawrence's terms this study will trust the tale rather than the teller.

The following chapter will discuss some of the concepts and attitudes which underpin the analytical method which is utilised in the readings of Part Two, as well as making some preliminary observations about the nature of Dickens's realism.

2 The Nature of Dickens's Realism

I

This study does not employ the documentary method, the crudest and most reductionist type of reflection theory. However, it does argue that Dickens's mature novels – the novels from *Dombey and Son* (1846–8) to *Our Mutual Friend* (1864–5) reflect the essential nature of his society, indeed of industrial society as a social type, and this chapter will make some general points about the manner in which Victorian society is reflected in these novels and about the nature of Dickens's realistic method.

The mature novels reflect not selected aspects of the surface of social life, but the *essential* condition of social relations within a *whole society*, which is seen as a social organism, a system of interrelated parts. The concern to depict society in its essential aspects is often regarded as characteristic of 'true realism' as against the superficial realism of the naturalist school.[1] Certainly, Dickens's realism is concerned with 'piercing through to the underlying meaning of the industrial scene rather than describing it in minute detail'[2] and his novels dramatise 'the experience of a society, not its isolable facts'.[3] We cannot reduce Dickens's social criticism to a collection of separable attitudes to money, speculation, prisons, urban slums, the Poor Law, etc., or a series of journalistic/propagandist pleas for reform of this institution or that social evil. Instead his social criticism is embodied in a vision of social experience in its generality – the essential quality of everyday social relations throughout the system, and the general possibilities for a fulfilling social life. And to the sociologist of literature this baring of the general and essential condition is, in the last instance, more important than a detailed documentation of the surface features of the age. Indeed, Raymond Williams asserts that this type of general, total vision of society 'is the kind of social criticism that belongs to literature and especially, in our civilisation, to the novel'.[4]

Society is not reflected in Dickens's later novels in a passive or mechanical fashion. Dickens's imagination works on his material to reflect social reality in a way which is both creative and critical. Although the mature novels were carefully written not to offend middle-class sensibilities, Lucien Goldmann's description of the nineteenth-century European novel offering 'a form of critical opposition to the ongoing development of bourgeois society'[5] is, as we shall see, highly relevant for Dickens's later work. However, it should be emphasised at this point that the critical nature of Dickens's realism is not articulated in an explicit political fashion, neither is it embodied in the words of a literary spokesman. There is no Vautrin in Dickens's novels. Orlick is anti-social but inarticulate. A character such as Gowan in *Little Dorrit* may utter words which have a greater significance within the world of the novel than he is aware, but his easy recognition of the market nature of social life is accepted with no personal consciousness of loss. Indeed, those characters in a Dickens novel who are consciously used as a moral touchstone or mouthpiece (e.g. Jarndyce in *Bleak House*, or Boffin in *Our Mutual Friend*) are inadequate to articulate the social insights of the imaginative core of the novel which transcend their middle-class platitudes.

Furthermore, we must not expect that Dickens himself would have been able to consciously formulate the insights of his mature work into a coherent body of social theory, critically opposed to contemporary society and its values. This point is worth developing in some detail. Recent critics of Dickens, particularly John Carey[6] who contends that Dickens is not primarily a social critic, have made much of the inconsistency and at times reactionary nature of the opinions expressed in Dickens's journalism, speeches and letters. This, they claim, proves that Dickens was not a social theorist. This conclusion fails to recognise that Dickens could be inconsistent and confused about contemporary social issues and yet at the same time capable, when the force of his imagination had worked on his material, of writing novels which contain insights into the workings of his society which reveal the very penetration and intelligence which is characteristically lacking in his reported views on current events.

As a thinker Dickens was not good at grasping the theoretical implications of issues or at organising his own ideas into systematic order. He was no conscious proto-Marxist, and was in no way drawn towards socialism, a systematic statement of which was lacking in Britain when Dickens died in 1870, anyway. Ironically at the very time his novels were revealing an increasingly critical and challenging social perspective Dickens's own opinions were progressively hardening into a conservative impatience with liberal opinion, for example, on the questions of capital punishment and the amelioration of prison conditions,[7] and the scandal involving Governor Eyre. This book is not concerned with what Dickens thought about society but with what his novels tell us about society. We are concerned with the novels and not with the man. At all times we must remember that 'when we speak of point of view in relation to creative literature we are referring to something somewhat different from a man's consciously held, or fairly easily abstractable, ideas'.[8] It will not invalidate the readings of the novels which follow in Part Two to recognise that Dickens would probably have been unable to articulate and organise the social insights embodied imaginatively in these novels into a coherent theoretical argument.

Indeed such a situation is not unusual. There are many precedents of a novelist not grasping the full complexities or ambiguities of the work he has created, or of a writer creating a novel which moves in a direction contrary to the social or political stance which was intended. Sociologists of literature, taking their lead from Engels's praise of Balzac as a writer whose conscious views were in contrast to his poetic vision, have developed the concept of 'dissociation' to account for this. Essentially, the theory of dissociation is 'the image of the poet as Balaam speaking truth against his knowledge or avowed philosophy'.[9] Lucien Goldmann asserts (in *The Hidden God*) that:

> The history of literature is full of writers whose thought was rigorously contrary to the sense and structure of their work (among many examples, Balzac, Goethe, etc.) . . . There is nothing absurd in the notion of a writer or poet who does not apprehend the objective significance of his own works.

However, it is not only the Marxist school which recognises the phenomenon. Raymond Williams, though in a more tentative fashion, testifies to it:

> It seems to be perfectly possible for a writer to hold ideas, even strong ideas, and to express them directly or through particular characters, while at the same time the actions he creates, the values and consequences he explores, bear in quite other directions: a case, we might say, where the writer's opinions outside his writings are different from the ideas he finally embodies in his work.[10]

Thus the reader should not expect a simple correlation between Dickens's social vision as it appears in the novels (the only concern of this study) and his reported opinions on contemporary social issues.

Another important consideration when defining the nature of Dickens's realism follows from the relation between environment and morality which exists in the novels. It is often said that Dickens's novels criticise mid-Victorian industrialism from a moralistic or humanistic point of view. This is true, but as the novels assert that the general quality of moral life and everyday social relations are both largely the product of social and economic institutions this criticism is also profoundly sociological. Dickens's novelistic attitude to environment is not simple, and its emphasis changes throughout his fiction, and even within the same book. Victorian capitalism is never seen as a *completely* deterministic environment, but in the mature work evil, greed, selfishness, materialism, crime are not abstract moral qualities but presented as the product of an historically specific environment, individual responses to the influence of a set of social conditions operating in mid-nineteenth-century England.

By the time he created Miss Wade, Magwitch and Bradley Headstone Dickens had come a long way from the view of environment which presented Bill Sikes's passion as moral evil independent of his environment and socialisation. The moral oppositions which characterise the mature work (e.g. between Woodcourt and Smallweed, Doyce and Merdle) are given a sound social basis. The relation between Dickens's morally based criticism of his society, and his recognition of the influence of the social/economic environment on the general character of everyday social life accounts for the special flavour of Dickens's social criticism. Thus within a few paragraphs of her critical work on Dickens, Barbara Hardy can call Dickens 'a moral novelist', and then assert that his novels reveal 'a sociological imagination'.[11]

The critical nature of Dickens's novelistic reflection of society implies not merely an observation of society (consistent with the documentary approach) but an imaginative judgement, which is necessarily bound up with a creative attempt to understand the nature of what was seen as a new and significantly different social system. Dickens's mature novels ambitiously try to analyse the nature of industrial society through the medium of fiction, to explore and define this new society rather than merely reflecting it passively. In Edgar Johnson's book *Charles Dickens: His Tragedy and Triumph* the chapter on *Bleak House* is entitled 'The Anatomy of Society' and this

could serve as a descriptive label for the whole sequence of novels
from *Bleak House* to *Our Mutual Friend.* Similarly, F. R. Leavis's
comments on *Little Dorrit* have a general relevance for the whole
body of the mature work. '*Little Dorrit* . . . offers something like a
comprehensive report on Victorian England – what is life, what are
the possibilities of life, in this society and civilisation, and what could
life, in a better society, be?'[12]

If we remember that the main concern of Dickens's realistic
method is a critical evaluation of the general social condition within
an industrial society it prevents us from regarding as faults aspects of
his realistic method which follow directly and functionally from his
chief artistic concern with society as a whole. For example, consider
Dickens's method of characterisation. A general criticism is that his
central characters are not psychologically interesting, and his peri-
pheral figures too exaggerated and grotesque. However, if Dickens's
chief artistic subject is society then it is also true that in a sense his chief
characters are social institutions – Chancery, the Circumlocution
Office, Expectations, Shares. As Grahame Smith points out 'For *Bleak
House* to have its Lydgate, its Madame Bovary, its Raskolnikov
would be a denial of its own existence. The novel's ultimate
protagonist is the Court of Chancery.'[13] Throughout the later novels
Dickens's attitude to characterisation is consistent – characters are
utilised to illustrate some truths about society, not human
psychology. (As we shall see, this is true even in Dickens's most
interesting psychological studies – e.g. Miss Wade and Bradley
Headstone, whose neuroses grow out of aspects of their social
environment.)

It is not difficult to see how Dickens's method of characterisation
has been criticised as exaggerated. As illustrations of social forces his
characters are presented in extreme terms that the essence of society
may be seen more clearly. The typical Dickens characters embody
essential aspects of their society, in their most highly developed and
concentrated forms. Lukács's theory of the type is directly relevant
to a discussion of Dickens's characterisation. To Lukács the creation
of 'types' which reveal the essential nature of a social/historical
situation or experience is one of the touchstones of literary greatness.
What constitutes a type is

> not its average quality, not its mere individual being however
> profoundly conceived; what makes it a type is that in it all the
> humanly and socially essential determinants are present on their

highest level of development, in the ultimate unfolding of the possibilities latent in them, in extreme presentation of their extremes.[14]

Dickens's method of characterisation produces a whole gallery of 'types', e.g. Bounderby, Mrs Clennam, Pancks, Wemmick, Podsnap. Thus the extremely defined, highly concentrated presentation of character is not a failing in Dickens's realism (as compared to the careful, intricate revelation of inner life which we find in the novels of George Eliot) but is a consequence of the social basis of his realistic method.

I have used the term 'social vision' frequently in this chapter. The term relates to the essential way in which the novels see society, a way of seeing which is both poetic and critical. The social vision is the artistically controlling view of the essential nature of the general experience, which provides the organising crux of each of the great novels. The social vision imposes a poetic unity on a confusing world, and although, as we shall see, the adoption of conventional closed, happy endings often contradicts the logic of the novels' social vision, the social vision itself is impressive in its coherence and imaginative clarity. The social vision in the mature novels is essentially pessimistic – indeed because it implies that things are not going to change it can be called a tragic vision. However, although the later novels reflect despair for society, hope for the individual life is never completely abandoned. The system is not totally deterministic. As we shall see, Dickens's artistic attitude to environment cannot be reduced to simple equations. 'His [i.e. Dickens] novels show a division between the society he rejects and the humanity he believes in, and that humanity, in different ways, is somehow preserved, frozen, shut off, and saved from the social pressure',[15] but only a vulnerable few escape the blighting effects of environment to attain fulfilment and happiness. Mid-Victorian capitalism is presented in the later novels as producing 'a universal process of degradation . . . to be escaped from only by a man or a woman here and there, through unusual courage or abnegation or grace'.[16]

II

It would be unwise at this point to offer too much detail about the characteristic properties of the social vision of the mature work. This will be fully described in the chapters on the individual novels. However, some of the crucial concepts which interrelate to make up this vision deserve to be briefly introduced. It will be demonstrated that in the later novels industrial society is seen as an oppressive and alienating system, external and hostile to the individuals within it, who function in themselves and through their relations with others as objects, machines, or things. Now the concepts of alienation and reification[17] have been used by sociologists of literature to describe the imaginative worlds contained in the fiction of various modern writers, but they have not been seen as relevant analytical tools for a study of novels within the nineteenth-century critical realist tradition. For Lucien Goldmann (who virtually ignored the English novelistic tradition) the fact that this was so was a problem.

> Although it is obvious that the absurd worlds of Kafka or Camus's *L'Etranger*, or Robbe-Grillet's world composed of relatively autonomous objects, correspond to the analysis of reification as developed by Marx and later Marxists, the problem arises as to why, when this analysis was elaborated in the second half of the 19th century and concerned a phenomenon that appeared in a still earlier period, this same phenomenon was expressed in the novels only at the end of World War I.[18]

In fact the mature novels of Dickens provide arguably the first literary illustration of a reified social world, tending to dehumanisation and mechanical, 'thing-like' existence.

Everywhere in the later novels we see the tendency for people in the grip of the mechanism of industrial society to become as objects, controlled or manipulated, or bought and sold. This will be emphasised in the readings which follow in Part Two. However, it is worth pointing out now that in *Hard Times* the whole factory population of Coketown is seen as living an objectified, mechanical life. For the factory workers life is a duplicated, automatic, clockwork existence. We are told that Coketown

> contained several large streets all very like one another, and many small streets still more like one another, inhabited by people equally like one another, who all went in and out at the same hours, with the same sound on the same pavements, to do the same work, and to whom every day was the same as yesterday and tomorrow, and every year the counterpart of the last and the next (p. 65).

It is this mechanical existence that Stephen Blackpool complains of to Bounderby asserting the essential humanity of the workers, crushed and threatened as it is, against the employers 'rating 'em [i.e. the factory workers] as so much Power, and reg'lating 'em as if they was figures in a soom, or machines: wi'out loves and likens, wi'out memories and inclinations, wi'out souls' (p. 182). In the later novels it is not an occasional fate for people to be dehumanised into machines. Here it is the lot of a whole class, and it is increasingly seen as the common lot of industrial society.

It is important to recognise that one of Dickens's favourite literary devices is directly related to this way of seeing society. This technique is Dickens's characteristic reversal of the relation between humans and things. The use of this common literary device is a stylistic expression of a crucial aspect of Dickens's social vision, representing an artistically successful marriage of form and content.

Dorothy Van Ghent, in her essay, 'On *Great Expectations*' in *The English Novel: Form and Fiction* (1953), was the first to emphasise how appropriate this literary device was to the Dickens world. She asserts that Dickens imaginatively grasped the process by which the human being was being exploited as a ' "thing" or an engine capable of being used for profit', and argues that:

> Dickens's intuition alarmingly saw this process in motion . . . and he sought an extraordinary explanation for it. People were becoming things, and things (the things that money can buy or that are the means for making money or for exalting prestige in the abstract) were becoming more important than people. People were becoming de-animated, robbed of their souls, and things were usurping the prerogatives of animal creatures – governing the lives of their owners in the most literal sense.[19]

Thus in Dickens's novels there is a reversal of the qualities of people and things. On the one hand we see a fairly constant use of the pathetic fallacy – the projection of human impulses and feelings upon the non-human, as upon houses, and furniture, and even clothes – while on the other hand

> people are described by non-human attributes, or by such an exaggeration of or emphasis on one part of their appearance that they seem to be reduced wholly to that part, with an effect of having become 'thinged' into one of their own bodily members or

into an article of their clothing or into some inanimate object of which they have made a fetish. . . . Many of what we shall call 'signatures' of Dickens's people – that special exaggerated feature or gesture or mannerism which comes to stand for the whole person – are such dissociated parts of the body, like Jaggers's huge forefinger which he bites and then plunges menacingly at the accused, or Wemmick's post-office mouth, or the clockwork apparatus in Magwitch's throat that clicks as if it were going to strike. The device is not used arbitrarily or capriciously. [20]

It could be argued that this literary device is present throughout Dickens's fiction, a trademark of his style in the early popular period as well as in the more pessimistic mature work. However, in the later novels the technique is used in imaginative contexts which are more sinister and ominous. In the early novels the reversal of the properties of humans and things is most often amusingly bizarre or convention- ally comic or incongruous. In the later novels the human properties of objects are less a source of comedy and increasingly more dangerous and malevolent towards the human world. Young Jerry Cruncher's impression that he is being chased down the street by live coffins is less comic than frightening. On the other hand, the thing-like properties of human beings are more ambiguous and sinister in the later novels. The mode of characterisation that in the early novels produced comic/grotesque eccentrics, in the later novels produces alienated men (e.g. Pancks and Wemmick). Frederick Dorrit and Miss Havisham are more painfully disturbing than grotesquely amusing. Humphrey House remarks:

> the eccentrics and monsters in the earlier books walk through a crowd without exciting particular attention: in the later they are likely to be pointed at in the streets, and are forced into bitter seclusion. . . . Silas Wegg and Mr Venus are at odds and ends with their world as Daniel Quilp was not. [21]

In the early novels this stylistic device, though an important element in Dickens's comic technique, appears structurally accidental, whereas in the later novels it functions as an integral part of a coherent imaginative vision of society (a successful modification and adap- tation of an old technique to the service of a newly conceived social vision.)

Organically related to the novels' exploration of alienation is the theme of the split-man. The increasing bureaucratisation of official life throughout the nineteenth century encouraged the separation of life into private and official spheres, destroying man's wholeness, rendering personality incomplete, and inducing a crisis of identity. The later novels contain a whole series of split or partial men (Morfin (*Dombey and Son*), Bucket (*Bleak House*), Pancks (*Little Dorrit*), Jarvis Lorry (*A Tale of Two Cities*), Wemmick (*Great Expectations*), and Riah (*Our Mutual Friend*)) and explore this social fact in a manner which demonstrates the human loss involved.

The single most important organising concept in the later work, and the core of the novels' social vision, is the obsessively recurring metaphor of society as one huge market-place. This is the most consistently voiced and strongly felt social theme of the later fiction, and it is impossible to over-emphasise its importance. All social relations, including marriage and friendship, are mediated through an economic frame of reference. Social behaviour in all areas of mid-Victorian society is presented in the novels as conditioned by a degraded market-place logic. In *The German Ideology* (1845/6) Marx had said of industrial society, 'In modern civil society all relations are in practice subordinated to the single abstract relation of money and speculation',[22] and it is precisely this insight into mid-Victorian capitalism which is central to the social vision of Dickens's mature fiction. His novels reflect the conditioning importance for the general relations of everyday social life of the relations of the economic sphere. In all areas of social life, so the later novels assert, social behaviour is in essence taking on the character of the new market relations of the economic sector.

Some theoretical principles of Lucien Goldmann's sociology of the novel are highly relevant here; thus I quote at length.

> The novel form seems to me, in effect, to be the *transposition on the literary plane of everyday life in the individualistic society created by market production*. There is a *rigorous homology* between the literary form of the novel, as I have defined it with the help of Lukács and Girard, and the everyday relation between man and commodities in general, and by extension between men and other men, in a market society.
>
> The natural, healthy relation between men and commodities is that in which production is consciously governed by future consumption, by the concrete qualities of objects, by their *use value*.
>
> Now what characterises market production is, on the contrary, the elimination of this relation with men's consciousness, its

reduction to the implicit through the mediation of the new economic reality created by this form of production: *exchange value.* . . .

If one wishes to obtain an article of clothing or a house today, one has to find the money needed to buy them. The producer of clothes or homes is indifferent to the use values of the objects he produces. For him, these objects are no more than a necessary evil to obtain what alone interests him, an exchange value sufficient to ensure the viability of his enterprise. In the economic life, which constitutes the most important part of modern social life, every authentic relation with the qualitative aspect of objects and persons tends to disappear – interhuman relations as well as those between men and things – and be replaced by a mediatised and degraded relation: the relation with purely quantitative exchange values. . . .

On the conscious, manifest plane, the *economic life* is composed of people orientated exclusively towards exchange values, degraded values, to which are added in production a number of individuals – the creators in every sphere – who remain essentially orientated towards use values and who by virtue of that fact are situated on the fringes of society and become *problematic individuals*; and, of course, even these individuals . . . cannot be deluded as to the degradations that their creative activity undergoes in a market society, when this activity is manifested externally, when it becomes a book, a painting, teaching, a musical composition, etc., enjoying a certain prestige, and having therefore a certain price. . . .

In view of this, there is nothing surprising about the creation of the novel as a literary genre. Its apparently extremely complex form is the one in which men live every day, when they are obliged to seek all quality, all use values in a mode degraded by the mediation of quantity, of exchange value – and this in a society in which any effort to orientate oneself directly towards use value can only produce individuals who are themselves degraded, but in a different mode, that of *the problematic individual.*

Thus the two structures, that of an important fictional genre and that of exchange proved to be strictly homologous, to the point at which one might speak of one and the same structure manifesting itself on two different planes.[23]

It is not necessary to accept a Marxist perspective or to agree with

Goldmann's ambitious but oversimplified theory of great works of literature giving coherence to the world vision of a social group to grasp the usefulness for the world of Dickens's mature fiction of the concept of exchange-value. Exchange-value is not just a technical economic description of market transactions, but is a value judgement about social relations. Hence relations of exchange-value apply not only to the relations of men and goods, but to the relations of men with each other. It is precisely the quantitative and mediated nature of social relations throughout the mid-Victorian system which the later novels repudiate. Of course, Dickens would not have been able to consciously articulate his imaginative insights into a systematic economic theory, but the social vision of his mature work is indeed structured around an imaginative consciousness that the essential nature of everyday social relations in mid-Victorian England is that of relations of quantitative exchange-value. If exchange-value does not totally dominate mid-Victorian England the exceptions are a few lucky or innocent individuals who successfully orientate themselves to qualitative relations with other people, in a struggle for happiness and authentic values. Certainly those collective movements aimed at improving the general quality of life (trade unionism, socialism, etc.) are ignored by Dickens. The struggle against exchange-values and alienation is individualistic, the work of a few, here and there, not organised together for any social purpose, and certainly not politically united. And this struggle is fought in the face of overwhelming odds. In all social areas ways of thinking and feeling, morality itself, is lapsing into economic rationale; marriage is a form of speculation; friends are treated as business assets, and people generally as pieces of merchandise, mere economic objects.

Some examples from *Dombey and Son* (1846–8) will give an idea of the way in which relations of exchange-value are dramatised in the novels. The loss of his first wife affected Dombey merely as the loss of a piece of valuable merchandise. Dombey 'had a sense within him, that if his wife should sicken and decay, he would be very sorry, and that he would find a something gone from among his plate and furniture, and other household possessions, which was well worth the having, and could not be lost without sincere regret' (p. 54). His second wife was bought, like an object labelled 'good blood', in what was a mere marriage speculation. ('He sees me at the auction, and he thinks it well to buy me', remarks Edith.) Both Edith and Alice Marlow, the prostitute, Mrs Brown's daughter, were appropriated and marketed by their own mothers as potential economic assets –

('She . . . thought to make a sort of property of me', complains Alice). All Dombey's relationships are mediated through an economic reference. 'Money . . . can do anything', he tells his son. And he selfishly regards his children solely as potential assets which can be invested, to boost his family pride and the status of his firm. Thus Florence — 'But what was a girl to Dombey and Son! In the capital of the House's name and dignity, such a child was merely a piece of base coin that couldn't be invested — a bad Boy — nothing more' (p. 51). Thus Dombey too makes 'a sort of property' of his children. Of course, as in the last example, it is possible (and indeed very frequent) for economic metaphors to be humorous and at the same time retain a critical relevance for the imaginative world of the novels.

The mature novels repeatedly identify the spread of a degrading business or money ethos into all areas of social life, a pervasive spread of a dehumanising philosophy located in the new economic realities of mid-Victorian England. At this point it is important to be clear about what is meant by the term 'business ethos'. We can't say simply that Dickens is anti-business: many of his heroes are either active or retired businessmen. Indeed, it will be argued in Chapter 3 that entrepreneurial middle-class values and ideals are used sympathetically to structure the novels. However, there is no doubt that a contextual study of the use of the word 'business' in the later novels would reveal that it seldom escapes pejorative connotations.

What Dickens is against in business is not merely a rigorous attitude to business and an eye for the main chance, as expressed, for example, by Jonas Chuzzlewit, 'Here's the rule for bargains, "Do other men, for they would do you." That's the true business precept. All others are counterfeits' (p. 241). What Dickens constantly repudiates throughout the later novels is an attitude to business which elevates it into the primary or sole concern of life, so that imaginative, spiritual, and religious life lapses into an extension of the economic, to be regarded in the same quantitative terms. When Arthur Clennam soberly admitted, 'I'm the only child of parents who weighed, measured, and priced everything; for whom what could not be weighed, measured, and priced, had no existence' (p. 59), he was talking about precisely this phenomenon. This shrinking of the whole of life to be encompassed in a narrow, sterile, business mould is seen by Dickens as unforgivable. It is anti-life in that, like the utilitarian statistical perspective, it is another aspect of the system which totally denies the values of heart and the emotions. It is a consuming ethos which, on the individual level, reduces life to a mechanical robot existence, and which, on the social level, produces a general impoverishment in the quality of social life.

Smallweed (*Bleak House*) and the official Pancks (*Little Dorrit*) are the mouthpieces for this hateful business/money ethos. A conversation between Clennam and Pancks (which will be discussed in greater detail later) is revealing.

> 'But I like business', said Pancks, getting on a little faster. 'What's a man made for?'
> 'For nothing else?' said Clennam.
> Pancks put the counter question, 'What else?' It packed up, in the smallest compass, a weight that had rested on Clennam's life; and he made no answer (p. 201).

This weight lies on the whole of mid-Victorian England too.

We have said that the word 'business' is increasingly used with pejorative connotations. We can see this happening as early as *Martin Chuzzlewit* (1843/4). Of Major Pawkins we are told,

> In commercial affairs he was a bold speculator. In plainer words he had a most distinguished genius for swindling and could start a bank, or negotiate a loan, or form a land-jobbing company (entailing ruin, pestilence, and death on hundreds of families), with any gifted creature in the Union. This made him an admirable man of business (p. 331).

The increasingly pejorative use of 'business' parallels the rise of joint-stock companies, and with them the passive, remotely controlling directors of mid-Victorian business, the large-scale investors and stock-market speculators. Mid-Victorian business is presented in the later novels as moving away from the traditional middle-class entrepreneurial business values — where thrift, industry and investment in a small privately owned and managed firm were seen as moral virtues. The values current in the mid-Victorian business world, however, are associated in the later novels unequivocally with spiritual and moral loss. It will be argued that what we shall call 'the business-ethos', not just a business code but a general way of thinking and feeling; an attitude to people; a judgement and evaluation of life's different goals, is a perversion of the entrepreneurial ideals of early Victorian capitalism.

III

We have identified some of the most important characteristics of the mature novels' social vision. The studies of individual novels will help the reader to decide to what extent we can call these novels challenging and radical. Over the years many left-wing critics have felt sympathetically drawn to the social world of Dickens's novels and have tried to claim him as a radical fellow-traveller. However, most have encountered difficulties in defining the quality of Dickens's radicalism. The experience of Shaw and Orwell is typical. Although both assert that Dickens can be regarded as a 'revolutionary' writer they are only able to accommodate Dickens within the category of 'revolutionary' by defining this in a severely qualified and highly general fashion.

Shaw saw Dickens as an unconscious revolutionary and made the by now common (if not notorious) comparison with Marx. In the introduction he wrote to *Great Expectations* in 1937 Shaw made explicit the revolutionary implications of Dickens's work.

> Dickens never regarded himself as a revolutionist, though he certainly was one. . . . The difference between a revolutionist and what Marx called a bourgeois is that the bourgeois regards the existing social order as the permanent and natural order of human society, needing reforms now and then and here and there, but essentially good and sane and right and respectable and proper and everlasting. To the revolutionist it is transitory, mistaken, objectionable, and pathological: a social disease to be cured, not to be endured. . . .
>
> The difference between Marx and Dickens was that Marx knew that he was a revolutionist whilst Dickens had not the faintest suspicion of that part of his calling.[24]

Shaw is employing a modified use of the concept of dissociation (i.e. Dickens did not fully grasp the implications of his own writing). Yet Shaw oversimplifies the position. Certainly the later novels do imaginatively assert that the system is 'a social disease to be cured', and Shaw's position may be justifiable given his terms and definition of 'revolutionary', but this definition is a highly qualified one. It obscures the fact that Dickens in his novels as well as his speeches and journalism was violently opposed to revolutionary methods as a political means to an end.

George Orwell was quite clear about this last point, but he too was confused when he came to define Dickens as a social critic. He asserts confidently that

> The truth is that Dickens's criticism of society is almost exclusively moral. . . . There is no clear sign that he wants the existing order to be overthrown, or that he believes it would make very much difference if it were overthrown. . . .
>
> It seems that in every attack Dickens makes upon society he is always pointing to a change of spirit rather than to a change of structure. . . . A 'change of heart' is in fact *the* alibi of people who do not wish to endanger the *status quo* ('Charles Dickens', *Inside the Whale*, 1940).[25]

Yet Orwell goes on to modify his definition of 'revolutionary' in an effort to accommodate Dickens:

> I said earlier that Dickens is not *in the accepted sense* a revolutionary writer. But it is not at all certain that a merely moral criticism of society may not be just as 'revolutionary' — and revolution, after all, means turning things upside down — as the politico-economic criticism which is fashionable at this moment. Blake was not a politician, but there is more understanding of the nature of capitalist society in a poem like 'I wander through each charter'd street' than in three-quarters of Socialist literature.[26]

Of course the problem of defining the nature of Dickens's radicalism is exacerbated by the fact that his social criticism is in the form of a general vision of society rather than concrete or constructive political proposals for social change. I do not believe that there is any meaningful sense in which we can call Dickens a revolutionary or socialist writer. However, I also believe that if a novelist reveals the essential forces within his society at work he has no additional duty to describe the manner of their resolution, or to produce a detailed blueprint of the future society which will result from this resolution. Indeed Engels himself believed that 'there is no compulsion for the writer to put into the reader's hands the future historical resolution of the social conflicts which he is depicting' (letter to Minna Kautsky), and interestingly he also asserted that a

> socialist-biased novel fully achieves its purpose . . . if, by conscien-

tiously describing real mutual relations, breaking down conventional illusions about them, it shatters the optimism of the
bourgeois, instils doubt as to the eternal character of the existing
order, although the author does not offer any definite solution or
does not even line up openly on any particular side.

It is equally clear that the fact that the mature novels contain both
explicit warnings of the fearful *possibility* of revolution, and implicit
imaginative pointers to revolution as the most *probable* result of the
existing social conditions (for the latter see the reading, in Chapter 4
of this book, of *Bleak House*), presents problems for the nature of
Dickens's realism. There was no revolution. The shadowy figures
lurking in the darkness of Tom's did not bring the system down.
Critics have adopted various strategies to deal with what might
appear a failure in Dickens's realistic vision. Robert Barnard talking
of *Bleak House* solves the problem by simply avoiding it — 'When we
read this novel we do not stop to meditate that Dickens was certainly
mistaken in his diagnosis — we simply enter his world, and accept his
vision.'[27] George Lukács, on the other hand, confronts the problem
but his attempts to explain away the tension between realistic literary
technique and correct historical prediction are not very clear or
convincing.

> Only 'prophetic' vision, or subsequent study of a completed
> period, can grasp the unity underlying sharp contradictions. One
> would misconceive the role of perspective in literature, though, if
> one were to identify 'prophetic' understanding with correct
> political foresight. If foresight were the criterion, there would have
> been no successful typology in nineteenth-century literature. For it
> was precisely the greatest writers of that age — Balzac and
> Stendhal, Dickens and Tolstoy — who erred most in their view of
> what the future would be like.[28]

Dickens lived and wrote in an historical situation. He exaggerated the
danger of revolution. The mid-Victorian English working class was
closer to the passive sufferers of Bleeding Heart Yard than to the Paris
mob which stormed the Bastille. The Hyde Park demonstrations of
1866 provided a good test case for the revolutionary potential of the
working class — there was political tension but no open class struggle.
However, although the confusion in the novels' treatment of the
working class as being politically apathetic and yet at the same time

potential agents of an imminent revolution is a weakness in the novels, the historically mistaken pointers to the danger of revolution do not invalidate the novels' depiction of the essential nature of the general experience within an industrial society (the relation of the individual and the system, the quantitative nature of everyday social relations, etc.). We come back to the point that if the novelist grasps the essential nature of the present he is not obligated to attempt to predict the future. The absence of a late-Victorian revolution does not destroy the credibility of the social vision of the mature work.

IV

We have stated that the social vision of the mature work was pessimistic, even tragic. This presents an interesting problem for the sociologist of literature. It is a critical commonplace to say that Dickens's imaginative vision darkened in his later novels. Yet why was it in the economically expanding and materially prosperous 1850s and 1860s and not in the troubled 1840s that the most critical, challenging and pessimistic novels were written? When a social historian contemplates the 1850s and the 1860s he thinks of a society where capitalism was burgeoning, a society characterised by vigour, enterprise, self-confidence, and stability, and not of a society which, for example, *Little Dorrit* (1855-7) presents as a huge prison. Of course, Dickens was concerned in his mature fiction with a general condition, and the general *quality* of social relations cannot simply be determined by statistics of economic growth, the mistake of a Gradgrind. But this does not remove the problem. Why was it that the novels became increasingly pessimistic about the general condition when the economy was expanding confidently and aggressively?

Dickens's early fiction of the 1840s is characterised by a casual, and often improvised, plot which offers full scope to show off a large gallery of comic or grotesque eccentrics. Social criticism takes the form of journalistic attacks on specific abuses, seen as isolated, self-contained problems in a basically healthy system. Significantly, this social criticism is embodied in self-contained passages (e.g. the Poor Law satire in the early chapters of *Oliver Twist* (1837)), almost arbitrarily dropped into the casually unified mix of melodrama, sentimentality, and comedy which Dickens stirred up for the reading public. Thus in the earlier fiction self-contained social problems are considered in virtually self-contained essays which intrude into the novels' loose structure.

Most critics see *Dombey and Son* (1846–8) as the watershed novel which heralds the more mature and artistically satisfying work. Society is now seen as a system of interrelated parts. The necessary connection between the different social worlds of the novel is expressed through the heavy-handed melodramatic plot link between Edith Granger and Alice the prostitute, as well as by an anticipation of the disease metaphor of *Bleak House*. (This last point will be developed in Part 2, Chapter 4.) In the novels which follow society will be seen whole, and social criticism will no longer be confined to self-contained issues. This development in the novels' view of society is paralleled by a development of form, technique, and organisational prowess. It was necessary for Dickens to divorce himself completely from the picaresque tradition and find new methods which could satisfactorily carry the brunt of his deepening social awareness. The use of emblems and controlled patterns of imagery to make generalised criticisms of society are formal expressions of the radical development in Dickens's novelistic way of seeing society.

But why did Dickens come to see society whole in an increasingly pessimistic and critical fashion in the 1850s and 1860s when the economy appeared to have successfully recovered from the crisis and depression of 1837–42, and not during the early or mid 1840s, a period characterised by fear, unrest, and working-class political agitation?

Obviously a very brief look at the social/economic background to the mid-Victorian period would be helpful. In 1840 it appeared to contemporaries that English capitalism was facing a crisis. Kitson Clark has pointed out that 'by 1840 the bounding prosperity which the new industry had conferred had very largely disappeared and had been replaced by deep depression and ruin and misery to those who had trusted to it for their living'.[29] The anxiety and strain of the 1840s was reflected in workers' agitation, viewed apprehensively from above. The years 1838–42 mark the time of greatest support for the Chartists, some of whom expressed a militant desire for revolution. However, by the end of the 1840s Chartism had clearly lost its momentum, the rejection by Parliament of the People's Charter for the third time in 1848 marking the effective end of the Chartist movement. Fear of revolution did not die with the end of Chartism, of course. As W. L. Burn remarks, 'For two or three generations the English mind was vitally affected by the idea of revolution (whether as the ultimate hope or the ultimate terror), by the prevalence of the revolutionary mystique.'[30]

However, despite the 'revolutionary mystique', for most contemporaries the 1850s and 1860s was a period of greater assurance and optimism than the troubled 1840s. Modern historians might disagree about the extent of economic recovery but contemporary opinion (despite the fluctuations of 1857 and 1866) was certainly reassured by what were seen as more socially stable and economically prosperous conditions. The threat of social disruption and working-class violence had dissipated and many critics of the system during the hungry and potentially violent 1840s were able to trade mid-Victorian complacency for the anxiety of the previous decade. Yet during this period of relative social calm and economic strength Dickens wrote novels which convey a sense of society collapsing and moving towards a crisis. Such a social perspective would seem more appropriate to the previous decade.

Two reasons can be offered to explain this paradox. One is a time-lag theory. As A. O. J. Cockshut has reminded us, 'New social facts take a long time to work down to those imaginative depths where artistic creation originates, and then to work their way back upwards into a finished artistic product.'[31] This does not make for a sophisticated sociological argument but it strikes me as probably being true. The pessimism of the later novels is not a response to current working-class political agitation, but the result of an imaginative grasping of the foundation and dynamics of the capitalist system, which had to be sufficiently and unambiguously developed before it could carry irresistible conviction to Dickens's imaginative consciousness.

It is easier to grasp the essentials of any process if it is progressing or developing with a steady momentum (as English capitalism was in the 1850s and 1860s) than if it is in a confused state of flux (as in the 1840s).

Dickens himself shows uncertainty and confusion in his novelistic attitude to industrialisation as late as the watershed novel, *Dombey and Son* (1846–8). Two apparently incompatible attitudes and reactions to industrialisation are revealed in the novel's treatment of the railway as a symbol for industrial progress. On the one hand the novel communicates Dickens thrilling enthusiastically to the energy, excitement, and promise of a new era. The power to transform whole areas (see the 'before' and 'after' descriptions of Staggs's Gardens) is described with awe. The railway is a symbol of progress – 'In short, the yet unfinished Railway was in progress; and, from the very core of all this dire disorder, trailed smoothly away, upon its mighty course of civilisation and improvement' (p. 121). Yet, on the other hand, the railway is also called (Chapter 20), a monster with potential for destruction, the 'way of Death' and 'a type of the triumphant monster, Death'. These two contrasting attitudes – of thrilling triumph and fear – stand side by side in the same novel.

However, in addition to the time-lag theory, there is an important sociological factor which helps to throw light on this apparent paradox. One of the social facts to which Dickens's imagination responded most productively and which was a crucial catalyst in the formation of the mature novels' social vision was the growth, development and transformation of the city of London. Now in this process *the 1850s marked the crucial turning point*.[32]

Recognition of the importance of the city in Dickens's later fiction is vital to an understanding of both the genesis and the nature of the mature realistic method. In his mature work Dickens imaginatively arrived at a critical understanding of industrial society through his observation of the city population and the city landscape.

Surface changes in the physical face of London which are also social facts (e.g. the disorderly, haphazard growth of an untidy suburbia), are reflected in the novels (for the growth of suburbia see *Dombey and Son* (pp. 555–7) and *Our Mutual Friend* (pp. 267–8)). However, the chief importance of the city in the mature fiction is as an emblem for industrial society as a type. From *Bleak House* onwards, argues Fanger, 'London achieved a unity it has never had before . . . it takes on its full significance as capital, as the head and symbol of national life.'[33]

In fact we can see this happening in *Dombey and Son* (but not before). We are told that Harriet Carker often looked at the stragglers wandering into London.

Day after day, such travellers crept past, but always, as she thought, in one direction — always towards the town. Swallowed up in one phase or other of its immensity, towards which they seemed impelled by a desperate fascination, they never returned. Food for the hospitals, the churchyards, the prisons, the river, fever, madnesss, vice, and death, — they passed on to the monster, roaring in the distance, and were lost (pp. 562–3).

Here the city is an emblem for the destructive machinery of the industrial system, fuelled like Chancery and the Circumlocution

Office by the helpless victims who approach it with mistaken hope and optimism.

Changes in the landscape and life of London not only helped Dickens to imaginatively grasp the workings of the system. He uses descriptions of the changing physical face of London as an important literary device to express his growing understanding. Descriptions of London's streets, buildings and locales function artistically in the novels as an index of the moral life of the whole society, and the quality of social relations within it. In characteristically describing London as a chaos, a desert, a wilderness, or waste-land Dickens is not merely describing the background scene with a reporter's eye, but is commenting on the general spiritual life and experience within the community and bringing this into focus in an impressively economic fashion, which takes us to the very core of the novels' meaning. 'It is astonishing how much of what Dickens has to say in the late novels is concentrated in the images by which London is variously evoked.'[34]

A good example of this is provided by the description in *Little Dorrit* of the City, as Arthur Clennam walks towards his mother's house.

As he went along, upon a dreary night, the dim streets by which he went, seemed all depositories of oppressive secrets. The deserted counting-houses, with their secrets of books and papers locked up in chests and safes; the banking-houses, with their secrets of strong rooms and wells, the keys of which were in a very few secret pockets and a very few secret breasts; the secrets of all the dispersed grinders in the vast mill, among whom there were doubtless plunderers, forgers, and trust-betrayers of many sorts, whom the light of any day that dawned might reveal; he could have fancied that these things, in hiding, imparted a heaviness to the air. The shadow thickening and thickening as he approached its source, he thought of the secrets of the lonely church-vaults, where the people who had hoarded and secreted in iron coffers were in their turn similarly hoarded, not yet at rest from doing harm; and then of the secrets of the river, as it rolled its turbid tide between two frowning wildernesses of secrets, extending thick and dense, for many miles, and warding off the free air and the free country swept by winds and wings of birds (pp. 596–7).

The images here of secrecy and crime, decay and prison, business and death, disease and wilderness do not merely anticipate the plot revelations of Merdle and Mrs Clennam, but define through their interrelation and the suggestiveness of their association the novel's way of seeing society. The chief thematic concerns of the novel are concentrated in this passage. All the details in the description, however negligently included they might appear at first, have a generalising weight of significance. For example, the phrase 'grinders in the vast mill' has relevance to the whole social world of the novel (especially, as we shall see, to Pancks, Clennam, and the inhabitants of Bleeding Heart Yard). A consideration of the closing words reveals the poetic density of this description. It culminates in a glance at the key thematic emblem of the novel, prison ('warding off the free air and the free country'), and a suggestion that Victorian capitalism, and its chief creation, the urban metropolis, involves a reversal of nature (trenchantly rejecting the forces of the natural world, 'winds and wings of birds'). A close reading of the whole passage offers the most economical route to the heart of the novel's social vision.

To argue that Dickens's artistic use of the city in his novels is mainly metaphoric is not to ignore the fact that he insists on a realistic topography (indeed, London always is given a wealth of concrete, sensuous detail), or that he ever ceased to enjoy the crowded streets as an imaginatively stimulating locale, or to be proud of his expert knowledge of London. It is interesting that in his journalism Dickens showed much interest in the development of a new popular culture, and writes of urban amusements, cheap plays, etc. But in his novels, with a few exceptions (Mr George's visit to the cheap theatre in *Bleak House*), this aspect of city life is ignored in favour of the opposite perspective – the city as destroyer of community, the producer of loneliness, isolation, and separation. Nadgett, in *Martin Chuzzlewit*, 'belonged to a class, a race peculiar to the city, who are secrets as profound to one another as they are to the rest of mankind'. In *A Tale of Two Cities* (1859) this theme, implicit in the presentation of city life throughout the later novels, is more fully articulated.

A solemn consideration, when I enter a great city by night, that every one of those darkly clustered houses encloses its own secret; that every beating heart in the hundreds of thousands of breasts there, is, in some of its imaginings, a secret to the heart nearest it! Something of the awfulness, even of Death itself, is referable to this. . . . In any of the burial-places of this city through which I pass, is there a sleeper more inscrutable than its busy inhabitants are, in their innermost personality, to me, or than I am to them? (p. 44).

Although it could also be argued that collective movements to forge a new community — Chartism, trade unionism, and socialism — were themselves born in the cities, to most contemporaries the fact of isolation was more strongly felt than the idea of community. The sense of religious community as well as social community was fragmented in the major cities — working-class indifference to religion and absenteeism from church in the cities was seen as a major social problem. The interconnection between classes insisted upon in the later fiction is expressed in parallel with a view of the city population as a stream of individual, separate units. This way of seeing the city as involving alienation and a breakdown of community, and encouraging individual selfishness and crime, was a catalyst for the pessimistic novelistic vision of society which characterises the later fiction. The mature social vision is thus organically bound up in the observed and experienced social development of London, its burgeoning and transformation throughout the *1850s and 1860s.*

Compare the mature vision of the industrial and urban experience with the treatment of industrialisation in *The Old Curiosity Shop* (1840–1). The impact of industrialisation is felt in those scenes when Nell and her grandfather pass fearfully and confusedly through towns in the Black Country and view, as if in a nightmare, scenes of urban squalor and working-class unrest, culminating in night-time 'errands of terror and destruction'. But it is possible to flee from the nightmare of these industrial pockets into the refuge of the neighbouring countryside. 'Industrial society is strictly localised; it is something you come to, and then rapidly pass through and escape.'[35] It was only in his later fiction that Dickens displayed an imaginative recognition that the consequences of living in an industrial society or urban environment reach all members and social groups and cannot be avoided or escaped from by a means as illusory as a fugitive journey. Only in the post-Dombey novels was England imaginatively defined as an industrial society rather than a country within which there were rapidly expanding industrial areas.

However, to fully understand the manner in which this new industrial society was reflected in Dickens's novels we have to remember the importance of the mediating influence of class values and class-bound literary conventions. It is to a consideration of the influence of middle-class norms and values on the imaginative world of Dickens's novels that we now turn.

3 Dickens as a Bourgeois Writer

As early as 1855 Dickens was identified by *Blackwood's Magazine* as a class writer, and this view has remained current to the present day.

> We cannot but express our conviction that it is to the fact that he represents a class that he owes his speedy elevation to the top of the wave of popular favour. He is a man of very liberal sentiments . . . one of the advocates in the plea of Poor *versus* Rich, to the progress of which he lent no small aid in his day. But he is, notwithstanding, perhaps more distinctly than any other author of the time a *class* writer, the historian and representative of one circle in the many ranks of our social scale. Despite their descents into the lowest class, and their occasional flights into the less familiar ground of fashion, it is the air and breath of middle-class respectability which fills the books of Mr Dickens.

Ruskin declared, on Dickens's death in 1870:

> The literary loss is infinite – the political one I care less for than you do. Dickens was a pure modernist – a leader of the steam-whistle party par excellence – and he had no understanding of any power of antiquity except a sort of jackdaw sentiment for cathedral towers. . . .
> His hero is essentially the ironmaster; in spite of *Hard Times*, he has advanced by his influence every principle that makes them harder – the love of excitement, in all classes, and the fury of business competition, and the distrust both of nobility and clergy (from a letter to Charles Eliot Norton, June 1870).

Certainly Dickens wrote for a middle-class reading public, and deferred to their standards of decorum (see Chapter 1) but his relationship with his literary public, and his imaginative commitment in his novels to their ideals and values was far more complex and problematic than either of the above views would indicate. Ruskin, in particular, offers a simplistic view of Dickens's essentially hostile attitude to industrial progress, probably because Dickens had no truck with mediaevalism.

This chapter will make some general points about the relationship between Dickens's novels and middle-class values or ideology. First, however, the experience of the middle class at the time when the mature novels were written must be considered briefly. Throughout the 1850s and 1860s there was much snobbery and jealously guarded degrees of privilege within the middle class itself, which was not a homogeneous group with a consciously held and coherent ideology. Within this 'class' there was a huge variety in levels of income and life-styles. The middle class would contain everybody from a Dombey to a Walter Gay, from a Rouncewell to a Guppy, from a Merdle to a Pancks. This is not to deny that there were certain values or ideals which were sufficiently widespread throughout the middle classes to be labelled 'middle-class' and that these values were recognised as 'middle-class' by contemporaries as the middle-classes developed, socially and economically throughout the nineteenth century — points to which we will return. However, these values were not organised into a systematic ideology which was embraced by the middle class as a whole, which separated this class from the aristocracy, and which was used to assert middle-class superiority as a class to the latter.

Indeed in the period under consideration the division between the upper reaches of the middle class and the aristocracy became increasingly messy and blurred. This period — the 1850s and 1860s — is popularly regarded as marking the triumphant rise to political power of the middle-class. However, although middle-class propagandists were celebrating the imminent demise of the aristocracy by the late 1840s the English aristocracy showed no intention of retreating from an industrial world in which it should have been an anachronism. It proved itself to be far more resilient and flexible than its critics had imagined and basic control and direction of political power throughout the mid-Victorian period remained chiefly in the hands of the old order. Now it is doubtful if the aristocracy would have been able to maintain its privileged social/political position without the continued emulation and respect for the aristocratic mode of life from the most successful members of the middle class exerting pressure from below.

Traditionally, the crown of the merchant's career had been a place in the country. Increasingly throughout the mid-Victorian period the successful businessman, rather than claim status in terms of traditional middle-class values and on behalf of his class as a whole, sought to use his wealth to gain status on aristocratic terms through the buying of land and through marriage into aristocratic families. The result was a fusion of classes (encouraged by the role of the public schools) which was accompanied in the higher reaches of the middle class by an adulteration of traditional middle-class values and increasingly by the adoption by the successful large-scale businessman of an imitative life-style expressing deferential regard for aristocratic customs and social habits. In terms of values and social ideals this marriage between the aristocracy and the upper middle class was contracted on aristocratic terms. As a result of this strategic amalgamation the social and political threat from the middle class was absorbed, while the aristocracy strengthened its own position and reserved for itself an important role in the future development of industrial Britain.

Although one of the most explicit dramatisations of the class relations of the mid-Victorian period – the meeting between Sir Leicester Dedlock and Mr Rouncewell, the ironmaster in *Bleak House* – is presented as a clash of irreconcilable social forces and ideologies[1] the mature work is generally most sensitive to the adulteration of the traditional middle-class values taking place at this time, especially in the upper reaches of the middle classes.[2]

For example, in *Hard Times* we are told of the Gradgrind school, the social/political theorists of the bourgeois interest:

> They liked fine gentlemen – they pretended that they did not, but they did. They became exhausted in imitation of them; and they yaw-yawed in their speech like them; and they served out, with an enervated air, the little mouldy rations of political economy, on which they regaled their disciples. There never before was seen on earth such a wonderful hybrid race as was thus produced (pp. 157–8).

The upper middle class compromise with the aristocracy weakens the argument that there was a coherent bourgeois ideology and thus undermines the claim that Dickens's novels reflect this.

However, if we cannot talk of a coherent mid-Victorian bourgeois ideology it is still possible to identify certain social values which traditionally owed their strength to a broad acceptance within the middle classes – and indeed these values have a great importance for Dickens's fiction. In all the mature novels certain middle-class values operate as moral positives in the novels' schematic design and function as important organising agents within the total structure.

The middle-class values which are chosen are the values tradition-ally associated with the middle classes in the earlier, entrepreneurial stage of English capitalist development – self-dependence, work as vocation, industry, thrift, earnestness, perseverance, patience, duty, etc. By the mid-Victorian period many of these had been perverted within the middle class itself into a blind desire for wealth and property for their own sake – not, as in the earlier, idealistic model, as an indication of the moral/spiritual qualities responsible for its accumulation (work, grace, etc.). Duty had become secularised into an obsession with business success; work, industry, thrift into worship of money, etc. It is a point of crucial importance that the middle-class values which were associated with what Lukács calls the heroic epoch of bourgeois development are utilised in Dickens's mature novels *as a means of criticising the contemporary social situation and behaviour of the mid-Victorian middle class itself.* The values of the entrepreneurial stage of capitalist development no longer accurately embody the essential nature of moral behaviour in a middle-class world dominated by Merdle, Podsnap, and Veneering. Furthermore, the earlier middle-class ideals implicitly recognised the moral superiority of the industrious worker to the idle aristocrat. Following the mid-Victorian alliance of aristocracy and bourgeoisie the traditional middle-class value stance was severely compromised. Thus the use of entrepreneurial values as structural agents in the later novels implies the very reverse of a novelistic loyalty to the contemporary mid-Victorian middle class – indeed, the mature fiction is characterised by an increasingly fierce opposition to the values and life-style of the mid-Victorian middle classes.

Lukács's reading of Balzac's *Lost Illusions* in *Studies in European Realism* is relevant here. Lukács argues that the illusions seen in the novel as empty are the ideals of the heroic stage of bourgeois development, now destroyed by the ongoing movement of their own economic base. Lukács's remark that the 'heroic pioneers' of the early stage of capitalist development had to make way for the 'humanly inferior exploiters of the new development, the speculators and the racketeers'[3] has direct relevance for Dickens's opposition of, for example, Merdle and the firm of Doyce and Clennam in *Little Dorrit.*

It is interesting that Dickens's earlier novels reflect a comparatively untroubled middle-class optimism: a belief in progress, in the direction in which the system was moving (though changes might be necessary to remove certain local abuses); an impatience with tradition; a contempt for those who idealise the Middle Ages; above all a critical opposition to the aristocracy, seen in the aristocratic caricatures of the early novels, e.g. Sir Mulberry Hawk, Lord Frederick Verisopht (*Nicholas Nickleby*), and in occasional passages such as the opening pages of *Martin Chuzzlewit*, with their satire on aristocratic preoccupation with birth and lineage. When middle-class values were utilised in the earlier novels as a positive moral basis for Dickens's social criticism the object of attack was chiefly the *aristocracy* but in the later novels it has widened to include as the main butt of the novels' criticism the contemporary middle class itself. It is not only the expanding social/political power of the Merdles, or the moral compromise attendant on the alliance of the upper reaches of the middle class and the aristocracy that disgusted Dickens. The entrepreneurial middle-class ideals were hardly characteristic of the other segments of the middle class in mid-Victorian England. The middle areas of this class produced the snobbery of Meagles and Mrs Pocket; the hypocrisy of Casby and Mr Pumblechook; Mrs Clennam's perverted economic evangelicalism; Vholes's obsession with respectability; the self-centred philanthrophy of Mrs Jellyby and Mrs Pardiggle, the egocentric 'mission' of Chadband, etc. The lower regions produced the greed of the Smallweeds; the vulgarity of Guppy; the paranoid concern for respectability of Bradley Headstone and Charley Hexam; and the inhumanity of the official business code of Pancks and Wemmick. Indeed, in the lower regions of the middle class, peopled by the clerical grubbers and grinders, the hollow men Dickens described so well, commitment to the degraded business and money ethos which he imaginatively detested (a perverted form of the earlier entrepreneurial ideals), was particularly strong.

The selected middle-class values which operate in the later novels form a loosely integrated moral touchstone, a means of judging character, behaviour and action within the crowded, superficially chaotic and disordered social world of the novels. Thus within these novels the critical social vision is presented in parallel with a set of loosely bound values which act as an *interpretive code* or framework — that these are traditional middle-class values, provides the reading public with a familiar and accessible route into the novels. However, the result is a complex situation in which a social vision which is essentially hostile to bourgeois society is to be read and interpreted by means of a mediation through traditional middle-class values. Indeed, the relation between the social vision and the interpretive code is crucial to an understanding of Dickens's mature fiction. The readings of individual novels will demonstrate the manner in which the social vision transcends the limitations of the interpretive moral framework. However, it is as well to recognise at this point that the relationship of the middle-class value index and the social vision is problematic and responsible for many of the contradictions within the novels. In so far as Dickens provides a decoding mechanism in conjunction with his basic social vision we consistently feel that he has, by mistake, given us the wrong or an inadequate code. The tension between the middle-class value index and the social vision takes different forms. Sometimes the middle-class code may act to reinforce the essential social vision; more often it obstructs or contradicts it, most often it dilutes or weakens it. If the sociologist of the novel concentrates on either of these elements at the expense of the other, the result is a partial and one-sided view of Dickens's fiction. By concentrating on the social vision alone the radical social criticism is given a coherence lacking in the novel as a whole, while a concentration solely on the middle-class moral framework might suggest that Dickens was merely a class-bound writer, the relevance of whose work is constricted by the limiting influence of his class position. What characterises the mature fiction is the tension between these two elements.

There are occasions on which the two structures – the social vision and the moral filter – are superimposed in such a way that the content of the social vision is reinforced, though this often happens in a manner which dilutes the imaginative impact of the latter. For example, consider the use made in the later novels of the concept of the ideal home, chiefly a middle-class product. [4]

In the ideal the home was seen as a walled garden, a shelter or refuge from the indifference of a business-orientated world. (The concept is given one of its most articulate and developed expressions in Ruskin's lecture *Of Queens' Gardens*.) The family fireside was not only a source of sustaining emotional support but a place where fancy and innocent play could thrive. Though there are some horrendous households in Dickens's novels (e.g. the Wilfers in *Our Mutual Friend*) and frequent examples of unnatural, perverted relations within the family (from Dombey to the reversal of roles in the 'family' relationships of Amy Dorrit/Maggy and the Doll's Dressmaker/her drunken father), much artistic capital is made of the myth of the ideal home in the later fiction (ironically at a time when Dickens's own family relations had deteriorated) – and when this occurs it almost always produces on Dickens's part an embarrassing slice of arch and sentimental coyness. The virtues of hearth and home are declared to the background accompaniment of the busy, cheerful 'little' woman (both playmate and housekeeper) jangling her housekeeping keys in a happy and dutiful manner.

However, the ideal house in Dickens's novels – Jarndyce's St Albans haven is an obvious example – also characteristically operates as an implicit criticism of the general condition within the total system. It is both a literal plot refuge from, and an idealised social alternative to, the system. The ideal home often operates as a microcosm of a social environment within which relations are healthy and qualitative, representing a radical criticism of the materialistic values and loss of community in the wider environment. Yet the fact that Dickens is utilising the middle-class myth of the Victorian hearth to clarify (by opposition) what is wrong with the system dilutes and emasculates his social criticism by cloaking it within a cosy, sentimental gloss so that the criticism becomes as comfortable as the tool used to convey it. The sting of the criticism is drawn by an alternative to a corrupt bourgeois society being framed in terms of one of the chief myths of the bourgeoisie.

Some more points about the nature of the middle-class value index might best be emphasised now. The values are chosen selectively and hold together in a loosely integrated form. There is no attempt to give coherence to and articulate a middle-class ideology. Often a value which is utilised as part of the middle-class value code is subject to implicit criticism elsewhere within the structure of the same novel, e.g. Jarndyce's private charity in *Bleak House*. And the moral framework itself does not remain constant from one novel to another. A middle-class concept or ideal utilised comparatively uncritically in one novel is often subjected to increasing criticism in subsequent novels. As this is an important point it is worth considering an example – the flexibility in Dickens's artistic use of the middle-class value of self-help and the ideal of the self-made man.

The concept of self-help is associated with Samuel Smiles but it was current among the middle classes for a considerable time before Smiles gave it most memorable articulation with the publication of *Self-Help* in 1859. His chief assertion was that 'What some men are, all without difficulty might be. Employ the same means, and the same results will follow.' He argued that it 'is not eminent talent that is required to insure success in any pursuit, so much as purpose – not merely the power to achieve, but the will to labour energetically and perseveringly.' It is difficult today to comprehend the strength of the concept of self-help within the Victorian middle class.

Of course, Dickens himself was a walking example of the Victorian self-made man and celebrated his own success in *David Copperfield* (1849/50). We are explicitly told that David Copperfield's success was due to his 'habits of punctuality, order and diligence', his 'perseverance', and his 'continuous energy'. (The last two are spoken of as the 'source of my [i.e. David's] success'.) In this novel the treatment of the concept of the self-made man is heroic rather than critical or ironic, and in his next novel *Bleak House* (1852/3) the portrait of Rouncewell the ironmaster reflects this middle-class ideal in a favourable, positive light. However, from this point Dickens's attitude to the myth and its social implications becomes increasingly ambiguous.

In *Hard Times* (1854) Bounderby with his vaunting boasts of heroic and independent social climbing is ruthlessly satirised in a way which casts aspersions on these concepts themselves (though Bounderby's boasts are not true). The novel also explicitly undermines the validity of universal application of the concept. It was crucial to Smiles's argument that 'what some men are, all without difficulty might be'. However, Book II, Chapter 1 of the novel provides an explicit rejection of this.

> This, again, was among the fictions of Coketown; any capitalist there, who had made sixty thousand pounds out of sixpence, always professed to wonder why the sixty thousand nearest Hands didn't each make sixty thousand pounds out of sixpence, and more or less reproached them every one for not accomplishing the little feat. What I did you can do. Why don't you go and do it? (p. 152).

In *Little Dorrit* (1855–7), however, Doyce is presented sympathetically and he is a classic embodiment of Smiles's ideal. Clennam regards Doyce as an 'honest, self-helpful, indefatigable old man, who has worked his way all through his life'. The details given of Doyce's life are strikingly similar to the classic pattern sketched out by Smiles in his *Lives of Engineers*, even to the detail of early parental help and encouragement in his vocation. Doyce was the son of a north-country blacksmith, and had originally been apprenticed by his widowed mother to a lock-maker; that he had 'struck out a few little things' at the lock-makers, which had led to his being released from his indentures with a present, which present had enabled him to gratify his ardent wish to bind himself to a working engineer, under whom he had laboured hard, learned hard, and lived hard, seven years. His time being out, he had 'worked in the shop' at weekly wages seven or eight years more; and had then betaken himself to the banks of the Clyde, where he had studied, and filed, and hammered, and improved his knowledge, theoretical and practical, for six and seven years more. There he had had an offer to go to Lyons, which he had accepted; and from Lyons had been engaged to go to Germany, and in Germany had had an offer to go to St. Petersburg, and there had done very well indeed – never better (pp. 232–3).

From humble beginnings through a long apprenticeship to actively managing his own firm, it is the classic middle-class myth, and Doyce has particular relevance for the mid-Victorian period for engineers were folk-heroes to the mid-Victorians. Dickens's portrait of Doyce, then, utilises the middle-class myth of the self-made man even more sympathetically than the portrait of Rouncewell in *Bleak House*, who at times betrays a glib, self-satisfied tone.

However, the portrait of Doyce must be seen in terms of its implicit criticism of Merdle (see Chapter 5) and in *Great Expectations* (1860/1) the emphasis changes again. Pip's boyhood yearnings for higher social status are seen as a perverse source of frustration. Pip would have been better off without them. For the working class as a whole a general expectation of upward social mobility was only likely to cause unhappiness and wretchedness, and the agony of frustrated aspiration. In *Our Mutual Friend* (1864/5) Bradley Head-stone and Charley Hexam are both successful in rising in the scale of society, but in both cases self-improvement is seen as a problematic gain leading to extreme social uncertainty and a neurotic anxiety over the stability of this all too vulnerable and fragile social achievement.

In addition, increasingly in these later novels outstanding examples of social achievement are portrayed unsympathetically as spiritually or morally suspect – think of Lady Dedlock, Bounderby, Merdle, Stryver and Veneering etc. It is as if success on society's terms is incompatible with moral goodness – thus the heroes of the later novels are either only successful on moderate terms or (in the interests of a happy ending) have the trappings of success gifted to them (a far cry from success being earned by work, perseverance, endeavour, etc.). Thus an excessive social ambition and an obsession with upward social mobility increasingly comes to be regarded in the novels as far from natural or laudable — indeed as morally ambiguous. Its relevance for promoting the health of the whole social organism and of all groups within it has been rejected. Instead of maintaining the efficient running of the machinery of society the ideal has come to be seen as having a socially divisive potential spreading unhappiness and social frustration throughout the lower orders.

The importance of the middle-class value index will be clear when we look at individual novels in Part 2. However, if the term bourgeois novelist can only be applied to Dickens's novels in an ambiguous and misleading fashion, is there another group (other than the middle class) which we can identify as providing through its value structure the key to an understanding of the imaginative world of Dickens's mature novels?

In his journalism Dickens frequently talked of 'us, the people' and identified with the popular interest. However, it is impossible to make out a case for Dickens being a 'popular' novelist either in the sense that he drew on the experience and values of the working classes to structure his novels, or that he helped to promote through his fiction a sense of identity and class consciousness amongst the urban masses. Dickens rarely shows us the working class in a working situation, and Shaw has commented quite accurately, 'But of the segregated factory populations of our purely industrial towns he knew no more than an observant professional man can pick up on a flying visit to Manchester.' Furthermore, Dickens's novelistic attitude to the working class reveals no sympathy with any of the popular appeals for working-class solidarity or for any form of collective action. The novels do express sympathy for the urban poor in their character of passive, suffering victims but 'the aggregate of distress and sorrow has only to move, collectively, to be converted into its opposite, and be seen as a howling mob.'[5]

The novels applaud the emotional solidarity and mutual help amongst the working class (e.g. Liz and Jenny in *Bleak House*). And Dickens is willing to make the gesture of moral equality to the deserving members of the working class — i.e. nature's gentlemen. But it will be argued that this is not a radical gesture, an implied criticism of the class system, a declaration of faith in the people as a class — but instead, a mere sentimental sop to his readers, with

conservative social implications. Moral gentility is only awarded to
the individual member of the working class who dutifully accepts his
allotted place in society, and the need to be governed from above. It is
a necessary condition to accept a passive, non-political role in society.
Although moral equality might be awarded, this operates within the
divisions of the existing class system. The natural gentleman was still
expected to defer to his social superiors. A true gentleman would not
push in where he was not wanted (think of Joe Gargery in *Great
Expectations*).

This can be illustrated by examining the role of Stephen Blackpool
in *Hard Times*. It is strongly implied that he is one of nature's
gentlemen. When Louisa offers him her gift of money we are told of
Stephen's behaviour — 'He was neither courtly or handsome, nor
picturesque in any respect; and yet his manner of accepting it and
expressing his thanks without more words, had a grace in it that Lord
Chesterfield could not have taught his son in a century' (p. 190).
However, Stephen's moral worth is organically linked to political
apathy. He refused to join the trade union for reasons which he
doesn't make clear, and in answer to Bounderby's question of how he
would put right the muddle he answers, 'I donno, Sir. I canna be
expecten to't. 'Tis not me as should be looken to for that, Sir. 'Tis
them as is put ower me, and ower aw the rest of us. What do they tak
upon themseln, Sir, if not to do't?' (p. 181). He is, throughout the
novel — and in this he is representative of all Dickens's good
working-class characters, 'cap-tweaking, foot-shuffling, and reassuringly un-revolutionary'.[6]

Dickens has often been viewed as a democrat, mainly on account of
his famous speech to the Midland Institute at Birmingham, Sep-
tember 1869. 'I will now discharge my conscience of my political
creed, which is contained in two articles, and has no reference to any
party or persons. My faith in the people governing is, on the whole,
infinitesimal; my faith in the People governed is, on the whole,
illimitable.' Forster, however, added a shrewd postscript when he
claimed that 'it may be suspected, with some confidence, that the
construction of his real meaning was not far wrong which assumed it
as the condition precedent to his illimitable faith, that the people, even
with the big P., should be "governed".' Dickens was no embryonic
socialist, and his view of the working class owes more to Carlyle than
Marx. In a *Latter-Day Pamphlet*, Carlyle portrayed the working class
as a 'dumb inarticulate' mass crying out for good paternalistic
leadership. 'Guide me, govern me! I am mad and miserable and

cannot guide myself.' In Dickens's later fiction the working class is often portrayed as a dehumanised object or animal in need of strong control and management – in *Bleak House* Jo and his like are described as blind oxen, badly guided and sorely goaded, but liable to do an injury to themselves and to innocent others if they unwisely attempt to find their own way. The political analogy is clear.

Also present in the treatment of working–class characters is an implicitly patronising element. The dignity of working-class characters is reduced or denied by their being presented as comic figures of fun, or childlike innocents (often at the same time). As a result the good workers come across as a very short distance removed from half-wits. Mr Bagnet, Mr Boffin, Joe Gargery etc. – all innocents abroad in a corrupt world where they are terribly vulnerable. This vulnerability, of course, is consistent with the necessity (for their own good) of government being imposed in a benignly paternalistic fashion from above. There is no way that Dickens can be regarded as a 'popular writer' in any political or progressive sense.

However, an interesting suggestion for our purposes is Perkin's assertion that within the middle classes there existed a class or sub-group with its own, however vague, ideal – not necessarily committed to the orthodox middle-class position, indeed, openly critical of it on occasions. This class was the professional middle class, which 'had a separate, if sometimes subconscious, social ideal. . . . Their ideal society was a functional one based on expertise and selection by merit'.[7] During the mid-Victorian period an attempt was made by a number of professions to gain respectability and/or gentlemanly status for their members, by exercising a more severe control over the recruitment, competence and conduct of their fellow professionals. Exams were instituted, parliamentary recognition and registration was sought, and a new and much larger wave of professional institutions came into existence.

Among Dickens's own friends there were many professional men. In so far as Dickens's mature novels offer an alternative social ideal to mid-Victorian capitalism, it is framed largely in terms of the talented and trained professional man with a social conscience – e.g. Woodcourt (*Bleak House*) and Doyce (*Little Dorrit*). It is as if men from the *new* professions are seen as being uniquely capable of responding to the problems of the new industrial society. (In his novels Dickens remains suspicious or hostile to members of the *old* professions, the law and the clergy.) But this social ideal is presented within a familiar framework. It is as if Dickens is saying that if all men were like Doyce and Woodcourt — especially if the political governors were talented, responsible, or efficient — then all would be well. Thus in a sense the new professional man is the equivalent in the later novels (as a representative solution to the problems of Victorian society) to the individual philanthropist of the earlier fiction — the latter a type whose methods and likelihood of success Dickens seems to have viewed with increasing doubt and ambiguity (despite the reappearance of Boffin in *Our Mutual Friend*). The new professional rather than the philanthropist comes to be the representative man in the moral society the latter novels contrast idealistically to the reality of industrial England.

But we must beware of making too much of the role of the professional man. For example, the role of a character such as Doyce is complex. He is a *new* professional man, an engineer, but also an embodiment of the traditional (*old*) middle-class ideal of the self-made man. The engineer might have been the folk-hero of the mid-Victorian period but Doyce's personal business ethos (anti-speculation) looks to the past, and seems more applicable to an earlier stage of English capitalist development. Though by profession he is a *new* man, in terms of attitudes and values Doyce is a relic from entrepreneurial capitalism standing in stark contrast to the new capitalist hero of the mid-Victorian period, represented in *Little Dorrit* by Merdle. Perhaps significantly, unlike the young and energetic Woodcourt, Doyce is physically older and more worn. It is worth remarking that although the entrepreneurial ideal is still important in structuring the experience of the hero in Dickens's later fiction (both Arthur Clennam and Pip end up as active partners in a small, independent firm) this is not completely divorced from the professional ethos, for, as Humphrey House has pointed out, the small independent businessman is 'a man whose work bears a relation to his income similar to that of professional people to theirs'.[8]

However, it is difficult to attribute any world vision (in Goldmann's sense) to this professional group and Perkin leaves the nature of the professional ethos unsatisfactorily vague. We can say that Dickens greeted the arrival on the social scene (and particularly in the area of urban sanitary and health reform) of the well-trained, talented, and dedicated professional man with both personal and artistic sympathy. He used professional men, particularly Woodcourt, as a hopeful emblem for a better future. But beyond this we cannot argue that his novels are a literary transposition of the values of the mid-Victorian professional class.

Indeed, when he wrote his best work Dickens's social situation was characterised by the *absence* of an unambiguous commitment or orientation towards any one contemporary class. The imaginative world of his later novels stubbornly refuses to be reduced to an expression of the point of view, ideology, or world vision of any one social group. And this absence of an ideological commitment to a closely bound social group operates along with the important social fact of the developing city to give Dickens's mature novels their peculiar brooding tone and strongly communicated sense of individual isolation and separateness within the social organism.

As his literary career progressed Dickens increasingly came to have no faith in any group platform or programme. In his private life he was unhappy: his marriage and family relations were suffocating; his affair with Ellan Ternan was frustrating and unfulfilling. His personal letters to friends in his later years reflect a frustrated yearning; a feeling of having missed the boat; of (like the widowed David Copperfield) never having met the one true friend who could have given him fulfilment; a desire to be recalled to life like the heroes of his later novels. His portraits of Skimpole and Gowan (representing polar positions of art as aesthetic beauty, or as a commercial commodity) reveal his scant sympathy with the most common attitudes of the contemporary literary/cultural circles. He had no political faith, either in a party, pressure group, or even in the basic system. As early as 1855 he had written to W. C. Macready: 'As to the suffrage, I have lost hope even in the ballot. We appear to me to have proved the failure of representative institutions without an educated and advanced people to support them. . . . I have no present political faith or hope – not a grain.' By 1870, the year of his death, he wrote to Lytton, 'I do not think the present Government worse than another, and I think it better than another by the presence of Mr Gladstone; but it appears to me that our system fails.'

In his later years Dickens experienced the strain of belonging and not belonging. As a rejection of society in his novels became more extreme, in his private life Dickens felt a proportionate need to remain socially acceptable (think of his public declaration of the reasons for separating from his wife). Though his novels repudiated the *existing* order, Dickens still felt a deep commitment to a social order of some sort against the disruptions which he feared were either concomitant with the democratic principle, or liable to erupt from the urban slums. C. P. Snow has acutely observed of the later Dickens:

In many ways he reminds one, at the time when he was writing the
dark novels of his last period, of a middle-aged American liberal of
the present day: who has had great hopes and found them eroded:
who doesn't like what he sees round him and can't find a place to
stand: who is nevertheless unbreakably bound to the society in
which he grew up.[9]

Lukács (in *Studies in European Realism*) makes the point that:

> the really honest and gifted bourgeois writers who lived and wrote
> in the period following the great upheavals of 1848 naturally could
> not experience and share the development of their class with the
> same true devotion and intensity of feeling as their
> predecessors. . . . And because in the society of their time they
> found nothing to support wholeheartedly . . . they remained
> mere spectators of the social process.[10]

The later Dickens is an outsider; he takes no partisan position. With
reference to his novels the position of spectator is a source of both
strength and weakness — it is a strength in that it frees him to criticise
the middle class, in which he occupies an esteemed but uneasy
position, but, on the other hand, the lack of ideological commitment
to a group contributes to many of the inconsistencies and contradictions within the novels' value stance and point of view.

We have said that Dickens was, in a sense, outside society. But the
later novels make it clear that this is an impossible position. Jarndyce
in *Bleak House* finds this out when fever, engendered in the slums of
Tom-all-Alone's, penetrates his refuge from the system at St Albans.
To claim that Dickens was not a committed member of any class or
group is not to say that he was not involved in society. 'The act of
writing and publishing serially for a particular public, and the
experience of pleasing them, is for Dickens to enact his own
involvement in English society'.[11] This involvement is both social
and economic.

Following Dickens's death, Trollope said this of him in *St Paul's
Magazine* (July, 1870):

> I remember another novelist saying to me of Dickens — my friend
> and his friend, Charles Lever — that Dickens knew exactly how to
> tap the ever newly growing mass of readers as it sprang up among
> the lower classes. He could measure the reading public — probably

taking his measure of its unconsciously – and knew what the public wanted of him. Consequently the sale of his books has been hitherto so far from ephemeral – their circulation has been so different from that which is expected for ordinary novels – that it has resembled in its nature the sale of legs of mutton or of loaves of bread. The butcher or baker will know how many of this or that article he will 'do' in a summer or in a winter quarter, and so does the bookseller know how many 'Pickwicks' and how many 'Nicklebys' he will 'do'.

Dickens's relations to his literary market are particularly interesting to the sociologist of literature.[12] In his novels Dickens repudiated a social system in which mediated and quantitative relations of exchange-value predominated. Yet as soon as his novels were released they themselves became market commodities, and highly remunerative ones at that. In his portrayal of Gowan, the artist in *Little Dorrit*, Dickens ruthlessly criticises the view of art which sees it merely as a potentially remunerative stand in the market. Yet Dickens, himself, was acutely sensitive to circulation figures and was willing to alter his artistic intent to give his readers what they wanted and so increase sales figures. When initial reaction to *Martin Chuzzlewit* was disappointing Dickens hastily sent its hero to America to exploit the widespread public interest in the life of the New World. At other times he tentatively sounded likely public reaction before committing himself to an important development of characterisation. Regarding the prospective change in Walter Gay (who was to go bad on similar lines to the elder Carker), he wrote to Forster, 'Do you think it can be done without making people angry?' Of course, the ending of *Great Expectations* was changed at Lytton's advice. Dickens himself (as he wrote to Forster) had 'no doubt that the story will be more acceptable through the alteration'. Dickens's editorial advice to a would-be contributor to his magazine reveals an important aspect of Dickens's attitude to his own fiction.

'I particularly entreat you to consider the catastrophe. You write to be read, of course. The close of the study is unnecessarily painful – will throw off numbers of persons who would otherwise read it, and who (as it stands) will be deterred by hearsay from doing so, and is so tremendous a piece of severity, that it will defeat your purpose.

When Dickens did include some tragic enormity in his own work it was usually cloaked in enough sentimentality to make it successful market fare. In *Fiction, Fair and Foul* (1880) Ruskin pertinently remarked that 'Nell, in *The Old Curiosity Shop*, was simply killed for the market as a butcher kills a lamb'. Another editorial remark by Dickens, as late as 1858, is of particular relevance to this question. He cautioned Wills, a member of his staff, 'I particularly wish you to look well to Wilkie's article . . . and not to leave anything in it that may be sweeping, and unnecessarily offensive to the middle class. He always has a tendency to overdo that.' Yet the novels he was writing at this very time revealed scant artistic sympathy for the middle class although he always deferred to middle-class canons of taste and propriety and accepted the obligation not to 'offend the Young Person'.

It is a measure of the complexity of the social context of the mature novels that a social vision which is critical of the current experience of the mid-Victorian middle class is framed in traditional middle-class values, expertly aimed at the contemporary middle-class reading public, and is presented in accordance with middle-class standards of decorum and taste. On the one hand the novels remorselessly expose and repudiate the market nature of society, but on the other hand they are themselves highly remunerative products in a very profitable literary market. Clearly the situation is too complex and messy for the label 'bourgeois novelist' to be an adequate or satisfactory summary of the mature work. The social tensions which give the novels their characteristic flavour can best be demonstrated by turning to the novels themselves.

Part Two

The Mature Novels

4 *Bleak House*, and the 'Springing of a Mine'

When Lady Dedlock, the most famous beauty of exclusive fashion-able society, dies dressed in the clothes of a brickmaker's wife, lying on the steps of a pauper's burial ground in one of the most depressed and squalid areas of London, we are directed to one of the chief strands in the novel's social vision. The first point to note about *Bleak House* is the almost obsessive manner in which through plot, theme, and emblem the novel asserts the necessary connection between different, apparently self-contained social groups, and argues that society is a system of organically related and interconnected parts. The novel shatters the cosy fiction that respectable society can have no connection at all with the wretched, ragged inhabitants of an urban slum, such as Tom-all-Alone's. It argues that we are all in this together, all members and groups necessarily connected as part of one total system.

The systematic nature of society is emphasised in different ways. One is by means of the plot itself. Just about every character in the novel is linked in various ways with almost every other character, and the role played in the novel by coincidence and surprising connec-tions is directly advertised, sometimes to an extent which seems artistically heavy-handed. In view of this it is surprising that some critics have seen the Lady Dedlock sub-plot merely as a melodramatic appendage to the novel. In fact it has the same function as, for example, the disease metaphor in emphasising the collective nature of social experience. Lady Dedlock's death, heavy in social irony, brings together in significant association Chesney Wold and the English aristocracy, and the brickmaker's cottage and the paupers' burial ground near Tom-all-Alone's. After Lady Dedlock, Jo the crossing sweeper probably has the most important emblematic function, wandering unthinkingly into the lives of members of all social classes, a point underlined when Jarndyce and Woodcourt reflect at Jo's death-bed 'how strangely Fate has entangled this rough outcast in the web of very different lives' (p. 703).[1]

The different social worlds of the novel are also suggestively linked by a whole series of verbal echoes and repetitions and by related patterns of imagery. However, the most memorable way in which the corporate nature of society is emphasised is through the great emblems of the novel – the fog of Chapter 1 (which engulfs all the inhabitants of London regardless of age or class in a collective misery), the suit of Jarndyce and Jarndyce (which involves, whether they like it or not, members from all social groups), and most imaginatively powerful of all, the metaphor of disease.

In *Dombey and Son* (Chapter 47) the concept of disease spreading from the slums 'to blight the innocent and spread contagion among the pure' is introduced but not fully developed in a way which is integral to the meaning of the novel. Dickens writes of 'the thick and sullen air' of the slums 'where Vice and Fever propagate together, raining the tremendous social retributions which are ever pouring down, and ever coming thicker!' (p. 738). In *Bleak House* this metaphor is given its most articulate and dramatically impressive formulation. In his treatment of the theme in *Bleak House* Dickens may well have drawn on a passage in Carlyle's *Past and Present* (1843). In the chapter 'Gospel of Mammonism' Carlyle refers to a story told in William Alison's *Observations on the Management of the Poor in Scotland* (1840). A poor Irish widow, after appealing unsuccessfully to various charitable establishments for help, contracts typhus fever and dies, but not before infecting seventeen others who also died.[2] However, if Carlyle was a literary source immediate inspiration came from the contemporaneity of the public health and sanitation issue, in which Dickens was directly involved in a practical journalistic fashion. Cholera had struck London in 1848–9, and was to return in 1854, a fact which makes the novel's warning prophetic. The disease metaphor in *Bleak House* is an example of documentary material being utilised artistically. Its significance for the novel transcends its literal meaning, without ever rendering its realistic meaning redundant.

In *Bleak House* the disease theme is introduced in the description of Nemo/Hawdon's burial in the paupers' graveyard. He is taken 'to a hemmed-in churchyard, pestiferous and obscene, whence malignant diseases are communicated to the bodies of our dear brothers and sisters who have not departed' (p. 202). Into this place 'they lower our dear brother down a foot or two: here, sow him in corruption, to be raised in corruption: an avenging ghost at many a sick bedside' (p. 202). These ideas are fully developed in the famous description of Tom-all-Alone's, the urban slum, in Chapter 46.

> But he [i.e. Tom-all-Alone's] has his revenge. Even the winds are his messengers, and they serve him in these hours of darkness. There is not a drop of Tom's corrupted blood but propagates infection and contagion somewhere. It shall pollute, this very night, the choice stream (in which chemists on analysis would find the genuine nobility) of a Norman house, and his Grace shall not be able to say Nay to the infamous alliance. There is not an atom of Tom's slime, not a cubic inch of any pestilential gas in which he lives, not one obscenity or degradation about him, not an ignorance, not a wickedness, not a brutality of his committing, but shall work its retribution, through every order of society, up to the proudest of the proud, and to the highest of the high. Verily, what with tainting, plundering and spoiling, Tom has his revenge (p. 683).

Disease is no respecter of class and person. It makes a mockery of the claims of any group to be a self-contained unit in society. In *Bleak House* disease is the link between the Two Nations, and the plot works in parallel with the disease emblem to reinforce this theme. The fever (probably smallpox) carried by Jo from Tom-all-Alone's penetrates the 'safe' middle-class haven from social injustice set up by John Jarndyce at St Albans and strikes at Charley and Esther Summerson, thus exposing the myth of a self-contained, private world within society. An analogy between disease and revolution suggested at the end of the passage — both forms of plundering and spoiling would shatter the complacent world of respectable society — emphasises the importance, indeed the necessity, of recognising the organic relation between the rich and poor, the respectable and disreputable. Revolution is the most extreme instance of the way in which one social group can affect the destinies of all the others within the system and, as we shall see when discussing the image of the springing of a mine, fear of revolution underpins the novel's social vision.

II

The social vision of the novel does not only assert that society is a system. It offers a critical evaluation of the quality of life and everyday social relations within the system. The key to the novel's social vision is provided by the portrayal of Chancery, not only at the heart of the fog of Chapter 1 but at the core of the meaning of the book. The Court of Chancery is the real organising crux of *Bleak House*. It is more important for the unity and coherence of the text than the much discussed symbol of the fog which has certainly received more than its due share of critical attention in recent years. The social criticism in the novel is not limited to a specific attack on the legal system but extends to a repudiation of a whole society and in its representative function Chancery operates as a social microcosm. An examination of Chancery reveals not merely the failings of the legal system but the essential condition of mid-Victorian English society as a whole. What are the characteristics of life in Chancery?

The answer will be clearer if we consider the two analogies through which the nature of life in Chancery is revealed. On the one hand, Chancery is seen as a cruelly indifferent and inhuman machine, an external thing grinding up the individuals it should serve. On the other hand it is portrayed as a business firm, dealing profitably in people as economic assets. This latter perspective is developed in the novel through an extended analogy between society and a giant market-place, the single most important theme in the later fiction. These two analogies take us to the core of the novel's meaning and are worth considering in some detail.

Chancery is presented as operating as a force in itself, an alien thing indifferent to the individual suitors caught up in its mechanism. It is an alienating social world, external and hostile to the luckless individual with whom it comes in contact. It is the best example of Shaw's claim that in the later novels the social system is 'a huge machinery which grinds to pieces the people it should nourish and ennoble'. Indeed, Tom Jarndyce's involvement in Chancery is described by himself as 'being ground to bits in a slow mill' (p. 102), and Jarndyce talks of 'dead suitors, broken, heart and soul, upon the wheel of Chancery' (p. 547). In a novel full of parasites the mechanism of Chancery feeding off Chancery suitors is the ultimate symbol of parasitic life. Chancery's capacity to swallow up its clients is like the appetite of an insatiable monster, and is suggested by the shape of the bags containing Vholes's legal documents, 'stuffed out of all regularity of form, as the larger form of serpents are in their first gorged state' (p. 605).

One of Esther's remarks about Vholes's relation to his client, Richard Carstone, is particularly significant. She felt 'as if Richard

were wasting away beneath the eyes of this adviser, and there were
something of the vampire in him' (p. 876). The application of this
remark is general. Krook the pseudo-Lord Chancellor stands over the
dead body of Nemo, the law-writer, another Chancery victim, 'with
his lean hands spread out above the body like a vampire's wings'
(p. 189). The mechanism of Chancery, vampire-like, sucks the life-
blood and humanity from its suitors – not only Richard, but
Gridley, who wastes away to death, and Miss Flite, who preserves her
touching humanity at the cost of madness. In view of the characteristic fate of Chancery suitors it is appropriate that Chancery should be
associated with slow or violent death, and torture. Snagsby's shop, for
example, is described as a 'storehouse of awful implements of the
great torture of the law' (p. 184). If Chancery is a machine, it would
not be misplaced to compare its cruel impersonality to the indifference of the world Meursault contemplates in Camus's novel
L'Etranger.

Within Chancery there is a crisis of individuality and identity. The
suitors are treated as mere instruments or objects of convenience, but
for the agents of the system too life has lapsed into mechanical
functioning, a condition nicely caught in the opening chapter
showing the court in action – 'Eighteen of Mr Tangle's learned
friends, each armed with a little summary of eighteen hundred sheets,
bob up like eighteen hammers in a pianoforte, make eighteen bows,
and drop into their eighteen places of obscurity' (p. 54). The lawyers
too act like mechanical cogs within a greater machine.

Some desperately seek a frame of reference in the behaviour of
others, and slavishly try to conform to a model. Conversation Kenge
'formed himself on the model of a great lord who was his client', and
for Young Smallweed 'to become a Guppy is the object of his
ambition. He dresses at that gentleman (by whom he is patronised),
talks at him, walks at him, founds himself entirely on him' (p. 327).
Snagsby surrenders his identity to the will of his wife, while the name
taken by Hawdon in his occupation as law-writer is appropriately
Nemo (Latin for no-one).

However, although Chancery is a machine with a will of its own
the legal profession profits from its turnings. 'The one great principle
of the English law is, to make business for itself. There is no other
principle distinctly, certainly, and consistently maintained through all
its narrow turnings' (pp. 603–4). In this respect Chancery operates as
a business firm, regarding suitors as business assets – remunerative
commodities valued solely in quantitative terms of exchange-value. A

good example of this is provided by the letter Kenge sends to Esther, communicating Jarndyce's plans for her. The legal language and abbreviations strip Esther of her humanity and reduce her to the level of an economic object or piece of merchandise. 'We have arrnged for your being forded, carriage free, p eight o'clock coach from Reading, on Monday morning next, to White Horse Cellar, Piccadilly, London, where one of our clks will be in waiting to convey you to our offe as above' (p. 74). The metaphor of Chancery as a business firm is extended to embrace a whole society where everyday social relations (including friendship and marriage) are increasingly being degraded into a form of economic speculation. The analogy between society and a market-place is of crucial importance in the novel's attempt to *understand* the workings of mid-Victorian capitalism and is the most important imaginative focus in the later novels. We can see an extreme case of what we have called the 'money/business ethos' as a governing frame of reference for everyday life by considering the Smallweeds. A lifetime's social orientation to economic logic has reduced Smallweed's wife to a deranged puppet – mentally brainwashed she mechanically associates any number or figure mentioned in her presence with money or some other form of capital, repeating the result out loud like a frantic automatically functioning robot.

Indeed, the market ethos which reduces morality to economic rationale can dehumanise even children. In a passage which anticipates the theme of childhood and fancy in *Hard Times* we are told that Judy Smallweed, prematurely acquainted with a harsh economic frame of reference, without ever knowing a childhood of fables and innocent play, is in the company of other children 'like an animal of another species' (p. 344).

The Smallweed view of imaginative literature is that it is economically irrational. Asked if he ever reads, Smallweed replies, 'No, no, no. We have never been readers in our family. It don't pay. Stuff. Idleness. Folly. No, no!' (p. 351). Similarly the Smallweed view of friendship degrades it into an economic investment. On hearing that young Bart Smallweed has been dining at Guppy's expense, Grandfather Smallweed exclaims, 'That's right. Live at his expense as much as you can, and take warning by his foolish example. That's the use of such a friend. The only use you can put him to' (pp. 345–6).

It is no surprise that the family dissolves as a cohesive, mutually sustaining unit in the face of such a market mentality. The

Smallweeds' home reflects not community but the principles of individualistic competition. Bucket asserts, 'Lord! there ain't one of the family that wouldn't sell the other for a pound or two, except the old lady — and she's only out of it because she's too weak in her mind to drive a bargain' (p. 897).

But the novel emphasises again and again that it is not just in the business sphere (represented by the moneylender Smallweed) that the money/business ethos (and quantitative relations of exchange-value in general) infiltrates and undermines social relations. The process is general.

For example, it governs the behaviour of the philanthropists. Mrs Jellyby, always 'full of business', treats her daughter, Caddy, as a clerk or employee, and makes her home into an office. Mrs Pardiggle, too, boasts of her businesslike approach to charity, which is reflected in her visit to the brickmaker's house. Esther criticises the impression she makes ('her voice had not a friendly sound, I thought; it was much too businesslike and systematic') and adds pertinently, 'I hope it is not unkind in me to say that she certainly did make, in this, as in everything else, a show that was not conciliatory, of doing charity by wholesale, and of dealing in it to a large extent' (p. 159). Jarndyce himself admits that too often 'charity was assumed, as a regular uniform, by loud professors and speculators in cheap notoriety' (p. 256), and by attempting to gain through the socially viable image of public benefactor a cheaply bought fame and status the phil-anthropists were implicitly viewing their charity work as a market speculation.

This is true also within the religious sphere where Chadband, too, is a 'speculator in cheap notoriety'. His religion is undermined by an economic frame of reference. In an anticipation of Mrs Clennam, Chadband keeps a profit and loss account of the balance between his good deeds and sins. This is no more than a form of moral/spiritual book-keeping. Thus to the regulation of his spiritual life Chadband applies a form of business organisation characteristic of capitalism. Remember Max Weber saw profit and loss book-keeping as one of the preconditions of capitalism. For example, when Jo yawns during his moral lecture, Chadband proclaims, 'I stumbled, on Sabbath last, when I thought with pride of my three hours improving. The account is now favourably balanced: my creditor has accepted a composition' (p. 325).

Market-place activity characterises the political world too. Sir Leicester deals in parliamentary seats like a political merchant.

In fact, as to this question of opposition, the fair Dedlock's observation was superfluous; Sir Leicester, on these occasions, always delivering in his own candidateship, as a kind of handsome retail order to be promptly executed. Two other little seats that belong to him, he treats as retail orders of less importance; merely sending down the men, and signifying to the tradespeople, 'you will have the goodness to make these materials into two members of parliament, and to send them home when done' (pp. 623–4).

On an individual level Skimpole and Turveydrop both invest in a false identity and exploit it to live comfortably at other people's expense. Skimpole's projection of his image as an irresponsible but innocent child, and Turveydrop's promotion of himself to his family as a 'model of Deportment' are both strategies of speculation for economic gain. This theme of investment in a socially viable surface is developed in *Little Dorrit* and *Our Mutual Friend*.

The extension of rights of property throughout society, possession of things increasingly being extended to possession of people, is another way in which the market mentality characterises the general quality of social life. Property is one of the great social gods of mid-Victorian society (later to be crystallised in the image of Podsnap's plate), and the desire to pursue it and protect it is one of the chief motivating forces within the system.

Grandfather Smallweed rushes to take possession of Krook's papers and belongings obsessively repeating 'like an echo, "the – the property! The property! – property!"' (p. 522). The politicians and theorists appropriate Tom-all-Alone's and the misery of the urban poor as subject for endless debate. The Chancery lawyers make their own (constantly accumulating) property out of the cases and miseries of their clients. Vholes appropriates vampire-fashion Richard Carstone's physical body (as well as his money). Tulkinghorn jealously guards his exclusive rights of property over aristocratic family secrets. Sir Leicester views seats in parliament as his own private property. The philanthropists make objects of property out of the recipients of their charity – Esther remarks that 'we both thought that Mrs Pardiggle would have got an infinitely better, if she had not had such a mechanical way of taking possession of people' (p. 159). Chadband exercises a right of property over those like the helpless Jo who listen to his sermons. As Bucket proceeds towards the end of his revelations about Tulkinghorn's murder in front of Sir Leicester, 'he seems imperceptibly to establish a dreadful right of property in Mademoiselle' (p. 797).

The essence of life in Chancery (and by extension throughout the whole system) is reinforced by various means; the descriptions of Chancery buildings, emphasising their rot and decay, and suggesting the spiritual quality of the lives of those living and working within; the use of representative characters (for example, the cold 'mechanically faithful' Tulkinghorn, who is 'indifferent to everything but his calling' and is consistently likened to a destructive machine, and the vampire-like Vholes, repeatedly associated with birds and animals of prey); and the metaphorical use of the suit of Jarndyce and Jarndyce.

Not only is the suit of Jarndyce and Jarndyce the quintessential Chancery case, but because Chancery itself is a microcosm of the whole system the suit (as Leavis points out) is a metaphor for the general quality of life in industrial society. To live within the boundaries of the suit is analogous to living within a generally corrupting social environment. 'No man's nature has been made the better by it' (p. 53), and we are told 'If two angels could be concerned in it, I believe it would change their nature' (p. 547). Being a party to the suit also means involvement in a competitive, free-for-all struggle for its spoils − an appropriate emblem for an individualistic, laissez-faire society. Ada tells Richard 'I am only grieved that I should be the enemy − as I suppose I am − of a great number of relations and others; and that they should be my enemies − as I suppose they are; and that we should all be ruining one another, without knowing how or why, and be in constant doubt and discord all our lives' (p. 108). And there is no way of divorcing oneself from this individualistic competition. As John Jarndyce says of the suit, 'We can't get out of the suit on any terms, for we are made parties to it, and must be parties to it, whether we like it or not' (p. 146). No man can deny his participation in society. The individuals born into the suit must accept their necessary involvement in something they cannot control. But Jarndyce does withdraw his involvement from the suit and escapes its corruption, and as we shall see, the method and success of Jarndyce's retreat results in a basic contradiction within the structure of the novel, typical of the tensions between plot and social vision which characterise the mature work.

III

Bleak House is a novel in which few characters make any real or meaningful contact with each other. Two classic cases of non-communication are Chadband's sermon to Jo, and Mrs Pardiggle's visit to the brickmaker's. The latter reflects not just isolation and separation between individuals but also the lack of communication between classes. Esther reflects, 'We both felt painfully sensible that between us and these people there was an iron barrier which could not be removed by our new friend [i.e. Mrs Pardiggle]. By whom or how it could be removed, we did not know, but we knew that' (p. 159). *Bleak House* presents the class extremes of mid-Victorian society.

Aristocratic society is presented in the novel as a world essentially as mechanical and automated as Chancery. Within it we find a clockwork observation of fastidiously cultivated surfaces, and a life of inflexible forms, stifling spontaneity and individuality and paralysing the imagination. All situations are interpreted through the same inflexible class-bound filter, what we could call Sir Leicester's creed of Wat Tylerism.

Bleak House presents aristocratic society as a world which has outlived its social utility and justification. There is no anticipation of the way in which the aristocracy might use strategic marriage alliances to maintain its privileged social position and its political influence. Instead the emphasis is on the ineluctable erosion of the traditional aristocratic powers and privileges. The floodgates of society which (according to Sir Leicester) will obliterate landmarks and uproot distinctions have already opened. When we first see Chesney Wold the landscape is obliterated under floodwater. In the street where the Dedlock town house is situated 'extinguishers for obsolete flambeaux gasp at the upstart gas' and 'even oil itself, yet lingering at long intervals in a little absurd glass pot . . . blinks and sulks at newer lights every night, like its high and dry master in the House of Lords' (p. 709). Yet the novel argues that an even greater threat to the aristocratic establishment than middle-class political influence is presented by the shadowy figures lurking in the darkness of Tom-all-Alone's.

If the fashionable world is peopled by dandified objects in emotional and spiritual isolation from each other the other side of the Two Nations divide exhibits a different sort of loss of humanity. Jo is the representative member of the urban poor and is consistently described as an uncomprehending animal.

> Jo, and the other lower animals, get on in the unintelligible mess as they can. It is market day. The blinded oxen, over-goaded, over-

driven, never guided, run into wrong places and are beaten out; and plunge, red-eyed, and foaming, at stone walls; and often sorely hurt the innocent, and often sorely hurt themselves. Very like Jo and his order; very, very like! (p. 275).

The urban poor have wrongs ('over-goaded, over-driven, never guided') but blinded by lack of education their own unsophisticated attempts at social improvement are liable to be disastrous, hurting both the working class themselves, and the 'innocent' middle class. The solution to their problems lies in responsible paternalistic government imposed from above.

The same political implication is present in the other metaphor applied to the lower classes in the novel – they are immature children, innocents abroad in a materialistic world. Dickens's good lower-class characters generally conform to this pattern of kind hearts but weak heads (see Chapter 3). Mr Bagnet is typical – kind and loyal, but virtually a simpleton, on an intellectual par with a helpless child. George Rouncewell also exhibits 'a certain massive simplicity, and absence of usage in the ways of the world' (p. 906) and when George and Bagnet set off to visit Smallweed we are told 'two more simple and unaccustomed children, in all the Smallweedy affairs of life' could hardly be imagined (p. 534). Of course, this is not a moral criticism but children are socially vulnerable and need protection.

This, in addition to a tendency to dilute the dignity of his lower-class characters by exploiting them for easy laughs as figures of fun and emphasising the absurdity of their speech and behaviour, implies a basic condescending and patronising novelistic attitude, contrasting ironically with the novel's praise of Woodcourt's ability to communicate with the poor (and break down the barrier so apparent during Mrs Pardiggle's visit to the brickmaker's house), by means of 'avoiding patronage and condescension, or childishness (which is the favourite device, many people deeming it quite a subtlety to talk to them like spelling books)' (p. 684).

Of course, Jo's alienation is not due to the effects of the industrial division of labour (we do not see the urban working class in a factory situation) but to extreme poverty and lack of education. He wanders through life an isolated observer of incidents he does not understand. But if we do not have a factory situation in the novel then we do have Tom-all-Alone's, a representative example of urban slum conditions.

As a documentary portrait of an urban slum Tom's offers very little concrete detail about the nature of the appalling conditions which

must have existed. However, without an explicit itemising of the
stomach-turning facts, the horror of conditions in Tom's is well
communicated to the reader by the shock and amazement experienced by Snagsby, a London dweller all his life, on viewing Tom's for
the first time – 'he, who had lived in London all his life, can scarce
believe his senses' (p. 364). Incidentally Snagsby's shock is not just a
mechanism to avoid offending his readers but reflects an important
truth. In Chadwick's *Report on the Sanitary Condition of the Labouring
Population of Great Britain* (1842) we are told that 'The statements of
the condition of considerable proportions of the labouring
population . . . have been received with surprise by persons of the
wealthier classes living in the immediate vicinity, to whom the facts
were as strange as if related to foreigners or the natives of an unknown
country.'

But Tom's is not intended to be merely a sociological report. It has
an important function and a generalising suggestiveness within the
novel's structure. Life in Tom's is a logical extreme of the dehumanisation which the novel describes as taking place throughout the
system. Thus Tom's can be read as a frightening model for a future
social condition to set against the idealistic social alternative represented by the new Bleak House, home of Woodcourt and Esther.

The question of responsibility for Tom's is dealt with in some
detail. 'This desirable property is in Chancery, of course. It would be
an insult to the discernment of any man with half an eye, to tell him
so' (p. 273). Tom's is born of Chancery corruption. That is – because
of Chancery's representative function – it is in the corrupt nature of
the whole industrial system that the genesis of the urban slum
problem lies. The development of Victorian capitalism has inevitably
produced bastard offspring like Tom's. However, within the system
there are various agencies with the potential power to relieve the
extent of the hardship suffered by the urban poor, failing to do so. In
an important passage in Chapter 46 these are accused – the political
system, the public institutions for social welfare, the utilitarian
political economists ('force of figures'), the aesthetic world of culture,
and all the religious denominations. Dickens concludes, 'in the midst
of which dust and noise, there is but one thing perfectly clear, to wit,
that Tom only may and can, or shall and will, be reclaimed according
to somebody's theory but nobody's practice. And in the hopeful
meantime, Tom goes to perdition head foremost in his old determined spirit' (p. 683).

The crucial point is that all these agencies for change concern themselves with the problem on the level of theory. In effect these groups and institutions are appropriating the evil and misery of Tom's to serve time as fuel for arguments and debates, and inner conflicts within each respective area. Utilising the metaphor of two different punishments to remedy a criminal the novel suggests an alternative course. (To set Tom right the question is 'whether he shall be set to splitting trusses of polemical straws with the crooked knife of his mind, or whether he shall be put to stone-breaking instead.' (p. 683)) To polemical straw-splitting is opposed stone-breaking, with implications of direct action and vigorous practical reform — perhaps even suggested by the term is the actual physical demolition of the urban slums. Yet within the novel there is a confusion in the treatment of the problem of urban poverty. On the one hand, the practical problem of Tom's can only be solved by vigorous and direct political/administrative action (sanitary reform, rehousing, etc.) This is a radical solution to counter the twin evils of disease and crime. In so far as Tom's is a test-case for method of social change the implication is that a social problem demands a social answer. Yet to the problem of poverty in the abstract Dickens offers through Jarndyce the conservative solution of private charity. Here the social problems of the system are given a moral solution (a moral change of heart experienced generally within the community). We will return to this.

One thing the novel does make clear, however, is that a social problem such as Tom's (or for that matter, Chancery) cannot be treated as a separate concern to be cured by some form of local surgery or amputation. This follows from the presentation of society as a system of interrelated parts, which fit together in such a way that they reinforce each other and support the total structure. For example, the legal system reinforces the existing class system dominated by aristocratic power and privilege because it 'gives to monied might the means abundantly of wearying out the right' (p. 51). Any reduction of aristocratic legal privilege resulting from Chancery reform would alter the balance of the class system by weakening the aristocratic position *vis-à-vis* other social groups. That is why Sir Leicester is 'upon the whole of a fixed opinion, that to give the sanction of his countenance to any complaints respecting it, would be to encourage some person in the lower classes to rise up somewhere — like Wat Tyler' (p. 61). The Dedlock political satire emphasises the close fit between the class system and the political system. Similarly any successful or permanent solution to the problem represented by Tom's must also come to terms with the legal and political systems which combined to produce Tom's, and continue to produce similar spectres.

In the earlier fiction social criticism was aimed at self-contained issues, but in *Bleak House* what is being criticised is a whole system, and the problem is how to bring about general change. Yet although Tom's is not seen as an isolated problem it is presented as the most crucial issue facing mid-Victorian society, because it is necessarily bound up with the great Victorian nightmare of revolution. In the Preface to a new edition of *Oliver Twist* published in 1851, a year before he started work on *Bleak House*, Dickens declared that without reform of slums and sanitation 'those classes of the people which increase the fastest, must become so desperate, and be made so miserable, as to bear within themselves the *certain* seeds of ruin to the whole community' (my italics). The threat was revolution and to a discussion of this theme in *Bleak House* we now turn.

IV

Throughout the novel there are frequent warnings that some form of sudden violent change is about to explode and shatter the respectable world of Victorian society. Forces are building up in the darkness and shadows of the urban underworld undermining the superficial social/economic prosperity until the moment when they will burst forth upon a smug and complacent, self-contemplating society.

The aristocratic world is especially threatened. 'Both the world of fashion and the Court of Chancery are . . . sleeping beauties, whom the Knight will wake one day, when all the stopped spits in the kitchen shall begin to turn prodigiously' (p. 55). This ominous note is echoed in the description of the crowd which gathers at Chesney Wold – 'For it is, even with the stillest and politest circles, as with the circle the necromancer draws around him – very strange appearances may be seen in active motion outside. With this difference; that, being realities and not phantoms, there is the greater danger of their breaking in' (p. 212). There is little doubt that these 'strange appearances . . . in active motion' are identical to the shadowy movements in the darkness of Tom-all-Alone's.

There is no one character in the novel who represents the urban poor in the role of agents of revolution. However, Jo's progress from Tom's to Jarndyce's respectable middle-class home at St Albans, carrying the fever which strikes at Charley and Esther, is analogous to the revolutionary process. Indeed, both are forms of 'spoiling and plundering' by which Tom's will have his revenge. When Jo was compared to a drover's dog the warning was given — 'Turn that dog's descendants wild, like Jo, and in a very few years they will so degenerate that they will lose even their bark — but not their bite!' (p. 275).

Apart from explicit warnings of the latent danger of revolution there is wedded into the imaginative structure of the novel a suggestive pattern of imagery which is organically related to this theme — the image of the springing or exploding of a mine or bomb. We are told of Tom's: 'Twice, lately, there has been a crash and a cloud of dust, like the springing of a mine, in Tom-all-Alone's; and, each time, a house has fallen. . . . As several more houses are nearly ready to go, the next crash in Tom-all-Alone's may be expected to be a good one' (p. 273). The 'next crash in Tom's' suggests the social crash of a revolution engendered in the urban slums which will explode on an unsuspecting society 'like the springing of a mine'. In this passage we are not being told what *could* happen unless certain measures are taken. The meaning is more positive and pessimistic. Given the existing social conditions ('as several more houses are nearly ready to go'), revolution is the probable if not inevitable social result. It is not surprising that this more pessimistic insight is expressed implicitly through Dickens's art, not via an explicit authorial intrusion into the narrative.

The imagery links 'the next crash in Tom-all-Alone's' to Boythorn's extreme solution to the problem of reforming Chancery. Remembering the representative nature of Chancery, remarks about Chancery reform embody a generalising suggestiveness for change of the whole system. Boythorn's solution is that

Nothing but a mine below it on a busy day in term time, with all its records, rules, and precedents collected in it, and every functionary belonging to it also, high and low, upward and downward, from its son the Accountant-General to its father the Devil, and the whole blown to atoms with 10,000 hundredweight of gunpowder, would reform it in the least! (p. 169).

What Boythorn is saying is that the only way to reform a system so corrupt as Chancery/Victorian society is by violent and total change. Partial or peaceful change is not possible. If Boythorn's statement was an isolated one in the novel and not part of a related scheme of

imagery we might regard it as typical eccentric Boythorn extremism
and receive it, as his audience does, with a laugh. However, the
common imagery emphasises its importance within the total
structure. It is the first unequivocal statement that peaceful change of
the mid-Victorian industrial system is impossible.

The same image is used to convey the special aristocratic
vulnerability to revolution. Probably the French Revolution with its
attack on aristocratic privilege was in Dickens's mind. One of the
pictures at Chesney Wold is of 'a Sir Somebody Dedlock, with a
battle, a sprung-mine, volumes of smoke, flashes of lightning, a town
on fire, and a stormed fort, all in full action between his horse's two
hind legs: showing, he supposed, how little a Dedlock made of such
trifles' (p. 588). In the days portrayed in the painting aristocratic
battlefields were abroad. But now the aristocracy is complacently
sitting on a domestic mine and indeed the novel suggests that the fuse
is already burning. The effect on the aristocracy as a class if the mine of
revolution is sprung is represented by the analogy of Sir Leicester's
personal stroke and collapse when the truth about his wife's past is
revealed by Bucket in Chapter 54, appropriately called 'Springing a
Mine'. Perhaps it is significant that Hortense, the murderer responsible for the crime which results in the shattering of Sir Leicester's
private world, is described earlier by Esther as 'some woman from the
streets of Paris in the reign of terror' (p. 373).

In addition to the suggestive image of the springing of a mine, the
most important contribution to the theme of revolution is the death
by spontaneous combustion of Krook, the pseudo-Lord Chancellor.
Dickens cited specific historical and medical evidence to defend this
incident against the criticism of G. H. Lewes. However, its real
significance lies in its symbolic suggestiveness. An analogy between
Chancery and Krook's house is clearly signposted in the novel. The
neighbours refer to Krook as the Lord Chancellor and to his shop as
Chancery. Krook himself accepts it ('There's no great odds betwixt
us, we both grub on in a muddle' (p. 101)), explaining the reasons for
his nickname — his muddled organisation and hoarding of goods that
decay and waste away, and his refusal to embrace any degree of
change or reform. Krook's house lodges Miss Flite and Nemo,
casualties of the system, and contains Krook's rapacious cat Lady Jane,
who permanently lusts after Miss Flite's caged birds and even had
designs on the newly dead body of Nemo. Like Chancery Krook's is a
microcosm, and Krook's death provides an image of a social structure
tearing itself apart from within. It is one of the most important

emblematic images in the book — and it is a revolutionary image. The language drives home the representative significance of the incident.

> Help, help, help! Come into this house for Heaven's sake! Plenty can come in but none can help. The Lord Chancellor of that Court, true to his title in his last act, has died the death of all Lord Chancellors of all Courts, and of all authorities in all places under all names soever, where false pretences are made, and where injustice is done. Call the death by any name Your Highness will, attribute it to whom you will, or say it might have been prevented how you will, it is the same death eternally — inborn, inbred, engendered in the corrupted humours of the vicious body itself, and that only — Spontaneous Combustion, and none other of all the deaths that can be died (pp. 511−12).

The social process analogous to spontaneous combustion is clearly revolution — 'inborn, inbred, engendered in the corrupted humours [i.e. Tom's] of the vicious body itself [mid-Victorian capitalism]'. The language stresses the general, universal nature of the process, one common to 'all authorities in all places under all names soever, where false pretences are made and where injustice is done'. Its relevance applies not just to the legal system, but to the political system, and the aristocratic world, with its hierarchy headed by 'Your Highness'. The crucial point is that what is being described here is an inexorable process, bound by some sort of causal law, in which spontaneous combustion (in social terms, revolution) is seen as the logical, inevitable, the ineluctable product of a general social corruption. Admittedly the details are vague and as a theory of social/historical development it is somewhat crude and unsophisticated. However, this does not alter the fact that Krook's death provides the strongest imaginative statement in the novel of the inevitable nature of revolution as the fate awaiting mid-Victorian England.

Michael Goldberg protests that in 'consigning Krook to the flames he [Dickens] is making a gesture of revolutionary impatience that is unmatched by any ideological statement to be found in his works',[3] and Arnold Kettle, after asserting that 'the spontaneous combustion image is a revolutionary image as opposed to a reformist one'[4] goes on to admit that 'though Bleak House is in this deep undeniable sense a revolutionary novel, there are no revolutionaries in it'.[5] Yet this should not surprise us. Dickens's portrayal of the mob in Barnaby Rudge and later in A Tale of Two Cities testifies to his Carlylean inspired hatred of revolutionary means. What is at work in the Krook passage is Dickens's imaginative consciousness. Krook's death is not a carefully wrought intellectual proposition put forward by a systematic or scientific political thinker. It embodies an *imaginative* insight into the nature of industrial society and it can be argued that this insight is in certain qualified respects of a Marxist nature, i.e. it sees capitalist society developing within itself the conditions which will lead to its demise. On the other hand set against this radical imaginative argument the novel also offers a moral alternative to revolution as a means of redeeming the system. The Marxist implications of the mature novels should not be emphasised at the expense of other elements within the same novels which directly contradict the revolutionary perspective.

Indeed the whole vexed question of social change involves a series of tensions and contradictions within the imaginative structure of *Bleak House*. It is clear from the Dedlock satire that there is little hope of productive change coming from the political system, dominated as it is by the influence of an aristocracy which has a vested interest in maintaining the social/political status quo. To redeem the whole system of Victorian society would need, it would seem, a miracle. In fact Esther (in a passage deleted only because of the demands of space) declares that Chancery was 'so flagrant and bad, that little short of a miracle could bring any good out of it to any one' (p. 378). The social vision of *Bleak House* then, is of the mid-Victorian system as a hostile piece of machinery, morally rotten (through permeation of market values), and on the verge of collapse (the images of the 'springing of a mine' and Krook's spontaneous combustion.) '*Bleak House* is not so much a warning to society to reform itself as a picture of a society long past the stage at which reform is still possible'.[6]

And yet few contemporary readers of *Bleak House* found the novel uncomfortable or subversive. This is because the social vision was qualified and compromised by the reassuring dual operation of two reinforcing structures — what we have called an interpretive code of middle-class values (see Chapter 3), and the closed 'happy' ending in line with contemporary novelistic conventions. The middle-class index is embodied in certain characters (Jarndyce, Esther, Woodcourt) whose experience is invested with a general social significance which, against the logic of the social vision, offers the sort of 'miracle' to save Victorian society which is needed. These elements which contradict, and to a certain extent defuse, the revolutionary implications of the novel must now be discussed at some length.

V

The 'miracle' comes in the form of a general moral change throughout society, an infusion of new values which will produce a 'hopeful change' in the general quality of social life. To a social problem a moral cure is offered. In a sense moral change (an inbred cure, a gradual spread of new values which change the quality of life from within) is a short-cut solution, the very reverse of revolution, for moral change makes change of institutions unnecessary.

The representative figure for this form of non-violent change is John Jarndyce, the only man who remains free from contamination by the suit of Jarndyce and Jarndyce. In the midst of a corrupt environment he attempts to orientate himself to the human qualities of people and to qualitative relations of use-value. We meet him mainly in Esther's narrative — and here it is very important to be aware of the distinction of tone and emphasis between Esther's first-person narrative and the third-person omniscient narrative. The brunt of the novel's *social vision* (especially the loaded descriptions of important locales — for example, Chancery, the fashionable world, and Tom's) is contained in the omniscient narrative, the tone of which (appropriately for a critical analysis of society) is consistently impersonal and objective. The tone and emphasis of Esther's narrative, however, is altogether more cheerful and optimistic, and through Esther's views and values and in the presentation of Jarndyce it reassuringly reflects middle-class values, perspectives and maxims. Against the overwhelmingly bleak background of the social vision and the omniscient narrative, Esther's narrative hopefully asserts that within a corrupt environment relations of use-value *can* be achieved in private life by selected individuals. The formal device of the double-narrative would appear to enable Dickens to have it both ways.

We have said that Esther's narrative is cosier, its implications less subversive than the omniscient narrative. There is an interesting exception, where the two narratives gell rather than collide. In her nightmare dreams when in the grip of fever Esther sees herself as a thing, a helpless, depersonalised, suffering part of a greater system. She imagines that

strung together somewhere in a great black space, there was a flaming necklace, or ring, or starry circle of some kind, of which *I* was one of the beads! And when my only prayer was to be taken off from the rest, and when it was such inexplicable agony and misery to be a part of the dreadful thing (p. 544).

This is one of the strongest images in the novel of the individual trapped in the indifferent machinery of the social system.

However, for the most part, Esther's narrative perspective is reassuring, showcasing such traditional middle-class values as hard work and duty, self-sacrifice, and housekeeping thrift and efficiency. Indeed, Esther's characteristic act is to disconcertingly jingle her housekeeping keys and to repeat merrily, 'Duty, my dear, Duty'. Jarndyce too is presented sympathetically in terms of entrepreneurial middle-class values. His career advice to Richard is an anticipation of Samuel Smiles. 'Trust in nothing but in Providence and your own efforts' (p. 232), he advises, emphasising the necessity of hard work and perseverance, and in lecturing Richard against an indecision of character, and a light-hearted, frivolous attitude towards his finances, Jarndyce reflects a middle-class approval of earnestness and responsibility (especially in money matters).

Yet within his role as an embodiment of traditional middle-class virtues there are interesting contradictions. Despite his recommendation of self-help and perseverance to Richard, Jarndyce is willing to enlist Sir Leicester's aid to smooth Richard's way and boost his career chances, and is disappointed when Sir Leicester refuses this appeal for patronage and nepotism. Jarndyce urges on Richard the importance of work, yet does no work himself. We have to assume that Jarndyce's present income was not totally inherited from his uncle but was to a considerable extent the result of past work and business success. Yet Jarndyce is defined in moral terms which makes materialistic success on society's own terms extremely improbable. Though earnestness and responsibility in money matters is urged on Richard, Jarndyce continues to indulgently tolerate Skimpole who 'artlessly' boasts of his incapacity to budget responsibly.

The social implications of Jarndyce's private charity are worth discussing at some length. It is often said that Jarndyce's private charity is the alternative to a political response to urban poverty. In fact individual philanthropy was firmly located at the centre of contemporary political theory as the most appropriate response to the problem of urban poverty.[7]

However, it was clearly a political gesture with conservative not radical implications. The philanthropist 'was expected to direct his activities so that they conformed with and if possible strengthened the existing social system'.[8]

The interesting thing about the novel's treatment of Jarndyce's philanthropy is that though in the scheme of the novel it is a moral positive, presented sympathetically, it is subjected to an implied critical comment from within the imaginative structure of the novel itself. Whenever Jarndyce meets social distress (as, for example, in Skimpole's house) 'we could not help hearing the clink of money' (p. 655). There is an ironic parallel to this in Snagsby's habit of leaving a half-crown whenever *he* encountered social distress. The consistently ironic tone applied to Snagsby's response reveals its inadequacy and serves as a comment on Jarndyce's analogous behaviour.

For example, when in the room occupied by the brickmakers' families he first encounters the appalling conditions in Tom-all-Alone's 'Mr Snagsby has to lay upon the table half-a-crown, his usual panacea for an immense variety of afflictions' (p. 368). At the bedside of the dying Jo 'Mr Snagsby, touched by the spectacle before him, immediately lays upon the table half-a-crown; that magic balsam of his for all kinds of wounds' (p. 702). Later he repeats 'that infallible remedy', and by the time he leaves there are four in the pile — 'he has never been so close to a case requiring so many' (p. 703). Now Jarndyce's charity is exactly analogous though the sums he dispenses are larger, extending to free board at Bleak House. But he can only accommodate half-a-dozen casualties in his home at St Albans and how many half-crowns will the whole corrupt system require if the individual benevolence of a Jarndyce or Snagsby is to provide effective relief? If Snagsby's response is inadequate, the significance of this touches Jarndyce too. The ironic parallel with Snagsby renders the novel's treatment of the theme more ambigous and inconsistent than is at first apparent.

There are also contradictions in Jarndyce's role as midwife for the sort of 'miracle' cure needed to redeem the system. There is little doubt that Dickens intends Jarndyce's transformation of the original Bleak House which he inherited from his great uncle, Tom Jarndyce, to be read as a metaphor for this general change. The condition of the house he inherited was much as Tom's is now. Tom's, Jarndyce admits 'is much at this day what Bleak House was then' (p. 146) and 'Although Bleak House was not in Chancery, its master was, and it was stamped with the same seal' (p. 147). The physical condition of the house as it was when Jarndyce inherited it is described:

In the meantime, the place became dilapidated, the wind whistled through the cracked walls, the rain fell through the broken roof, the weeds choked the passage to the rotting door. When I brought what remained of him home here, the brains seemed to me to have been blown out of the house too; it was so shattered and ruined (p. 146).

The rotten structure facing imminent collapse parallels the moral and social condition of mid-Victorian England as the novel's social vision presents it. But Jarndyce inherited the house and restored the ruin to healthy, vigorous life, transforming the moral climate by his own kindness and generosity, bringing to Bleak House what Esther describes as a 'hopeful change' (p. 146). This 'hopeful change' was no doubt intended as a model for the general change of heart necessary for the regeneration of the mid-Victorian system. The novel is called *Bleak House*, not *Tom-all-Alone's* – in fact many of the possible titles on the short list which Dickens considered made mention of Tom's. This choice draws attention towards the redemption of the house and implies a note of optimism. We will come back to this important metaphor later, however, for if the intended meaning is clear its objective significance moves in a different direction.

Apart from this analogy there is little detail given about the way in which this 'miracle' cure will work its effect. How will the new morality spread? It is unrealistic to expect such a change to be a sudden, all-in-a-moment phenomenon. Yet the nurturing of new moral values and their spread is only possible if individuals can retain these new values and social relationships under pressure from the wider social environment. Of course the novel asserts that although this is difficult it *can* be done – the model for such a survival is Jarndyce's ability to remain unaffected by Chancery contamination despite his involvement in the suit of Jarndyce and Jarndyce. However, the argument suffers badly here from a further series of tensions and contradictions which undermine Jarndyce's moral survival.

How is it that Jarndyce survives the suit's otherwise all-embracing corruption? Esther provides the answer. Jarndyce is successful because 'he is an uncommon character, and he has resolutely kept himself outside the circle' (p. 581). Yet earlier Jarndyce himself had said, 'We can't get out of the suit on any terms, for we are made parties to it, and *must* be parties to it, whether we like it or not' (p. 146). The whole novel emphasises the corporate nature of the system. There is no way an individual can keep himself 'outside the circle' of society. Indeed the novel argues that within the system of society there is no such thing as an isolated, self-contained private world. The effectiveness of Jarndyce's sanctuary is exposed from within the imaginative structure of the novel itself when Bleak House is penetrated by the fever, bred in the London slums, which strikes at Charley and Esther, two of the social victims Jarndyce had drawn protectively into his retreat. Of course, the charity which Jarndyce extends to selected victims of the system is itself dependent on his private fortune which was certainly not gained from being 'outside the circle of society'. If retreat to a private world is necessary for Jarndyce's moral survival this further undermines his representative role – this strategy is only a practical possibility for those few who are as economically independent as Jarndyce. Is the spread of the new morality to be confined to the rich and the handful of victims which each rescues?

If we turn once again to the metaphor of Jarndyce's transformation of Bleak House we discover a further confusion. Closer consideration reveals that the objective significance of this episode is at odds with the intended meaning. The first thing that Jarndyce did after inheriting the house was to embark on a vigorous course of structural rebuilding. The ruin was repaired and restored to functional utility. This necessarily preceded the change in moral climate. Thus the implications of Jarndyce's regeneration of Bleak House are that a system at the stage of imminent collapse must first be countered by direct structural change before a moral rebirth can be attempted. Of course, practical repair corresponds to the recommended remedy for the test-case of Tom's ('stonebreaking'), while to offer *only* a general moral change as a solution to the problems of the system is to grasp the issue in the theoretical terms Dickens rejected when considering responsibility for the continued existence of Tom's. Furthermore, direct structural rebuilding of a corrupt environment is the very thing Jarndyce rejected by his strategic retreat from Chancery to St Albans. Thus the meaning of the two analogies involving Jarndyce – the tactic of non-involvement and retreat which enabled him to escape Chancery corruption, and his positive, vigorous redemption of Bleak House – operate in completely opposite directions. The novel's contradictions are indicative of Dickens's own confusion about the problem of social change.

Of course, Jarndyce is not the only character in the novel who asserts the human value of people against their market value. There are also the Bagnets, Caddy Jellyby, Mr George. But all these characters have a childlike innocence and simplicity which may protect them like a cocoon from materialistic values but which leaves them extremely vulnerable to the Smallweeds of society. Their social survival is fragile and perilous. Caddy is duped by Mr Turveydrop after being exploited by her mother; George is manipulated by Smallweed and Tulkinghorn; and the Bagnets are merely helpless observers of the situation which threatens to bankrupt them. Furthermore these figures are not powerful enough to provide an imaginative counter to the pessimistic social vision of the novel. Thus it is to the two Bleak Houses — Jarndyce's St Albans home, and its miniature copy into which Esther and Allan Woodcourt move in Yorkshire — that we must turn for the chief representative expression of humanistic, qualitative values as a reference for social action.

Though neither of these locales provides a viable model for peaceful means of total social change they do offer abstract models of an ideal alternative society. However, neither is totally successful in realising its function.

Jarndyce's redeemed Bleak House is clearly the weakest in this respect, suffering from all the inconsistencies we have discussed in Jarndyce's role. The intention is clear enough. The roles of Jarndyce and Esther within the house are analogous to the functions of social and political institutions in an efficiently governed society. Jarndyce's role (remember he wishes to be called 'Guardian') corresponds to the protective function of the Lord Chancellor and the legal system, while Esther's role as housekeeper, responsible for orderly and efficient government within the system, corresponds to the governing function of the political system. Skimpole says of her, 'You appear to me to be the very touchstone of responsibility. When I see you, my dear Miss Summerson, intent upon the perfect working of the whole little orderly system of which you are at the centre, I feel inclined to say to myself . . . that's responsibility' (p. 587). In this sense Jarndyce and Esther are in their domestic roles ideal opposites of Chancery lawyers and aristocratic politicians. However, it is a serious flaw in the ideal nature of Bleak House that, when we first see it, it indulgently harbours Skimpole (the chief individual parasite in the novel) and is always hospitably open to the philanthropists. In addition to the other inconsistencies involving Jarndyce there is the moral irresponsibility of his east-wind fiction. This 'pretence to account for any disappointment he could not conceal, rather than he would blame the real cause of it, or disparage or depreciate any one' (pp. 130–1), is a form of moral cowardice, inconsistent with Jarndyce's protective 'Guardian' role. By indulging Skimpole Jarndyce allows him to prey on other members of society — in time

Skimpole introduces Richard to Vholes. All the contradictions in Jarndyce's role – including his curious willingness to assist Richard into taking up the law as a profession despite what he knows about Chancery – reduce the artistic integrity and coherence of Bleak House as an idealistic social microcosm.

The new Bleak House of Esther and Woodcourt is more successful, as 'a small-scale model of construction' following 'the anatomy of destructiveness',[9] yet even here the attempt is not entirely convincing. Certainly the new Bleak House does not tolerate a Skimpole or support the philanthropists. Within it there is an implied system of qualitative value which puts the market values of a Smallweed in their place, subordinated to humanistic life values. Esther admits, 'we are not rich in the bank' (p. 934), but listing the respect, affection, and love with which her husband is held in the community she adds, 'Is not this to be rich?' (p. 935). Furthermore, the new Bleak House does not imply retreat from the evils of the system. Woodcourt is no revolutionary but in contrast to Jarndyce he has a specialised job – and this job is given clear social implications which involve a direct reformist confrontation with social injustice and misery. Woodcourt is a public medical attendant for the poor in an area in the industrial north. His capacity to communicate with members of the working class stressed in his dealings with Jo implies that not only will he improve the quality of life for working men in that area but will also help to break down the 'iron barrier' between classes so apparent to Esther in the brickmaker's cottage. Woodcourt's role implies not only social relief but social control through mutual understanding. As a member of one of the newly recognised professions Woodcourt is felt to be particularly well qualified to deal with the problems of the new industrial society and hence an ideal choice for the representative man in this small-scale utopian social alternative.

The marriage of Esther and Woodcourt is to be read as the symbolic union of the doctor and the housekeeper – duty and skilled social service (Woodcourt) allied with duty, order, and responsible government (Esther, who retains the same symbolic role as she filled in the old Bleak House). However, if it is being suggested that a corrupt social system can be cured by internal doctoring of the unhealthy areas (Woodcourt) or internal spring-cleaning of the dirty parts of the structure (Esther), then this flies in the face of the imaginative logic of the novel's social vision. The systematic nature of society means that diseased parts of the structure cannot be dealt with separately as self-contained problems for local surgery. Esther and Allan do not point the way to the manner in which general change can take place – at best they make up an ideal alternative to the existing system, and thus by opposition throw into light its chief failings.

However, the social implications of Esther and Woodcourt are diluted by their marriage being incorporated into the general happy ending. The new Bleak House as a social ideal operates as an implicit criticism of existing society but it is also a cosy embodiment of the middle-class myth of the ideal home (and thus an ending consistent with the tone and implied middle-class values of Esther's whole narrative). Thus it is no surprise that Dickens's language when describing the house is altogether too cute and sentimental. The house is 'a cottage, quite a rustic cottage of doll's rooms' (p. 912), and though Woodcourt's appointment is for an economically developing area ('a thriving place . . . streams and streets, town and country, mill and moor' (p. 872)), what is strongly emphasised in the description of the house is the countrified, tranquil, idyllic surroundings, vaguely suggesting a romantic escape from the urban horrors of Tom's into the innocent, pure and natural world of the country.

Of course, Esther's marriage is just one part of a sentimental happy ending tailored to satisfy contemporary expectations. However, as is the case with most of the later novels, the ending is problematic. Dickens intervenes to produce by main force a closed happy ending out of his material. In fact he overdoes it. Not only does Sir Leicester share in the sentimental handout but there is even a tentative suggestion on the closing page that Esther's facial scars have disappeared.

The novel opened with the objective probing tone of the omniscient narrative laying bare fog-bound Chancery. It ends with Esther's narrative, her marriage, and the confident suggestion that her future domestic happiness is assured. Chancery and Tom's are forcibly pushed into the background. Not surprisingly, few critics find the ending satisfactory. Barbara Hardy points out that in a novel which tells us of society that parts cannot be separated from the whole, we can only endorse the ending by cutting it off and isolating it (as a part) from the whole structure.[10]

The real problem is that neither in tone nor content are the two narratives satisfactorily resolved. Esther's narrative is given a closed ending, which coincides with the ending of the novel as a whole thus implying that the whole structure of the novel has been satisfactorily closed. But the marriage and future happiness of Esther and Allan is not resolved with the bleak social vision contained in the omniscient narrative. Chancery and Tom's are merely ignored at the end. The omniscient narrative in fact has an implicitly open ending.

Furthermore, the experience of the hero and heroine is closed in such a way as to contradict the imaginative logic and integrity of the social vision, thus seriously weakening the artistic coherence of the novel as a whole. The social vision has depicted the essential relations of the individual and the system of industrial society. The individual is shown in tension and conflict with his society, which is often seen as an external, hostile thing. But in the close of Esther's narrative the relations between the individual and society are not felt as problematic. Dickens forcibly intervenes to suggest a spurious harmony. The closed ending to Esther's narrative implies that Esther and Allan are no longer at odds with their environment, the demands of self and community have been reconciled and they are now integrated within the society whose dominant values they have denied and opposed. Yet the position they occupy — integration without moral compromise — seems desired rather than convincingly achieved.

It is true of Dickens's later novels generally that the material — his tragic view of society — demands an open form. The closed form (tying up the social issues of the plot in conveniently tidy fashion) denies (or at least severely compromises) the problematic nature of the social world as described in the novel's social vision. The mutually reinforcing relationship between a closed ending and the middle-class value index cannot be emphasised too strongly. The successful operation of a middle-class interpretive code implies the *necessary existence* of a closed ending, to remove doubts about the future, and reward (hence legitimise and celebrate) the moral position of hero and heroine, defined in middle-class terms. The dual operation of these two imaginative structures helps to explain why novels which stand in critical opposition towards Victorian society were acceptable to a middle-class reading public. However, in so far as the Jarndyce, Esther, and Woodcourt themes are a conscious attempt to relieve the gloom of the bleak social backcloth and suggest that the system can be redeemed by a moral change of heart, this attempt is artistically unsuccessful, thematically muddled, and lacking in imaginative power (Jarndyce's 'hopeful change' lacks the imaginative power of Krook's spontaneous combustion).

Above all it goes in the face of the imaginative awareness that the quality of moral life throughout the system increasingly takes on the character of the relations of the economic sphere – an insight contained in the developed metaphor of society as a market-place in which everyday social relations take on a quantitative and mediated character. The moral life of the community in *Bleak House* is seen less in terms of abstract moral qualities than as the product of social institutions and economic forces. Yet in suggesting that a general moral change can redeem society (without change of social/economic institutions) Dickens is confusingly going back to a view of morality as independent of the environment more characteristic of his earlier fiction. The basic contradiction between a social environment in need of total change and the capacity of innocence to develop miraculously and survive in the midst of the universal corruption underlies the whole of the later fiction.

Many of these problems of unity and resolution of themes and insights – especially the tensions between the conservative and revolutionary responses to social change, and between moral optimism and social realism – will be encountered in the other novels. However, the next novel to be considered, *Little Dorrit*, embodies a particularly impressive degree of overall structural coherence making it probably Dickens's most unified and successful mature work.

5 *Little Dorrit* – Alienation and the Market

I

When Arthur Clennam, the lonely brooding hero of *Little Dorrit*, returns to London (in Chapter 3) he contemplates the city on a depressing Sunday evening in a passage which touches on many of the chief concerns of the novel. Clennam's horror at the living conditions surrounding him makes further artistic capital out of the contemporary public health issue. 'Fifty thousand lairs surrounded him where people lived so unwholesomely that fair water put into their crowded rooms on Saturday night, would be corrupt on Sunday morning' (p. 68).[1] The Thames has been polluted and contaminated by its contact with the city. 'Through the heart of the town a deadly sewer ebbed and flowed, in the place of a fine fresh river' (p. 68). Dickens is to return to this social fact of the Thames pollution as an emblem for the contamination of the industrial system in *Our Mutual Friend*. However, the novel's concern here goes beyond contemporary anxiety over public health. The quality of life experienced by the urban masses has a generalising significance for the world of the novel. The urban dwellers live in 'miles of close wells and pits of houses, where the inhabitants gasped for air' (p. 68), suggesting a claustrophobic urban environment which in its constraining and suffocating effects is explicitly seen as a prison. Clennam

> sat in the same place as the day died, looking at the dull houses opposite, and thinking, if the disembodied spirits of former inhabitants were ever conscious of them, how they must pity themselves for their old places of imprisonment (p. 770).

Of course, the image of the prison takes us to the organising crux of the novel. As most critics have emphasised the prison is the chief thematic concept in *Little Dorrit* giving a unity and coherence to the total structure of the novel in a manner similar to Chancery in *Bleak House*. Such is the obvious resonance of the prison for the world of *Little Dorrit* that for many critics a reading of the novel takes on the character of a 'spot-the-prison' contest.

Without in any way exhausting the mine of verbal references to prison and imprisonment it is possible to point to the actual prisons in the landscape of the novel (Marseilles, and the Marshalsea), places described as if they were prisons (the quarantine quarters at Marseilles where Meagles refers to the passengers as 'jail-birds'; the 'dreary red-brick dungeon at Hampton Court' where Mrs Gowan lives; the Convent of St Bernard in the Alps, which even Amy Dorrit regards as 'something like a prison') and tell-tale verbal associations of imprisonment (as in Merdle's characteristic gesture of 'clasping his wrists as if he were taking himself into custody' (p. 445)).

The prison imagery permeates every social world in the novel. It cannot be escaped from. Prison imagery constantly attends the Dorrits on their travels through Europe, culminating in a developed analogy between life in the Marshalsea and the genteel society of the Anglo-Italians which starts, 'It appeared on the whole, to Little Dorrit herself, that this same society in which they lived, greatly resembled a superior sort of Marshalsea' (p. 565). Furthermore, the prison metaphor widens in scope throughout the novel. From the single room in which the paralysed Mrs Clennam lives 'in prison, and in bonds here' it extends to the whole of life as men have made it in an industrial world. 'Far aslant across the city, over its jumbled roofs, and through the open tracery of its church towers, struck the long bright rays, bars of the prison of this lower world' (p. 831). The novel is to explore the possibilities of living in a social environment seen as generally imprisoning and yet, as an individual, escaping its taint and achieving authentic and fulfilling social relationships.

Yet to leave the discussion of the prison with the bare assertion that in *Little Dorrit* Dickens portrays mid-Victorian England as a huge prison is to beg a series of important questions – both sociological and artistic. How meaningful is the remark that industrial society is a prison – a trite generalisation or a penetrating social insight? It is clearly part of the novel's concern to depict a social environment which constrains and suffocates personal will and individuality. Clennam's remark to Meagles at the beginning of the book, 'I have no will. That is to say . . . next to none that I can put in action now' (p. 59) could well be applied to the whole social world of the novel, for of all Dickens's books *Little Dorrit* is the one in which action is most passive and control of destiny most minimal. We see individuality stifled in all the social worlds of the novel – in business (Clennam's own history and Pancks's official life), in High Society (under the guidance of Mrs General), Bleeding Heart Yard, the Circumlocution Office – and so on. However, the concept of society as a prison implies a completely deterministic structure and the prison of the will in the novel is not complete. This is the whole point of Amy Dorrit's role. The prison tendencies of the system may be overwhelming but they never totally deny the will or freedom of the individual. If society is a prison then it appears that some people (admittedly very few) are not subject to its overmastering authority.

Another problem arising from the prison emblem is that when a social or economic historian thinks of mid-Victorian capitalism he does not think of a prison but of a system bourgeoning and expanding in a confident and aggressive fashion. However, in the novel Dickens is not primarily concerned with the surface prosperity or material well-being of the system. He is concerned with the general quality of life, with a general condition and the possibilities of fulfilment within it, and these cannot be determined by statistics of economic growth.

However, the most important thing about the prison analogy is what artistic use is made of it. In fact seeing society whole as a prison has many benefits for the organisation of the novel and the successful realisation of other deeper, more interesting social insights, and these benefits exist independently of the strength of the prison idea as a value-judgement about society. In particular the prison emblem is a device which aids the novelist in conveying the spiritually impoverishing effects on the individual of the alienation and isolation which the novel sees as characteristic of developing industrial society. The effects of living in a crowded world, cut off from others and defensively turning inwards to embrace reassuring fictions is seen in the novel as the equivalent of being in solitary confinement in prison.

Alienation is strongly linked in the novel to feelings of isolation and separateness. Critics have commented on the pervasive feeling of loneliness in the novel. Arthur Clennam is Dickens's most lonely, self-communing, and passive hero. On returning to London at the beginning of the novel he 'could not have felt more depressed and cast away if he had been in a wilderness' (p. 203). A sense of isolation within a crowded city takes many forms in the novel, and is present even in the concluding paragraph of the qualified 'happy' ending. For most of the novel Amy Dorrit's condition parallels that of Clennam's – lonely in her unexpressed love for Clennam and resigned to its failure she travels unhappily throughout Europe in an unreal existence which offers no pleasure. Pancks's eccentricity cannot prevent him from being alienated by his work as Casby's Grinder, and Flora's bizarre, if individualistic, language cuts her off from meaningful communication with others so that she lives in her own solitary universe, like the pathetic Frederick Dorrit, who exists almost on the verge of non-being, and Affery in her separate world of waking dreams (she exists in a 'ghostly, dreamy, sleep-walking state'). Even in the midst of the feasts given in his honour Merdle walks his own separate and joyless way, obsessed with his 'medical' complaint and frightened by his Chief Butler. His role in this anonymous world, surrounded by unnamed persons with trade/professional titles, is passive and solitary.

The most interesting way in which *Little Dorrit* reflects a general alienation is through the manner in which almost all the characters in the novel wilfully assert myths and fictions about themselves, their social position, or about the nature of social reality itself in order to bring justification, meaning, or consolation to their life. The point is that people who are alienated from their environment need illusions (sometimes harmless, sometimes damaging) to live by. This need to turn away from painful reality into a self-created fiction is a direct response to the alienating nature of the system. (Life in a prison can only be acceptable if the prison nature of reality is obscured or distorted by a strategic use of fictions.) Thus the concept of the prison informs the experience of most of the individuals within the novel – another example of method of characterisation being tied up with a controlling and critical way of seeing society. The richness of this theme in the novel is one of the undisputed artistic benefits of the prison emblem.

This use of reassuring or comforting myths is itself a form of voluntary imprisonment. Thus in an impressive variety of ways the characters in the novel offer an image of their society. Mrs Clennam's world view in which she has a duty to be God's instrument of punishment for sin legitimises her spite and vindictiveness. Pancks, alienated in his official life, needs his fiction of the 'Whole Duty of Man in a commercial country' which reduces all life to a mechanical performance of business tasks to justify his continued existence as Casby's Grinder. William Dorrit in the Marshalsea utilises 'the miserably ragged old fiction of the family gentility' and cannot live outside the protective walls of his self-image of being Father of the Marshalsea. Indeed the social outcasts of the Marshalsea Prison in general conspire to honour the myth that the Marshalsea is a place of rest and true freedom. Clennam believes his own suffocating conviction that he is too old for love, 'an older man, who had done with that tender part of life' (p. 432). Mrs Gowan needs to assert the fiction that her son's infatuation with Pet Meagles is the result of the machinations of the girl's parents.

Some forms of self-deception in the novel are comparatively harmless, like Meagles's image of himself as a 'practical man'. On the other hand, Miss Wade's neurotic suspicion that everybody wishes to patronisingly taunt her with knowledge of her illegitimacy is also perversely a source of pain and torment to herself. The paranoia of Miss Wade's 'History of a Self-Tormenter' is not merely an excellent case-book of an individual neurosis but is a typical product of an alienating social system – she too cannot bear to see society as it is. The courage of Clennam's position at the end of the book – he sees society as it is without abandoning the search for authentic relations or capitulating to society's values – must be seen against the failure of other characters (almost universal in the novel, for even Amy Dorrit carries with her a false image of her 'father as he was') to confront the nature of social reality and their position in it with honesty and realism. *Little Dorrit*'s characteristic turning from reality into comforting fiction is an integral part of the novel's social criticism – within the structure of *Little Dorrit* the social vision and the method of characterisation are organically related through the prison emblem.

This must be remembered in view of criticism that the prison symbol in *Little Dorrit* is 'thinly intellectual, more obviously worked out',[2] and offers an excessive evidence of authorial design (Barbara Hardy talks about the 'tiring explicitness').[3] We must balance this by recognising that the prison motif acts as midwife for many of the richest elements of the social vision and promotes an impressive overall degree of artistic control and coherence.

The concentration of critical interest on the prison is particularly unfortunate in that the strength and depth of the novel derive from the fact that the material is organised in a variety of ways which overlap. And in the relation between these organising principles – the prison, surfaces, the Circumlocution Office, the market, manners, and mechanism – lies the key to the understanding of the novel's meaning. What *Little Dorrit* tells us about society is too complex and sociologically interesting to be satisfactorily reduced to the unquali- fied critical tag 'Society is a prison'.

The relation between the prison and the Circumlocution Office is particularly important. The Circumlocution Office, as was discussed in Chapter 1, is the novel's institutional emblem for the nature of the system. It is an inhuman piece of machinery, hostile to the individuals who apply to it for aid ('troublesome convicts who were under sentence to be broken alive on that wheel' (p. 596)). Its running parts have been clogged up with red tape but it still grinds on, out of control. It is a Frankenstein monster with a mind of its own; an external social force which constrains the individuals who have created it to serve their interests. Unlike the rather vague concept of the prison the Circumlocution Office is given a lot of concrete detail. We see it provoking the anger of Meagles, frustrating the individual aspirations and talents of Doyce, resisting the attempts of Clennam to make sense of its structure and impose some direction over its wayward machinery.

Indeed, an integral part of the mature novels' social criticism and repudiation of the industrial system is the portrayal of life lapsing into mechanism. This is especially true of *Little Dorrit*. The Circumlocution Office, the representative social institution in the novel, 'went on mechanically, every day'. Panck's official identity is consistently described as that of 'a little labouring steam-engine', while Rugg refers to himself in conversation with Clennam as 'a professional machine'. Within fashionable, genteel society a mechanical life is induced by the operation of the inflexible code of manners, represented by Mrs General, a lady 'whose manner was perfect, considered as a piece of machinery'. Within Mrs Clennam's house Flintwinch's presence is brought to bear on its paralysed owner 'daily like some eccentric mechanical force'. Indeed, the quality of life within the house is that of a mechanical existence. 'Morning, noon, and night, morning, noon, and night, each recurring with its accompanying monotony, always the same reluctant return of the same sequences of machinery, like a dragging piece of clockwork' (pp. 387–8). In the description of Casby's house the repetition of the word 'ticking' (applied to a clock, a bird, the parlour fire, and Casby's watch and eyebrows) suggests that the house is one large clockwork mechanism the component parts of which (both people and things) function in synchronised fashion. Even Baptist is regarded in Bleeding Heart Yard as if he was 'a mechanical toy'.

Concentration on the prison motif has also deflected attention away from an equally important element within *Little Dorrit*'s critical evaluation of social life – the analogy between society and the market-place, which must be discussed at some length.

II

Social relations in every sphere, including friendship and marriage, are encompassed within the principles of economic marketing. Individuals characteristically try to promote a socially valued image of themselves in order to gain status or material advantage, (as if they were economic goods to be labelled, advertised, and profitably sold). Skimpole and Turveydrop did this in *Bleak House* but the tactic is general within the social world of *Little Dorrit*.

Gowan cynically admits to Arthur Clennam that in his painting he is an imposer ('Buy one of my pictures, and I assure you in confidence, it will not be worth the money' (p. 358)) but he legitimises this by maintaining that his behaviour is general throughout society. 'They all do it. . . . Painters, writers, patriots, all the rest who have stands in the market' (p. 358). Though Gowan's cynicism is presented unsympathetically there is no doubt that it is an accurate representation of the social world of the novel. For example, Gowan's belief 'So great the success, so great the imposition' (p. 358) is true of Merdle, as well as Casby and William Dorrit. Rigaud openly admits his stand in the market and he too asserts that this is a general strategy. He tells Clennam in the Marshalsea,

I sell anything that commands a price. How do your lawyers live, your politicians, your intriguers, your men of the Exchange? How do you live? How do you come here? Have you sold no friend? . . . Effectively, sir, . . . Society sells itself and sells me: and I sell Society (p. 818).

William Dorrit's stand in the market is an attempt (for the most part successful) to promote an image of himself as Patriarch or Father to the other Marshalsea prisoners whom he views in an implicitly mercenary light as potential sources of testimonials. He is even willing to pervert his relation with Amy into an economic proposition by encouraging her to receive John Chivery's amorous attentions in order that the special privileges and perks he enjoys from the Chief Turnkey, John's father, might not be lost.

Casby's stand in the market is defined by Pancks. 'What do you pretend to be? . . . What's your moral game? What do you go in for? Benevolence, an't it?' (p. 869). Under his benevolent mask Casby's values are 'Bargain and sale, bless you! Fixed Principles!' (p. 871). The nature of Casby's deceit is conveyed significantly through a metaphor

of false advertising in a commercial or business enterprise. Arthur
Clennam remembers rumours that 'Christopher Casby was a mere
Inn signpost without any Inn — an invitation to rest and be thankful,
when there was no place to put up at, and nothing whatever to be
thankful for' (p. 190). When Pancks unmasks Casby he takes up this
analogy.

> Why! The worst-looking cheat in all this town who gets the value
> of eighteenpence under false pretences, ain't half such a cheat as this
> sign-post of The Casby's Head here! . . . It's a mighty fine sign-
> post, is The Casby's Head, . . . but the real name of the House is
> the Sham's Arms (pp. 870—1).

This is related to the theme of surfaces, another important strand in
the novel's fabric. Certainly given the way mid-Victorian England is
presented in the novel, the 'Sham's Arms' is a representative signpost
for the whole country, as appropriate as the fact that the crime of
Merdle, representative hero of his time, is fraud.

If Gowan, Rigaud, William Dorrit, and Casby are individuals who
have stands in the market, then the Barnacles as a family have a class
stand in the market through their privileged monopoly of the
Circumlocution Office. The Barnacles practise the art of government
for what they can get out of it. On an individual level they gain
sinecure positions, and as a class they use their political influence to
help maintain the aristocracy's privileged social position. Ferdinand
Barnacle 'fully understood the Department to be a politico —
diplomatic hocus pocus piece of machinery for the assistance of the
nobs in keeping off the snobs' (pp. 157—8). It is not too much to say
that the Barnacles speculate in government for aristocratic survival.

Mrs Clennam has a stand in the market both as partner in the
family business firm and through her religion. Her house is permeated
by market values. In direct contrast to the Victorian middle-class ideal
of home as a refuge from the business world her house is both a
private home *and* a business office, the centre from which the
operations of the family firm are directed. Her harsh business
orientation to life is reflected in the economic and materialistic spirit
of her religion, which illustrates Weber's famous link between
Protestantism and capitalism. In a development of the case of
Chadband (*Bleak House*) her religion is a form of profit and loss book-
keeping. She 'was always balancing her bargains with the Majesty of
heaven, posting up the entries to her credit, strictly keeping her set-

off, and claiming her due' (p. 89). Clennam himself says of his parents, 'Their very religion was a gloomy sacrifice of tastes and sympathies that were never their own, offered up as a part of a bargain for the security of their possessions' (p. 59). In attacking Mrs Clennam's brand of religion Dickens was pointing in particular to a middle-class phenomenon. 'By the 1850s the Economic Evangelicalism of 1830 has become essentially a middle class point of view'.[4] However, Dickens probably felt that in a commercial society all types of religion will tend to this adulterated form, for he signposts the general relevance of Mrs Clennam's religious book-keeping. 'Thousands upon thousands do it, according to their varying manner, every day' (p. 89).

In a manner similar to Old Smallweed in *Bleak House* Pancks gives articulate expression to the business/money ethos which Mrs Clennam has adhered to under the religious guise of evangelicalism. 'Take all you can get, and keep back all you can't be forced to give up. That's business' (p. 324) asserts Pancks. Like Smallweed Pancks denies the imaginative life. When Clennam asks him if he reads, Pancks replies, 'Never read anything but letters and accounts' (p. 202). The only taste or inclination Pancks will admit to would have been approved by Smallweed too. 'I have an inclination to get money, sir . . . if you will show me how' (p. 202). Pancks's commitment to such a view has left him a hollow man whose life is a stiff mechanical performance of a daily business round. 'I am a man of business. What business have I in this present world, except to stick to business? No business' (p. 322). A contemporary version of the celebrated seventeenth-century devotional pamphlet 'The Whole Duty of Man' put forward unironically by the official Pancks in conversation with Clennam reveals the extent to which the dominant business/market mentality has influenced the quality of everyday life in mid-Victorian industrial England.

'But I like business', said Pancks, getting on a little faster. 'What's a man made for?'
    'For nothing else?' said Clennam.

Pancks's reply has a generalising significance:

'What else? . . . What else do you suppose I think I'm made for? Nothing. Rattle me out of bed, set me going, give me as short a time as you like to bolt my meals in, and keep me at it. Keep me always at it, and I'll keep you always at it, you keep somebody else always at it. There you are with the Whole Duty of Man in a commercial country.' (pp. 201−2).

Duty has become secularised. The primary aim in life is not individual salvation but business success. Work is seen not as a means of achieving grace but as a means of creating wealth and attaining social respectability. The philosophy of Pancks, Casby's Grinder, corresponds to the real experience of the majority of the urban working population. While Pancks sadly admits, 'What has my life been? Fag and grind, fag and grind, turn the wheel, turn the wheel' (pp. 870−1), the tenants of Bleeding Heart Yard appeal to Pancks on a different occasion, 'Poor as you see us, master, we're always grinding, drudging, toiling, every minute we're awake' (p. 202). Clennam too admits that his whole business life abroad was 'always grinding in a mill I always hated' (p. 59). In addition, in the description of the City by night (Book II, Chapter 10) discussed in Chapter 2 of this book, the whole working population of the City is described as 'dispersed grinders in the vast mill' (p. 596). The majority of the working population, whether manual workers like Plornish or clerical officials like Pancks, are a species of toiler or 'grinder' in the social mill − creating wealth but being themselves ground in the process. The mill is one of Dickens's favourite images in the later novels for the destructive machinery of the system. In his official existence Pancks is a mechanical part of a greater machine. His humanity has been perverted into a slavish, unfulfilling robot existence, and the imagery of machinery is constantly applied to him (even his speech is a form of 'mechanical revolvancy').

However, though in his official capacity as Casby's grubber, Pancks gives explicit articulation to the business/money ethos, in his private life he attempts to realise his latent humanity by researching into unclaimed inheritances so that, in effect, he can give money away. 'I belong body and soul to my proprietor. . . . But I do a little in the other way, sometimes; privately, very privately, Miss Dorrit' (p. 334). On the night when he has completed his case on the Dorrit inheritance we see Pancks playing leap-frog with Rugg (another 'professional machine' in his official life) in the Marshalsea yard, the first time Pancks breaks out of his straitjacket of mechanical behaviour and reveals the energy of natural, spontaneous life.

Of course, Pancks is a first draft for Wemmick (*Great Expectations*) but he also develops the contrast between Mr Bucket's private affability and companionship, and the impersonal, scientific methods of procedure he rigorously follows in his official role as police detective (a role which, because he is an agent of a corrupt system, involves him in such acts as harassing destitute children such as Jo). Mr Bucket is Dickens's first study of the split-man.

Max Weber has described the necessary separation of private and official life attendant on the bureaucratic process. This process, being the best fit with the needs of industrial society, was spreading in the mid-Victorian period to influence the working lives of an increasing number of people. One of the possible consequences of this separation was the growth of two distinct identities and personalities, and the division of life into two unreconciled spheres, each governed by opposing sets of values and norms of behaviour. Dickens's later novels provide one of the first literary dramatisations of this social process, and consistently point to the human loss involved.

However, as we shall see when discussing the ending of the novel, the spiritually denying opposition of Pancks's private and official selves is resolved in a rather artificial and unsatisfactory manner.

Of course, Pancks's advice to Casby, 'What you want is a good investment and a quick return' (p. 198), is applicable in all of the social worlds in the novel, not just the business sphere. For example, in fashionable genteel society marriage is a form of speculation in people. Mrs Merdle, who is described as if she were 'thinged' into her bosom, was purchased by Mr Merdle as an object of decorative value, for ostentatious display. 'It was not a bosom to repose upon, but it was a capital bosom to hang jewels upon. Mr Merdle wanted something to hang jewels upon, and he bought it for the purpose' (p. 293). Mrs Merdle herself is regarded as the best authority on Society and its expectations, and knows that in genteel society marriage is an economic investment.

> As to marriage on the part of a man, my dear, Society requires that he should retrieve his fortunes by marriage. Society requires that he should gain by marriage. Society requires that he should found a handsome establishment by marriage. Society does not see, otherwise, what he has to do with marriage (p. 441).

If the analogy with the market is implicit here it is later made explicit. Mrs Merdle

> knew what Society's mothers were, and what Society's daughters

were, and what Society's matrimonial market was, and how prices ruled in it, and what scheming and counter-scheming took place for the high buyers, and what bargaining and huckstering went on (p. 444).

In considering the market nature of society we must return to Gowan. In mid-Victorian England art has become, it would seem, merely another commercial activity like the buying and selling of Merdle's shares. Gowan only recognises the quantitative value of his work. 'But what I do in my trade, I do to sell. What all we fellows do, we do to sell. If we didn't want to sell it for the most we can get for it, we shouldn't do it' (p. 453). To Gowan art is a commodity. Though in its critical stance towards Gowan the novel implicitly proposes an exalted view of literature as a vocation it is well to remember that despite his elevated view of his own position as literary artist Dickens himself had a self-conscious stand in the literary market of the day (see Chapter 3). He too wrote to be read, and this has a crucial influence on the nature of his work.

The concept of the market is tied up in the structure of the novel with the prison emblem. It is through stock-market speculation that both William Dorrit and Clennam end up in the Marshalsea. Of course, the adulteration of everyday social relations by market values is one of the chief spiritually imprisoning forces in society. But the market and the prison are also linked through crime. The business dealings of both Mrs Clennam and Merdle involve them in crime. Mrs Clennam's suppression of the will involves her, in Rigaud's words, with 'the stolen money', while Merdle's whole business empire is founded on criminal fraud. Merdle is representative of the change in the economic climate which had taken place by the 1850s. The individual owner/manager of the small independent business had given way to the corporate capitalism (and the large-scale joint-stock companies) represented by Merdle. In the early novels (as House has pointed out) the representative 'bad businessman' tended to be the usurer, who was opposed by the ideal firm, representative of 'clean' capitalism, or capitalism with a heart – the small business firm where relations between employer and workers were personal and paternalistic (e.g. the Cheeryble brothers in *Nicholas Nickleby*). In the later novels, however, the representative bad businessman is the remotely directing capitalist or financier, and the speculator who plays the market. What is interesting is that he is still opposed by the ideal firm in the form of a small independent owner/manager concern, represented in *Little Dorrit* by the firm of Doyce and Clennam, a throwback to an earlier entrepreneurial stage of capitalism.

III

The novel's treatment of manners and class (like the creation of Merdle) is rooted in the Victorian social experience of the 1850s. To most contemporaries the system appeared to be becoming more fluid and offering greater opportunities for individual upward mobility, though in a certain sense it was also hardening – the something which made a man a gentleman was more than ever sought after and more highly prized.

The problem of social definition, and the difficulty of an individual being certain of where he stood in the class system (and of how others regarded him) is one of the chief themes in the later novels – from the gallery of characters concerned with social definition in *Little Dorrit*, through Pip's experience in *Great Expectations*, to Bradley Headstone and Charley Hexam in *Our Mutual Friend*. Their predicament belongs peculiarly to the mid-Victorian period. It was during this time (and not in the 1840s) that the great Victorian debate about gentility and snobbery was vigorously, and at times paranoically, engaged through journalism, novels, and general conversation. Most of the chief social concerns of the mature work surface in the debate on gentility which is imaginatively engaged throughout the later novels.

Of course, all social aspirers must understand the nuances of the surface manifestations of class if their claims for a higher status are to be successful. The satire on the High Society of the Merdles, Mrs Gowan, and Mrs General focuses on these surface manifestations of gentility, their value and their strategic use. The utilisation of manners in a time of widespread social mobility cuts both ways. Social climbing depends on the award of social acceptance from those above. Thus the would-be riser will adopt the mannered surfaces and consumption patterns of the higher status group as a means to subsequent acceptance. An individual must appear to belong – to have the correct social credentials – before he will be generally accepted as belonging (Veneering's tactic in *Our Mutual Friend*). Dickens says of Casby 'in the great social Exhibition, accessories are often accepted in lieu of the internal character' (p. 191) and the application is general to the world of the novel. In contrast to this aggressive individualistic use, manners and snobbery can also be utilised as a defensive mechanism by a higher status group to keep social climbers in their place.

An example of both uses of manners is provided by Rigaud. He asserts his claim to gentility ('A gentleman I am! And a gentleman I'll live, and a gentleman I'll die!' (p. 47)) in order to mix on terms of social equality within fashionable society. But he also exploits genteel surfaces to socially intimidate Baptist as Turveydrop does to his son in *Bleak House*. The power of genteel surfaces is illustrated in the opening scene of the novel. Rigaud's self-confident promotion of his gentlemanly status overcomes Baptist's natural repugnance and the latter acts as his servant.

The manipulation of genteel forms as a means of social acceptance is illustrated by a whole gallery of characters, none of whom can define his place in society with certainty or confidence. All aspire to gentility though they define this in different ways. Merdle has money and a reputation as a financier and speculator with the golden touch, but his appearance is described on various occasions as 'common' and his lack of urbane charm or sparkling manners is total. His response to this social situation was a typical bourgeois strategy. To counter aristocratic disdain for business as low and vulgar he made a strategic marriage with the socially expert Mrs Merdle. Her contribution to her husband's acceptance by fashionable society is clear from his remark, 'You supply manner, and I supply money' (p. 447).

Gowan's social position is also ambiguous. He stands uneasily on the borderline between two classes – a professional artist with a blood connection with the Barnacles. Though economically dependent on his income from painting, his cynical devaluation of artistic merit and his disparagement of his fellow-professionals separates him from them. This separation is reinforced by his stress on his own birth and his mocking claim that he is more of an amateur than a professional, which touches on the traditional aristocratic acceptance of art as an amateur pastime but not as a necessary means to a living. Thus Gowan attempts to maintain an uneasy and contradictory social position by appealing to his fashionable patrons in a manner which conceals and distorts his essential relation of economic dependence. 'I have not quite got all the Amateur out of me yet . . . and can't fall on to order, in a hurry, for the mere sake of sixpences' (p. 562). To Rigaud a total refusal to sully himself by manual work of any kind, and an exaggerated gallantry towards women, are the distinguishing marks of a gentleman. Though in fashionable society he is suspected of not being what he claims through the characteristically tasteless excess of his protestations of chivalry towards women he is never directly challenged. The success of his imposition is also reflected in the willingness of social inferiors to defer to him. 'Swagger and an air of authorised condescension do so much, that Mr Flintwinch had already begun to think this a highly gentlemanly personage' (p. 400).

William Dorrit in the Marshalsea, not unlike Gowan, asserts his gentlemanly status in direct proportion of the extent that he is economically dependent on others. The Dorrits systematically produced 'the family skeleton for the overawing of the College' beginning 'at about the period when they began to dine on the College charity' (p. 277). Of course, when released Dorrit is able to emulate Merdle in gaining social acceptance through his money and his acquisition of Mrs General. Associating the family with Mrs General's unimpeachable social qualifications as master of the proprieties is an equivalent strategy to Merdle's marriage and takes the vulgar gloss off Dorrit's money.

Before considering the defensive use of manners by fashionable society in Little Dorrit, it should be recognised that although the fusion of aristocratic birth and bourgeois money produced a blurred social grouping it is aristocratic values which are in the ascendance in this alliance.

In a sense Merdle's elevated position is a triumph for money power over birth but on the level of values aristocratic repugnance to business still operates. Mrs Merdle tells her husband, 'There is a positive vulgarity in carrying your business affairs about with you as you do' (p. 447), and the business origins of Merdle's wealth have to be patriotically distorted and elevated into the character of national benefits before they are acceptable. (Merdle's 'immense' undertakings 'bring him in such vast sums of money that they are regarded as — hum — national benefits' (p. 537).) The incident of Merdle's suicide is particularly revealing. It smacks too much of middle-class earnestness to be consistent with good taste. Earlier Mrs Merdle had encouraged her husband to 'care about nothing — or seem to care about nothing — as everybody else does' (p. 447). The Chief Butler is so disgusted with Merdle's 'low' death, incompatible with aristocratic boredom and indifference, that he resigns his post, remarking significantly, 'Sir, Mr Merdle never was the gentleman, and no ungentlemanly act on Mr Merdle's part would surprise me' (p. 774).

In considering the function of manners in this group the representative character is Mrs General. The mannered code as applied in High Society both distorts the nature of reality and dehumanises individuals by inducing a frozen and fastidious indifference. When in the grip of Mrs General's surfaces Amy Dorrit's capacity to be of use and help to others ceases to exist, and when she looks sympathetically at vagrants she is told, 'They should not be looked at. Nothing disagreeable should ever be looked at' (p. 530). Apart from the inhumanity of this advice, it reflects a wilful desire to distort the nature of the class realities of Victorian society. It is against this refusal to recognise the existence of Tom's or Bleeding Heart Yard that the social interconnections of the later novels are emphasised. The operation of the mannered code also substitutes a mechanical reflection of received opinions in place of individual thought. 'Mrs General had no opinions. Her way of forming a mind was to prevent it from forming opinions' (p. 503). It is significant that through Mrs General 'whose manner was perfect, considered as a piece of machinery' (p. 486) the mannered code is associated with a mechanical form of life. This imaginative and intellectual imprisonment of thought and will implicit in Mrs General's surfaces connects the world of High Society with the prison motif.

This relation is made explicit by Little Dorrit herself but her articulation of the connection is superfluous. Quite apart from the fact that throughout the Dorrits' European sojourn in genteel society prison imagery surrounds them, recognition of an essential similarity between fashionable society and the Marshalsea is implicit in the presentation of the latter. The Marshalsea, like the greater society outside its walls, contains a class hierarchy within which snobbery and patronage operate. There is just as much concern for social definition within the prison as outside it. In the prison yard there is an 'aristocratic or Pump side' where Mr Dorrit walks, occasionally crossing to the poor side (where there are no pretensions of gentility) to magnanimously bless the young children. Indeed Mr Dorrit's relations to the other prisoners, and in particular old Nandy, are an ironic parody of aristocratic privilege and patronage in mid-Victorian England. 'Mr Dorrit was in the habit of receiving this old man [i.e. Nandy] as if the old man held of him in vassalage under some feudal tenure' (p. 415). Within the Marshalsea, as in Mrs General's world, manners are used by Mr Dorrit to distort reality, in particular the economic obligations involved in the Testimonial question, which is made an opportunity for display of gentlemanly sensitivity and good breeding on the part of the giver. Clennam's refusal to give anything, following his promise to Little Dorrit, condemns him in point of

gentlemanly delicacy. 'His [i.e. Clennam's] obtuseness on the great
Testimonial question was . . . regarded as a positive shortcoming in
point of gentlemanly feeling' (p. 300). Indeed so clear is the parallel
between the social rituals embodied in Dorrit's role as Father of the
Marshalsea and the equally empty rituals of fashionable society – so
strong is the irony when Dorrit switches to his former role during
Mrs Merdle's dinner – that there is no need for the explicit
underlining of the analogy in Book ii, Chapter 7.

In *Little Dorrit* we see the mannered code being used by the
fashionable world *as a group* to maintain social distance and keep the
groups pressing from below in their place. To handle and manipulate
the code it is necessary to have a conscious state of initiation through
informal socialisation and specialised education. Meagles, for
example, representative of the respectable middle classes, admits to
Mrs Gowan that he cannot utilise the code of what he calls 'genteel
mystifications' with her skill and aplomb. Rigaud's exaggerated
aping of genteel manners fails to convince the experienced observer
because of its characteristic excess. It is not too much to argue that the
aristocracy's success in maintaining the high social valuation of these
forms which *as a class* they were uniquely well qualified to utilise and
in asserting these defensively *as a class* was a crucial factor in
aristocratic social survival as a privileged group. Ferdinand Barnacle
explained Merdle's success to Clennam in these terms,

> Pardon me, but I think you really have no idea how the human
> bees will swarm to the beating of any old tin kettle; in that fact lies
> the complete manual of governing them. When they can be got to
> believe that the kettle is made of the precious metals in that fact lies
> the whole power of men like our late lamented (p. 806).

He might as well have been talking of Rigaud, or William Dorrit in
the Marshalsea, or Casby etc. And certainly his words are relevant for
aristocratic survival. Consider the case of the Barnacles. Society
accepts their surfaces and forms at the aristocratic valuation of
'precious metals'. This is true, for example, of Meagles who as a
retired businessman might be expected to assert a counter set of
middle-class values in opposition to aristocratic manners. However,
he is so far from doing this, that, despite his personal experience of the
inefficiency of the Circumlocution Office, staffed by the Barnacle
family, he glories in the grand Barnacle company round his dinner
table when he marries Pet to Gowan, a man he suspects of being a
scoundrel. His snobbery is clearly meant to be read as typical of the

middle classes (Clennam observes that 'his good friend [i.e. Meagles] had a weakness which none of us need go into the next street to find' (p. 248)), and this snobbery helps to prop up the Barnacles' privileged position.

Of course, the working class as a group is even less qualified through socialisation and education to manipulate the learnt forms of genteel society. Yet they too accept them at their aristocratic valuation. Indeed the inhabitants of Bleeding Heart Yard accept the values of fashionable society for all the world as if they were pupils of Mrs General. It is worth remembering that within the Marshalsea the myth of William Dorrit's gentility originates in the turnkey's admiration of Dorrit's genteel accomplishments – he speaks foreign languages (a factor Magwitch was later to admire in Pip) and can play the piano. To Plornish it is a mark of William Dorrit's social greatness that his family must hide from him the knowledge that they work for a living. When news of Merdle's wealth penetrates Bleeding Heart Yard, instead of inspiring social resentment or frustration, or even awareness of relative deprivation, it is enjoyed vicariously by the inhabitants who vie with each other to exaggerate the size of his fortune. Indeed Merdle is lionised as much in Bleeding Heart Yard as in High Society, and his wealth is ironically a source of comfort to the grinders who live in the former. Clearly Bleeding Heart Yard is under the ideological control of the dominant social classes. There is no evidence of an emerging working-class social or political consciousness.

None of Dickens's good working-class characters ever threatens the political status quo. Plornish, for example, is politically passive and apathetic. His consciousness that something is wrong in society inspires only a dull puzzlement, in the best traditions of Stephen Blackpool.

> As to who was to blame for it, Mr Plornish didn't know who was to blame for it. He could tell you who suffered, but he couldn't tell you whose fault it was. It wasn't his place to find out, and who'd mind what he said, if he did find out? He only know'd that it wasn't put right by them what undertook that line of business, and that it didn't come right of itself (p. 184).

In place of a political response there is a cheerful stoicism – 'there was ups you see, and there was downs. It was in vain to ask why ups, why downs; there they was you know' (p. 799). The social forces which pressurise him cannot be understood or controlled. They have to be accepted and borne. Even when Plornish growls he does so 'in a prolix, gently-growling, foolish way'. And yet paradoxically this political passivity and apathy worried contemporaries. In a letter to Austen Layard in 1855 Dickens warned:

> There is nothing in the present time at once so galling to me as the alienation of the people from their own public affairs. . . . And I believe the discontent to be so much worse for smouldering, instead of blazing openly, that it is extremely like the general mind of France before the breaking out of the first Revolution, and is in danger of being turned by any one of a thousand accidents . . . into such a devil of a conflagration as never has been beheld since.

A social historian might protest that a general alienation from public affairs is not an historically accurate summary of working-class political life during the period, and point to the development of trade unions and co-operative societies. He might also assert that Chartism had helped to forge a greater degree of working-class class conscious-ness than is evident in Bleeding Heart Yard. Furthermore, these historical inaccuracies are combined with a basic contradiction in the presentation of the working class in the novel — their problematic identity as politically passive and yet a revolutionary danger.

Explicit warnings to act before it is too late, often authorial intrusions thrust into the narrative, are common to most of the later novels. For example, in *Hard Times* the fact-finding utilitarians had been sternly told 'in the day of your triumph, when romance is utterly driven out of their souls, and they [i.e. the Coketown hands] and a bare existence stand face to face, Reality will take a wolfish turn, and make an end of you' (p. 192). The only suggestion in *Little Dorrit* that the cap-doffing of the Plornishes might lead to stone-throwing is a description of destitute children in Covent Garden (Miserable children in rags . . . like young rats, slunk and hid, fed on offal, huddled together for warmth, and were hunted about') which carries the postscript, 'look to the rats young and old, all ye Barnacles, for before God they are eating away our foundations, and will bring the roofs on our heads!' (p.208). This directly relates to the collapse of the rotten foundations of Mrs Clennam's house (an episode which will be discussed later) as well as to Miss Wade's remark during quarantine conversation at Marseilles, 'If I had been shut up in any place to pine and suffer, I should always hate that place and wish to burn it down, or raze it to the ground' (p. 61). The urban masses of London had been explicitly described in Chapter 3 as living in 'places of imprisonment' from which there is 'no escape between the cradle and the grave'. But will the inhabitants of Bleeding Heart Yard ever fully recognise the imprisoning nature of their environment while they continue to defer ideologically to genteel society? In the treatment of the working class in *Little Dorrit* there does seem a confusion and lack of resolution between their *actual* character (passive, docile, deferential, and non-political) and their *latent* character as destructive agents of revolutuon, which corresponds to the great Victorian nightmare (most fully articulated by Carlyle).

Just as there is an ambiguity in the treatment of the working class, there is also an ambiguity in the novel's final position on the subject of manners. The way manners are utilised in High Society is attacked but the novel does not deny that there is value in the mannered code (in addition to, though not as a substitute for, the values of the heart) when the code is a symptom of real courtesy, consideration, and respect, and not a tool to be manipulated as a weapon in class competition. Dickens's experiences in America had hardened his dislike of a social life without a respectful use of civilised forms and a right and proper concern for the proprieties. (In *American Notes* (1843) and *Martin Chuzzlewit* (1843/4) the vulgarity and barbarism in American life was ruthlessly satirised.) This respect for the intrinsic qualities of manners is reflected in the sympathetic portrait of Clennam's concern with courtesy:

> 'Not to deceive you, sir, I notice it', said Mrs Plornish, 'and I take it kind of you. . . . It ain't many that comes into a poor place, that deems it worth their while to move their hats', said Mrs Plornish. 'But people think more of it than people think.'
>
> Clennam returned, with an uncomfortable feeling in so very slight a courtesy being unusual, Was that all! (p. 178).

The charm of Ferdinand Barnacle, frank and open but always polite, is also sympathetically presented, in a manner which anticipates Herbert Pocket and contrasts with Gowan's use of frankness and openness to wound Clennam. Within the novel's scheme of values it is Clennam and not Rigaud, Gowan, Merdle, or William Dorrit who is the ideal gentleman.

There is some play on the concept of natural gentility in *Little Dorrit*. Amy Dorrit, writing to Arthur Clennam, remarks of her sister Fanny, 'It is natural to her to be a lady' (p. 522). In Society's sense of the word this is true, for Fanny has always been selfish and indifferent to others. However, the novel implicitly suggests that it is Amy, who says of Society's expectations on the subject of gentility, 'I find that I cannot learn', who is the 'natural lady'. Through Amy an alternative *moral* definition of gentility is proposed – a definition not incompatible with working-class origins or manual labour. But how substantial is this award of natural gentility? In fact, typically in the later novels the concept of natural gentility is used to put a sentimental gloss on the class realities of mid-Victorian society. Just how empty and hollow this gesture is will be seen during the discussions of *Great Expectations* and *Our Mutual Friend* – two novels in which the award of 'true' gentility to a character has an important role within the novel. However, in *Little Dorrit* there is a good instance of Dickens's guard slipping to reveal the limitations of his radical stance. John Chivery shows such 'chivalrous feelings towards all that belongs to her[i.e. Amy]' that Clennam says, with cordial admiration, 'You speak, John, . . . like a Man' (pp. 795–6). The same tribute, with the addition of the adjectives 'gentle' and 'Christian', is to be paid to Joe Gargery in *Great Expectations*. But how much respect and dignity is John Chivery awarded throughout the novel? He is mercilessly exploited as a figure of fun, and in an earlier passage it would seem that his social origins condemn him despite this sentimental sop. Following his proposal to Amy Dorrit (despite his delicacy presented as something essentially comic and absurd) John Chivery breaks down – 'the heart, that was under the waistcoat of sprigs – mere slop-work, if the truth must be known – swelled to the size of the heart of a gentleman; and the *poor common little fellow*, having no room to hold it, burst into tears' (p.263) (the italics are mine).

IV

The social vision of *Little Dorrit* then presents mid-Victorian industrial England as an alienating and imprisoning environment. It is worth examining the novel's treatment of the idea of environment. In contrast to other Victorian novels with a social purpose, 'Dickens's writings convey a sense of the pressure of environment on the inner, as well as the outer, lives of the characters'.[5] The moral failings within the Marshalsea prison are seen as a product of the environment –

always kept before us is the Marshalsea 'stain' and its 'shadow'. Dickens emphasises William Dorrit's spiritual 'jail-rot', and the Marshalsea 'taint' on Tip's love for Amy. Tip himself appeared 'to take the Prison walls with him' in his unsuccessful attempts to find stable employment. Even the innocent Maggy is corrupted, and when Arthur Clennam is imprisoned he admits to Amy. 'I well know the taint of it clings to me' (p. 829). Only Amy escapes the corruption – the environment is not completely deterministic – but it testifies to its power that Amy's survival of innocence is associated with a unique continuation of childhood into adult life. This utilisation of the romantic concept of the child is another legacy in Dickens's attack on industrial society of the earlier romantic social critics, Wordsworth and Blake. Not only is Amy an exception to the general power of the environment to mould character but Rigaud, in a throwback to the villains of the earlier novels, is also presented as an embodiment of evil, which Iago-like, is independent of environment.

However, although at each end of the human scale (the extreme innocence of Amy, and the extreme malice and evil of Rigaud) character may be independent of environment, for the vast majority of people within these extremes environment is the decisive influence on character. The original prospective title of the book was *Nobody's Fault* and indeed in *Little Dorrit* moral failings are in the main presented as the product of the nature (and the failings) of the system. The fact that moral infection spreads from Merdle, an individual, might seem to contradict the association of moral corruption with a poisonous environment. However, Merdle is only successful because he appeals to the characteristic market principle for action in everyday social life – itself a product of the social/economic environment. Thus Merdle's success is not a cause of moral infection, but a symptom of the general condition.

Of course, if the social environment was regarded as totally deterministic there would be serious consequences for the novel form, for in a corrupt society there could be no heroes. It is because struggle against the environment is possible that most nineteenth-century novels are characterised (in Lukács's terms) by the presence of problematic heroes. Arthur Clennam is one of Dickens's most artistically successful heroes. While Amy's struggle loses some conviction because like Christ in Milton's *Paradise Regained* given her nature her temptations are not really tempting, Clennam is both vulnerable and fallible, and on occasions succumbs to the power of the environment. He makes the moral compromise involved in accepting the speculation principle, and unlike Amy, when imprisoned in the Marshalsea he lapses into an untidy state of depression and lethargy. The difficulty of his struggle to free himself from his past and attain authentic relations makes it artistically convincing. In this struggle he is helped not only by Amy but also by Doyce, a very important character in the value scheme of the novel.

The virtues of both Amy and Doyce are located within a framework of traditional middle-class values. Amy's response to her Marshalsea situation is in terms of work, perseverance, thrift, and duty, while Doyce reflects the traditional middle-class virtues of individualism and enterprise, as well as perseverance and work, and his business career conforms to the entrepreneurial ideal of the self-made man (see Chapter 3). Within *Little Dorrit* the traditional middle-class values of entrepreneurial capitalism are used to criticise not only the aristocratic Barnacles and the Circumlocution Office, but also the contemporary mid-Victorian experience of the middle class — represented in Mrs Clennam's form of religion (economic evangelicalism), Meagles's snobbery (the middle class as a fringe on the aristocratic mantle), Casby's business principles and hypocrisy, and Pancks's official worship of business. The traditional entrepreneurial values are seen as no longer applicable to the middle-class social situation, which has involved a series of social, moral, and ideological compromises.

Doyce's role in the criticism of the contemporary middle-class stance is particularly important. Clennam's rejection of his role in the family firm defined his essential moral position in opposition to the money/business ethos of his parents. His business partnership with Doyce does not involve moral compromise because the firm of Doyce and Clennam is explicitly presented as an ideal type of 'clean' capitalism, an historical throwback to an earlier state of entrepreneurial capitalist development. Doyce's business values are those of what Lukács would call the heroic phase of capitalist development. It is significant that Doyce rejects the speculation principle, the means by which Merdle's profits materialise as if by magic. Doyce's objection to speculation ('If I have prejudice connected with money and money figures . . . it is against speculating' (p. 736)) is a moral one, but it helps to define his representative social role in the novel. He represents the heroic entrepreneurial capitalist values in opposition to Merdle, the passive financier and speculator, the representative capitalist hero of the mid-Victorian period.

Within the firm of Doyce and Clennam human, qualitative relations can exist between employer and employee. There is a place in the firm for both Pancks and Baptist. In fact, the firm operates rather like Jarndyce's St Albans home as a refuge for victims of the system. Within the artistic scheme of the book Doyce's work stands in opposition to Pancks's alienating role as Casby's Grinder, and Gowan's purely quantitative, mediated valuation of his art. Doyce's work is fulfilling and creative, and it is valued qualitatively for its own sake. 'Daniel Doyce faced his condition with its pains and penalties attached to it, and soberly worked on for the work's sake' (p. 569). Indeed, Doyce can be read as a paradigm for the creative artist in any field whose work transcends its status as a marketable object. Dickens would have been thinking in particular of the literary artist. As an ideal model of capitalism with a heart, Doyce's firm operates as a critique of the way things are in mid-Victorian England – but it is important to recognise that Doyce's firm is not being offered optimistically as a microcosm for a practically realisable better future. In its nature and values it looks back to the past and the economic clock cannot be reversed. *Little Dorrit* contains no optimism for a general social reform. It is a novel about the way things are in an industrial society, and implies that things are not going to change.

It must also be pointed out that Doyce's role is not without its artistic problems. Doyce's business success abroad, necessary as a plot device for delivering Clennam from the Marshalsea, contradicts the logic of the social vision of the novel. It has been emphasised, especially in the experience of the Dorrits abroad, that the condition of life within the industrial system cannot be escaped from by a journey, a mere geographical movement from place to place. Doyce's European success after his years of frustration at the hands of the Circumlocution Office smacks of a fairy-tale resolution, out of place in the grimly realistic world of the novel. It is common to most of the later novels that money (elsewhere a chief agent of moral corruption) is necessary as a plot mechanism for the conventional happy ending – in this case Doyce's financial gain from working abroad which will put the firm back on its feet again and safeguard the future of Doyce, Clennam, Pancks, and Baptist. While in conflict with the Circumlocution Office Doyce seemed a problematic social figure. However, at the end of the novel, following his business success abroad, Doyce appears to be less in tension with his environment. Although his values have not been compromised, Doyce has been integrated back into Victorian society. A successful future for the firm of Doyce and Clennam is suggested, which will bring social respectability and economic comfort. The collapse of his old-fashioned firm, brought about by its contact with the characteristic new form of economic activity, stock-market speculation, could have been read as an appropriate metaphor for the historical development of Victorian capitalism – in which case, the firm's recovery and future success seems as artistically inappropriate and unlikely as that of Sol Gill's firm in *Dombey and Son*.

Any discussion of the ending of *Little Dorrit* must engage the question of whether a general social significance should be taken from the apparent liberation of certain characters from their self-imposed spiritual prisons. In the closing chapters Arthur Clennam is freed from the Marshalsea and rejects his own fiction that he is an older man whose opportunities for love and marriage are past and lost; Pancks rejects his spiritually impoverishing role as Casby's Grinder; Affery breaks out from the influence of 'the two clever ones' – ('I have broken out now, and I can't go back'); Tattycoram breaks free from her suffocating (probably lesbian) relationship with Miss Wade; and perhaps most important of all Mrs Clennam temporarily fights free from her physical paralysis and her domestic prison. The chapter headings of the last three chapters ('Going', 'Going!', and 'Gone') could be read as a pointer towards a general progression or liberation from society's prison. If the condition of individual characters is microcosmic then their individual releases might suggest that the prison nature of society is breaking down. The decisive action of Pancks and Mrs Clennam might also be seen as a movement away from mechanism towards spontaneous life. However, this optimistic interpretation of the ending cannot be justified from a closer reading of the text.

The releases of Affery and Tattycoram are not problematic, but are much less important than the escapes of Pancks and Mrs Clennam, both of which present problems of interpretation. Consider Pancks's release. To bring his private and official lives into line and resolve his crisis of identity he resigns from Casby's service. ' "I have discharged myself from your service", said Pancks, "that I may tell you what you are".' (p. 869). Momentarily he is no longer a split-man but this is only through the suicidal and self-defeating gesture of denying himself an official existence altogether. Because it is economically necessary for him to work, and because the values associated with Casby's business are presented as representative of the Victorian business world, Pancks's resignation would be a very temporary reprieve for him before he seeks work in another firm in conditions over which he can have little control, and which, in all probability, will reproduce the conditions of his official life under Casby (thus involving him once again in a split existence). However, at this point the firm of Doyce and Clennam is used as a convenient plot device to make good Pancks's escape from Casby. Dickens sets himself a problem but then artistically resolves it through the plot in a way which sidesteps its implications. Certainly this is no representative or general solution for the whole class of Grinders which Pancks represents, as the firm of Doyce and Clennam is unique in the world of the novel — a highly idealised exception to the existing reality of mid-Victorian business. The problem of Pancks will later be re-examined via Wemmick, but for the split-man of *Great Expectations* the plot offers no such artificial resolution of the private and official spheres.

Mrs Clennam's escape is problematic too. It is presented with a sentimental, quasi-religious gloss which gives it a vague representative flavour. Following her confession to Amy, Mrs Clennam and little Dorrit cross the river at sunset and mingle with the crowds enjoying the summer evening. The London scene is described, for the only time in the novel, in tones of peace, calm, and serenity. 'From a radiant centre, over the whole length and breadth of the tranquil firmament great shoots of light streamed among the early stars, like signs of the blessed later covenant of peace and hope that change the crown of thorns into a glory' (p. 862). This description is clearly intended to be compared with the earlier description of the Marshalsea that same morning when the sun 'struck the long bright rays, bars of the prison of this lower world' (p. 831). Does the association with the classic case of imprisonment being turned to triumph — Christ at Easter — imply that a general resurrection is imminent for the prison inhabitants of London, and industrial England? Such an impression would clash with the whole force and tone of the book, not least the sober, qualified ending of Arthur and Amy's marriage, which will be considered in a moment. It is not surprising that Dickens should reach for religious, sentimental language to convey cheaply a reassuring impression which has not been artistically worked for. Generally when we encounter religious imagery in the later novels it is a sign that Dickens is in artistic trouble, and wishes to achieve an emotional, unthinking response from his readers.

Furthermore, using Mrs Clennam as a representative figure for this spiritual liberation seems inappropriate, in view of the fact that the nature of her 'escape' from her spiritual prison is very limited and incomplete. Certainly, she does admit her past deception to Amy ('You know, now, what I have done'), and asks forgiveness ('Forgive me. Can you forgive me?'). But to the last she still deceives herself that her past motivation was religious duty not vindictively personal spite. She still insists to Amy, 'I have set myself against evil; not against good. I have been an instrument of severity against sin' (p. 860). She is still willing to deceive Arthur about his birth, and to buy off Rigaud. That her spiritual liberation is incomplete makes it appropriate that she should set off to *return* to her old domestic prison of her invalid years and though it collapses before she returns, Mrs Clennam herself reverts back to her mechanical existence. Paralysed and dumb, for three more years 'she lived and died a statue' (p. 863).

Most modern critics read the collapse of Mrs Clennam's house as an important emblematic episode, not an arbitrary plot resolution conveniently killing off Rigaud as some contemporary critics suggested. Indeed, Mrs Clennam's house can be read as a social microcosm – all the concepts and images which interrelate to produce the novel's social vision are concentrated in Mrs Clennam's house and its inhabitants (prison, crime, market, alienation, etc.). Like Dickens's best emblems it is given a rich variety of surface detail. It is described as a 'debilitated old house in the city, wrapped in its mantle of soot, and leaning heavily on the crutches that had partaken of its decay and worn out with it' (p. 220). If the house's collapse is to be given a general social suggestiveness, it is not as a symbol for the crashing down of society's surfaces and forms once truth and self-knowledge is admitted (as some critics have suggested) though it is connected with the existence of these surfaces and forms, in particular the mannered genteel code of fashionable society. The vision of society in *Little Dorrit* is of a corrupt system being propped up in its present form by the operation of snobbery and ideological deference. Meagles's snobbery reinforces the Barnacle position, as Bleeding Heart Yard's habitual admiration and deference does for the fashionable world as a whole. Both together make a crucial contribution to the survival of the system, albeit in a corrupt and degraded form. If an analogy is accepted between the rotting crutches which prop up the ruined architecture of Mrs Clennam's house and the social forms embodied in snobbery which work to support the social/political status quo, then the collapse of the house takes on an ominous general suggestiveness. Sweep away the genteel surfaces of

Mrs General and the result would be the collapse of the whole social structure, for it is only the continued valued recognition of Mrs General's forms in Bleeding Heart Yard that stands between society and the revolutionary nemesis identified with the ragged children in Covent Garden. Thus there is a basic ambiguity in the novel's treatment of the use of manners. Though the social/political utilisation of manners in fashionable society is seen as a social and moral evil, in a sense it is a necessary evil if revolutionary collapse is to be indefinitely postponed. Clearly this depressing perspective is far removed from the vague optimism conveyed in the description of the London evening which preceded the house's collapse. The throw-away glimmer of social hope is also out of tune with the sober and qualified implications of Clennam and Amy's marriage which closes the novel.

The ending of *Little Dorrit* is altogether less cosy and reassuring than Esther and Allan's country cottage conclusion to *Bleak House*. It is also a more open ending, and hence more appropriate to the tragic vision of society contained in the novel, which imaginatively demands a relatively open ending. *Little Dorrit* is a novel about the way things are in an industrial society, and does not offer the hope that change for the better in the near future is possible. The Marshalsea is still standing and the Circumlocution Office is still grinding on at the novel's conclusion. In *Little Dorrit* there is no equivalent of the attempt in *Bleak House* to suggest, however artistically unconvincingly, through Jarndyce's transformation of Bleak House that a hopeful change for the whole social system is possible. Yet we must not exaggerate the pessimism of *Little Dorrit*. John Wain has argued that the novel portrays Victorian England as 'a place where genuine happiness is impossible'.[6] He is wrong. The social environment is not presented as completely deterministic. If the novel offers no hope for the redemption of the *system*, there is still, in a qualified but important sense, hope for the *individual* life. Clennam and Amy achieve a real and authentic level of happiness at the close of the novel. However, this type of fulfilling, qualitative relationship is only possible in opposition to the dominant market morality of Victorian society, and Clennam's relationship with Amy is given no general or representative social significance. The uniqueness of their bond, its vulnerability, and the difficulties of the path which lies ahead are all suggested in the novel's closing paragraph. The newly married pair

'Went down into a modest life of usefulness and happiness. . . . They went quietly down into the roaring streets,
inseparable and blessed; and as they passed along in sunshine and
shade, the noisy and the eager, and the arrogant and the forward
and the vain, fretted and chaffed, and made their usual uproar'
(p. 895).

What is striking here is the qualification and reservation contained in
this tribute. There is the minimum of concession to contemporary
taste. Critics are agreed in finding the close of *Little Dorrit* Dickens's
most tactful and artistically successful ending, totally consistent with
the dominant mood of the book. There is a sense of balance and
proportion which is missing from the conclusion of the other novels.

On the one hand, Clennam and Amy choose a life of self-limitation
('a modest life'), and yet on the other hand, they are bravely
affirming self at the expense of community. They go down into the
streets where they will live apart from the jostling crowd. A sense of
loneliness, separateness, and non-communication pervades the book.
It is significant that the last image in the book is of the city crowd as a
stream of separate and solitary units.

What is important about Clennam's final position is that he stands
upright without benefit of supporting myths (in contrast to most of
the characters in the novel) and sees society for what it is. Tragic man,
according to Lucien Goldmann, confronts the world without
illusions as to its nature. He accepts the world as it is in order to fight
on for authentic values as an individual. This corresponds to
Clennam's position at the close of *Little Dorrit*. He does not attempt to
retreat into a private world, like Jarndyce, but goes 'quietly down
into the roaring streets'. Jarndyce, too, had seen society (i.e.
Chancery) for what it was, but had then retreated from this
confrontation into a private world where, through his east-wind
fiction, he distorts the nature of his immediate reality. Clennam's final
stance in the novel involves less compromise than that of any other
Dickens hero. If Clennam is Dickens's most successful tragic hero,
there is no doubt that the novel as a whole embodies a unified and
coherent tragic vision of mid-Victorian English capitalism. The
world will not be changed and authentic values realised on a general
level. Clennam's struggle with the Circumlocution Office had
provided an emblem for the individual's unsuccessful attempt to
change his environment. But though Clennam is resigned to the

condition of society at the novel's close, he does not capitulate to its dominant market values, and through his relationship with Amy maintains his struggle for authentic relationships. At the end of *Little Dorrit* we do not feel that Clennam has achieved a spurious integration within his society. The conflict between the individual and the system has not been artificially resolved.

6 *A Tale of Two Cities* – Revolutionary Madness and Moral Rebirth

I

A Tale of Two Cities (1859) is usually regarded by critics as being a curiosity, lacking the social vision and themes common to the other completed later novels, a sport or holiday fiction outside Dickens's main novelistic line of development. One critic has called it 'superficially . . . the least Dickensian of all the novels Dickens wrote',[1] and most critics in attempting to marry it into the Dickens canon stress the links with *Barnaby Rudge* (1841), the earlier tale of London mob violence during the 'No Popery' Gordon riots, rather than *A Tale's* relation to those novels which precede and follow it.

However, without denying the link with *Barnaby Rudge*, this reading emphasises the essential similarities in the way in which society is seen in *A Tale* and the other later novels. It is best not to read *A Tale of Two Cities* as a historical romance in the traditions of Scott, or simply as an adventure tale of individual heroism and self-sacrifice, but primarily as a novel which through the distancing medium of a historical melodrama, critically evaluates the condition of contemporary mid-Victorian England and imaginatively explores one of the possible consequences of that condition. Though the novel opens in 1775 the imaginative world created in the scenes set in England is, in its *essential* characteristics (rather than surface detail), that of England in the 1850s. English society is presented in terms of the by now familiar concepts and images of prison and death, secrecy and crime. Dickens's imaginative response to his society in *A Tale* is at one with those later novels which have more obvious or explicit social themes.

Throughout the mid-Victorian period Dickens's insistent imaginative analysis of society touched on the danger of revolution – not as the result of escalating surface political agitation, but as the inevitable consequence of a general corruption throughout the system. In the revolutionary image of Krook's spontaneous combustion Dickens proposed a crude social/historical cause and effect relation, i.e. a general unrelieved corruption within a system will lead inevitably to the explosive destruction of that system. This is developed in *A Tale of Two Cities* where the novel puts forward a positive, if unsophisticated, theory of historical dynamics to account for the outbreak of the French Revolution. The emphasis is similar. Any social explosion like the French Revolution has social causes engendered in the corrupt nature of the system itself.

The Revolution was not a freak or historical accident – the novel reveals a contempt for those who 'talk of this terrible revolution as if it were the one only harvest ever known under the skies that had not been sown – as if nothing had ever been done, or omitted to be done, that led to it' (p. 267).[2] Indeed it is precisely because the Revolution was the inescapable product of definite social facts that Dickens sees the experience as relevant for mid-Victorian England, also represented in the later novels as a system within which much is 'omitted to be done'. The tenement building where Defarge kept Dr Manette, and which reveals the misery of the Paris poor on the eve of revolution (a 'great foul nest', filthy and polluted, stinking from decomposing refuse on every landing as well as the 'intangible impurities' of 'poverty and deprivation') invites comparison with Tom-all-Alone's. The scenes set in revolutionary Paris offer an imaginative exploration of a possible future awaiting Victorian England. 'Crush humanity out of shape once more, under similar hammers, and it will twist itself into the same tortured forms' (p. 399).

We have said that despite the historical tag of the last quarter of the eighteenth century the scenes set in England reflect the novelist's imaginative grasp of the general condition within his society at the time when he was writing. Consider the opening scene. A coach is travelling down the Dover Road on a cold November night. Following the remarks associating separateness, secrecy and death with the nature of life in a great city, quoted in Chapter 2 (and which are directly inspired by the mid-Victorian expansion of London) we are asked to take an interest in one of the passengers – Jarvis Lorry, a clerk in Tellson's Bank, the representative social institution in the novel. As he sits dozing, Lorry's thoughts confusedly slide between his official existence at Tellson's (the bank) and a train of thought provoked by the history of Dr Manette, the victim he is on his way to help recall to life (images of the grave and prison). The way in which this passage brings business, death, and prison together in a suggestive relation is typical of the later novels — the connection having more than just plot significance but contributing to a way of seeing society.

We see *A Tale*'s contribution to the developing social awareness of the later novels in two imaginatively weighted descriptions of the London scene — one of the city as an urban wasteland, and the other of Tellson's Bank.

The former occurs when Sydney Carton walks out of Stryver's house in the early morning.

> When he got out of the house, the air was cold and sad, the dull sky overcast, the river dark and dim, the whole scene like a lifeless desert, and wreaths of dust were spinning round and round before the morning blast; as if the desert sand had risen far away, and the first spray of it in its advance had begun to overwhelm the city.
>
> Waste forces within him, and a desert all around, this man stood still on his way across a silent terrace, and saw for a moment, lying in the wilderness before him, a mirage of honourable ambition, self-denial, and preseverance (p. 121).

Of course, the scene mirrors Carton's inner condition, but his loneliness and isolation in a blighted landscape, the total absence of contact with other people, are all strongly reminiscent of Clennam's night walk through a deserted London towards his mother's home in *Little Dorrit*, while the whirling dust and the image of the city as an urban wilderness or wasteland introduces ideas which reach maturity in *Our Mutual Friend*.

Tellson's Bank has a role in this novel not unlike Chancery and the Circumlocution Office in theirs. It is the representative national institution — a respected and long-established bank which, like the somewhat different firm of Dombey and Son, communicates essential things about the national life.

The novel signposts the representative significance of Tellson's.

> Any one of these partners would have disinherited his son on the question of rebuilding Tellson's. In this respect the House was much on a par with the Country; which did very often disinherit its sons for suggesting improvements in laws and customs that had long been highly objectionable, but were only the more respectable (p. 83).

But the analogy goes much further than this. Tellson's functions as a
social microcosm and the description of the Tellson's building works
to suggest the operation of a complex and ominous set of social forces
beneath the prosperous surface of mid-Victorian society.

Tellson's is 'very small, very dark, very ugly, very incommodious.'
It contains

> the dingiest of windows, which were always under a shower-bath
> of mud from Fleet Street, and which were made the dingier by
> their own iron bars proper, and the heavy shadow of Temple Bar.
> If your business necessitated your seeing 'the House', you were put
> into a species of Condemned Hold at the back, where you
> meditated on a misspent life, until the House came with its hands in
> its pockets, and you could hardly blink at it in the dismal twilight.
> Your money came out of, or went into, wormy old wooden
> drawers, particles of which flew up your nose and down your
> throat when they were opened and shut. Your banknotes had a
> musty odour, as if they were fast decomposing into rags again.
> Your plate was stowed away among the neighbouring cesspools,
> and evil communications corrupted its good polish in a day or two.
> Your deeds got into extemporised strong-rooms made of kitchens
> and sculleries, and fretted all the fat out of their parchments into the
> banking-house air. Your lighter boxes of family papers went
> upstairs into a Barmecide room, . . . where . . . the first letters
> written to you by your old love, or by your little children, were
> but newly released from the horror of being ogled through the
> windows, by the heads exposed on Temple Bar with an insensate
> brutality and ferocity worthy of Abyssinia or Ashantee. . . .
>   Cramped in all kinds of dim cupboards and hutches at Tellson's,
> the oldest of men carried on the business gravely. When they took a
> young man into Tellson's London house, they hid him somewhere
> till he was old. They kept him in a dark place, like a cheese, until he
> had the full Tellson flavour and blue-mould upon him (pp. 83 – 5).

It is characteristic of Dickens's method that important criticisms of
society can be made through the medium of comedy without losing
any of their bite. Tellson's is both prosperous and respectable – like
mid-Victorian England – but the imagery relentlessly qualifies and
undermines this prosperity.

Tellson's respectability is tainted by the imagery of crime and
prisons – the 'iron bars', the 'Condemned Hold', the heads of

executed prisoners on Temple Bar. Merdle's business respectability was founded on crime, and the association is a key element in the design of Dickens's next novel, *Great Expectations*. The French scenes in the novel warn that barbaric abuse of authority results in a barbaric backlash. Thus, it is significant that Tellson's, pillar of English respectability, expressly approves of the heads on Temple Bar. 'But indeed, at that time, putting to death was a recipe much in vogue with all trades and professions, and not least of all with Tellson's' (p. 84). Jerry, Tellson's odd-job man, provides another link between business, crime, and death. In his private life (in contrast to this official position at Tellson's) he sets up as a 'businessman', selling dead bodies to the surgeons. Yet he refers to this illegal traffic in death as 'business' and to himself as an 'honest tradesman'. Like Tellson's the respectability he lays claim to is tainted.

The various items of wealth — money and banknotes, deeds etc. — hoarded in Tellson's are consistently given unpleasant, sinister, and provocative associations, which suggest that this wealth is based on repugnant and unsavoury social sources which the respectable world would recoil even from mentioning (another anticipation of *Great Expectations*). This is especially so of the plate, associated with the neighbouring cesspools, corrupting source of disease and contamination. Other forms of wealth are verbally associated with worms and rags.

Furthermore, the description also suggests that all this imposing wealth, material evidence of a bourgeoning society, has an existence paradoxically insecure and vulnerable. As evidence for the flourishing health of the system it is false and misleading. The money is held in parasite-ridden drawers slowly being eaten away. In a day or two the cesspools have tarnished the plate. The banknotes are described as if fast decomposing into waste and refuse (the anticipation here of *Our Mutual Friend* and its association of money and rubbish is striking). The multiple degrading associations of wealth not only work to tarnish the much-warranted respectability of the house, but also extend to the wider social system. The suggestion that the material wealth of the prosperous classes is based on unsavoury and insecure foundations is directly relevant to the scenes in revolutionary Paris which reveal the methods by which this insecurity could most strikingly be demonstrated. Thus John Gross is wrong to say that 'Tellson's, musty and cramped and antiquated, makes an excellent Dickensian set-piece, but is scarcely followed up'.[3]

There is another representative way in which Tellson's is associated with death. The bureaucratic mentality which shrinks a man to an official role is literally a denial of life. Esther's comment that Chancery is a 'dry, official place' could equally be applied to Tellson's. It is significant that the chief representative of the House is described as if he was an object ('the House came with its hands in its pockets, and you could hardly blink at it'), and that Lorry sees himself as a 'speaking machine'. The official life of the clerks in Tellson's is an enforced imprisonment of vitality and youth in 'dim cupboards and hutches'. The novel comments further on the official nature of the system through the representative character of Jarvis Lorry.

Lorry is not only a representative 'man of business' but also another study in Dickens's gallery of split-men, though in his case, overruling reference to his official role is the result of a sense of duty and an affectionate loyalty to the firm of Tellson's. However, this does not mean that his wilful identification of self with social role has not involved an alienating loss.

There is clear evidence of this in the scene where Lorry reveals to Lucie Manette that her father, whom she always believed dead, is in fact alive, though very ill and wasted. In this scene Lorry behaves as a comic oddity but his deprecatory references to himself, though they are only true of his own official self, reflect an essential truth about his society.

> Miss Manette, I am a man of business. I have a business charge to acquit myself of. In your reception of it, don't heed me any more than if I was a speaking machine – truly, I am not much else. . . . These are mere business relations, Miss; there is no friendship in them, no particular interest, nothing like sentiment. I have passed from one to another in the course of my business life, just as I pass from one of our customers to another in the course of my business day; in short, I have no feelings; I am a mere machine. . . . Feelings! I have no time for them, no chance for them. I pass my whole life, Miss, in turning an immense pecuniary mangle (pp. 54–5).

And yet Lorry does not mourn the emotional straitjacket imposed on him by his official business life, but believes, as a loyal representative of Tellson's should, that business is 'a very good thing, and a very respectable thing'. In modern terms Lorry is the complete company man. He tells Carton in the Old Bailey, 'We men of business, who serve a House, are not our own masters. We have to think of the House more than ourselves' (p. 113). Even in shaking hands with a customer self is abdicated. 'He shook in a self abnegating-way, as one who shook for Tellson and Co.' (p. 172).

This loss of individuality in his official role is countered by the gradual growth of a warm private friendship with Dr Manette. The opposition of private and official experience is not so extreme as for Pancks and Wemmick, and Lorry does not find the lack of resolution a dislocating experience. However, this does not alter the fact that when the novel opens Lorry too is 'buried alive' — by the emotionally suffocating effects of surrendering his complete self to a social role — and that his awakening private friendships represent *his* 'recall to life'.

Thus through the atmosphere and imagery of the English scenes; the generalising significance of the description of Tellson's Bank; and the representative use of Jarvis Lorry, we see Dickens engaging his society in the novel on those aspects of social life which characteristically charge his social vision in the later fiction. If Dr Manette's comfortable retreat in Soho invites comparison with Jarndyce's St Albans sanctuary the way in which the cosy family scene in Soho is shattered by revolutionary currents which bring all the members close to death is part two of the Jarndyce lesson. Respectable society cannot retreat into the safe and self-contained isolation of private life, and achieve immunity from the social forces of disease/revolution breeding in the urban slums. The novels prior to *A Tale* had condemned Victorian capitalism as a structure on the verge of collapse. *A Tale* explores both what would be involved in the nature of that (revolutionary) collapse and whether it is possible for individuals within such an environment to be spiritually reborn as a means of redeeming the total structure — a theme reworked in greater detail in *Our Mutual Friend*.

II

In turning to the scenes in revolutionary France one point must be emphasised at the outset. While the novel unequivocally presents revolution as the inevitable consequence of an unjust social system the portrait of the Paris mob during the Terror is the best evidence that even the later fiction completely rejects revolutionary means to a social end. The descriptions of the mob in *A Tale* are strikingly similar to those of the Gordon rioters in *Barnaby Rudge*. The same metaphors are used — the Paris mob is likened to devils, madmen, wild beasts, and savages.

It would be tedious to list all the examples, but special attention should be paid to the Carmagnole dance, which is given the generalising significance of what the novel regards as constituting the essence of revolution in the abstract. The dancers are described as 'dancing like five thousand demons'. At first the dance appears wild and formless, but then

> some ghastly apparition of a dance figure gone raving mad arose among them. . . . No fight could have been half so terrible as this dance. It was so emphatically a fallen sport – a something, once innocent, delivered over to all devilry – a healthy pastime changed into a means of angering the blood, bewildering the senses, and steeling the heart. Such grace as was visible in it, made it the uglier, showing how warped and perverted all things good by nature were becoming. The maidenly bosom bared to this, the pretty almost-child's head thus distracted, the delicate foot mincing this slough of blood and dirt, were types of the disjointed time (pp. 307–8).

The details of the dance are types of revolution in the abstract – a nightmarish reversal of all things natural, innocent and good.

In the novel, revolution is presented as a classless inferno lacking social or moral law; a bestial level of anarchy and arbitrary violence; a form of social cannibalism. The representative figures of revolution, of course, are the Defarges, the Vengeance and perhaps most of all Jacques III, of St Antoine, a 'life-thirsty, cannibal-looking, bloody-minded juryman' (p. 345).

There is not one word about the mob that might suggest that revolution is either constructive or beneficial. To fail to recognise this it is necessary to wear political blinkers like T. A. Jackson who, in *Charles Dickens: The Progress of a Radical* (1937), incredibly claims that the novel reflects 'a complete and whole-hearted sympathy with the revolutionaries; and, up to a point, an entire agreement with, and admiration for, their methods of setting to work'.

In an important sense *A Tale* exposes the Revolution as futile and self-defeating. The destruction of a prison, the Bastille, was the spark for a revolution to create social justice, and yet the conditions and quality of life it produced are those of the prison. La Force is the symbolic home of revolutionary France – a prison for all generations and classes. 'Two score and twelve were told off. From the farmer-general of seventy, whose riches couldn't buy his life, to the seamstress of twenty, whose poverty and obscurity could not save her' (p. 376). The Revolution might have been seen as a symbolic end to prisons, but instead it has repopulated them.

III

The novel tries to understand the French revolutionary experience because of its relevance to contemporary England. Will the inequalities within the mid-Victorian industrial system inevitably provoke the same revolutionary holocaust? In a somewhat problematic fashion, *A Tale* optimistically suggests that a general process of individual rebirth or resurrection can provide a preventative social counter to revolutionary hatred and violence. Social redemption through love and spiritual rebirth is not being offered as a solution to revolutionary France, but consistent with where the real interest in the novel lies, is being prescribed as a preventative cure for mid-Victorian England in the tradition of Jarndyce's 'hopeful change'. The physical struggle between Miss Pross and Madame Defarge is thus not only an opposition of moral values but a contrast between alternative methods of social change – moral redemption through love, and revolutionary change of the system.

The theme of rebirth (and the words 'recall to life') are kept before the reader insistently. There is the somewhat unstable resurrection of Dr Manette, as well as Darnay's two close escapes from imminent death. Jerry Cruncher's nocturnal profession of 'Resurrection-Man' keeps the theme before us on a comic level, while an ironic twist is supplied by the twin recalls to 'life' of Foulon and Cly, each from a faked death.

The best-known example of individual rebirth through self-sacrificing love is provided by Sydney Carton. As we might expect, his moral rebirth is charted by means of his orientation to traditional middle-class values. The mirage which Carton momentarily sees before him in the London wilderness is very much a middle-class creation – 'a mirage of honourable ambition, self-denial, and perseverance'. However ambiguous Dickens's ideas about social rising were at this time (and we see the ambiguity and complexity in his next novel, *Great Expectations*), and although the successful social climber, Stryver, is presented unsympathetically as an aggressive bully, there is no doubt that Carton is criticised for lacking earnestness and the ambition and perseverance to match his talents. Significantly, his double and moral opposite, Charles Darnay, is a paragon of middle-class virtues, despite his aristocratic birth. His moderate prosperity is self-made and the result of hard work ('He had expected labour and he found it, and did it, and made the best of it' (p. 160)) and diligent perseverance ('So with great perseverance and untiring industry, he prospered' (p. 160)).

Carton's rebirth involves a positive response to middle-class values. Although his sacrifice is given a general social significance, in Carton's own mind it is localised and domestic in scope – honouring an individual promise, and preserving the integrity of a domestic household which is presented in terms of the middle-class Victorian ideal. Thus his sacrifice reflects a positive orientation to middle-class values – honour, truth, duty and the home. Though he dies, he is in a sense morally integrated back into Victorian society. Like most of Dickens's heroes he is made to appear, at the close of the novel, no longer a problematic person. Thus in *A Tale* we again see the operation of an interpretive framework of middle-class values. Scenes of anxiety in England and social nightmare in France make up the social backcloth of the novel. In the foreground are the reassuring figures of Lorry, who thinks that business is good and respectable, and Carton and his twin Darnay, two figures whose human value lies in proportion to their positive orientation to middle-class values. Of course, in addition, the novel reflects an interpretation of the French Revolution general amongst the Victorian middle class, whose spokesman on the subject, Carlyle, was Dickens's chief literary inspiration for the novel.

We feel that had Carton been consistently developed as a character he would have died not at peace, looking 'sublime and prophetic', but in the very spirit of the revolution – in a frustrated rage at a world which regarded the gap between his talents and achievements with indifference.

The details of Carton's prophecy direct us to an even greater problem in both the themes of revolution and resurrection. Carton's prophetic thoughts run,

> I see a beautiful city and a brilliant people rising from this abyss, and in their struggles to be truly free, in their triumphs and defeats, through long years to come, I see the evil of this time and of the previous time of which this is the natural birth, gradually making expiation for itself and wearing out (p. 404).

Now if revolution is a state of madness and moral disease, etc., then there is no reason why the destructive process should not go on indefinitely; but history forces Dickens to recognise that the revolutionary madness did end, and a hopeful future was born out of the revolutionary disorder. Once again we are directed to the problem of the open or closed nature of the ending, although in this novel the situation is somewhat different. History forces Dickens to add a historical footnote to what otherwise would have been an open ending – the novel closing pessimistically with a fundamental and unresolved opposition between the rampaging mob and the necessary demands of an ordered and peaceful social condition, represented by the moral qualities of Lucie, Miss Pross, etc. Were it not for the assurances of Carton's prophecy, the domestic, private theme would have been left relatively open too – Lucie, Dr Manette, and Darnay presumably safe but their futures left unknown. Of course the historical nature of the material forces Dickens to come to terms on some level with the problem of historical dynamics. The very fact that the novel views the revolution as the inevitable result of aristocratic oppression and indifference involves Dickens with a theory of history, however primitive. In Carton's prophecy the revolutionary condition is the 'natural birth' of aristocratic mismanagement. The implication of this cause/effect relation is to suggest a similar historical relation in which revolution is seen as the historically necessary means to achieve the 'beautiful city and a brilliant people' (the latter being the 'natural birth' of revolution). Such a suggestion would oppose the novel's conscious intent, for Dickens clearly wishes to repudiate revolution as a means to an end and certainly not legitimise or justify it through consideration of a wider historical context.

Of course, recognising the social progress made in post-revolutionary France, in effect is an admission that the whole society *was* recalled to life. Yet the prison nature of revolutionary France could only be broken down by the operation of forces which the novel represents as having no place in such a society – another contradiction. Thus at the heart of the novel there is a failure to resolve the awareness of historical dynamics with the portrayal of the revolutionaries. If revolution is a sick and cruel madness (if the Defarges and Jacques III are typical revolutionaries) then it is inconceivable that it could result in any ordered form of society, let alone the social progress Dickens is inescapably forced to concede. Thus Dickens's attempt at an objective view of historical change compromises the imaginative truth of his very subjective description of the mob. However, just as Krook's spontaneous combustion carried far greater imaginative impact than Jarndyce's 'hopeful change' of Bleak House, the scenes of revolutionary violence in *A Tale* contain a far greater imaginative force than those dealing with the alternative means of changing a sick society – by individual moral rebirth. In *A Tale*, as elsewhere in Dickens, the dark side of the picture is rendered with greater imaginative conviction than its optimistic counterpart.

7 *Great Expectations* — Tainted Respectability and True Gentility

Having just visited Newgate with Wemmick to pass time while waiting for Estella, Pip reflects:

> how strange it was that I should be encompassed by all this taint of prison and crime, that in my childhood out on our lonely marshes on a winter evening I should have first encountered it; that, it should have reappeared on two occasions, starting out like a stain that was faded but not gone; that, it should in this way pervade my fortune and advancement (p. 284).[1]

Pip's whole life had been mysteriously connected and tainted with 'prison and crime' – his fatal meeting with Magwitch who forces him to rob Joe; his part in the chase and recapture of Magwitch and Compeyson; the two meetings with the convict entrusted with Magwitch's first gift (in The Three Jolly Bargemen, and on the stagecoach); the convict's leg-iron used as a weapon against his sister; his London association with Jaggers, whose office stands under the shadow of Newgate and his visits to the latter with Wemmick – all prefigure the momentous discovery that his 'expectations' to live a gentlemanly life of idle luxury were founded on the labour and money of the convict Magwitch. The connection between Pip's newly gained but complacently held respectability and the world of convicts and crime (even though Magwitch's labour in Australia is honest) takes us to the very heart of *Great Expectations* (1860–1). As Ross Dabney remarks, 'That Pip's money comes from Magwitch is a discovery fertile in class ironies and in reflections on the source of unearned incomes'.[2]

During the narrative, Pip remarks that in each individual life there is a 'long chain of iron or gold' which from the forging of the first link binds one to a certain and unique course. The applicability to Pip himself later becomes clear – his chains of gold (the money which constitutes his expectations) are irretrievably bound up with chains of iron (and the criminal world). The novel strongly suggests that this is also true for the whole society, bound together by chains of gold (material wealth – enjoyed by some and founded on the labour of others) and chains of iron (crime). Indeed crime is the link between the Two Nations in this novel as disease is in *Bleak House*, prison in *Little Dorrit*, and revolution in *A Tale of Two Cities*.

Thus the systematic nature of society is implicit in the plot which reinforces a familiar message in the later fiction – the existence of the respectable and prosperous 'nation' within society cannot be separated from the existence of the other miserable or disreputable one. One cannot have Miss Havisham without Magwitch.

II

Pip's 'expectations' are crucial to all the major themes of the novel. They form – rather like the suit of Jarndyce and Jarndyce or the Circumlocution Office – a social environment which constrains the individual in a manner analogous to the wider social system. Pip's 'expectations' are representative in another sense too – they embody the whole power of money and class in mid-Victorian England. The presentation of these expectations in the novel illustrates Dickens's technique of portraying abstract social forces as if they were objects or concrete things. Pip experiences his 'great expectations' as an external pressure or a thing – like force which in its essential operation dehumanises him.

From the moment of Jaggers's announcement of Pip's expectations the tendency towards dehumanisation prefigured by Pumblechook appropriating him as an object of patronage is exacerbated. The town's tradesmen regard Pip as a valuable piece of merchandise. 'Mr Trabb measured and calculated me, in the parlour, as if I were an estate and he the finest species of surveyor' (p. 178). Earlier, by setting Pip up to love the unattainable Estella, Miss Havisham had utilised him as an object to be broken as her revenge on the male sex. Now she uses his expectations (and the popular belief that they originated with her) to goad her parasitic relatives. Once again Pip is a mere object of convenience. He comes to realise that he was 'only suffered in Satis House as a convenience, a sting for the greedy relations, a model with a mechanical heart to practise on when no other practice was at hand' (p. 341).

Indeed Miss Havisham on a personal level reproduces the destructive social processes which elsewhere in the novel (for example in the experience of Magwitch and Wemmick) are seen as the alienating pressure of the social system on the individual. Miss Havisham stands in classic opposition to Jarndyce. She pulls selected individuals into her private world not to protect or fulfil them but to dehumanise them. Satis House, unlike Bleak House, is not a haven from the system, but a microcosm which reproduces its evils, a fact strongly anticipated by its description. The windows are either 'walled up' or 'rustily barred' associating the house with a tomb or prison; the neglected garden 'was quite a wilderness'; the brewery is no longer functional or useful. Within Miss Havisham's private world, Pip and Estella are dolls, manipulated as instruments of personal revenge, passive objects, devoid of personal will and initiative.

The most significant way in which Pip's expectations dehumanise him is by reducing him to an ostentatious object, bought over by Magwitch for display as a supreme act of class one-upmanship over his fellow colonists.

> The blood horses of them colonists might fling up the dust over me as I was walking; what do I say? I says to myself 'I'm making a better gentleman nor ever you'll be!' When one of 'em says to another, 'He was a convict, a few year ago, and is an ignorant common fellow now, for all he's lucky', what do I say? I says to myself, 'If I ain't a gentleman, nor yet ain't got no learning, I'm the owner of such. All on you owns stock and land; Which on you owns a brought-up London gentleman?' (p. 339).

From the moment of his return Magwitch asserts ownership of Pip. His characteristic gesture is revealing. 'Once more, he took me by both hands and surveyed me with an air of admiring proprietorship' (p. 348). When Pip reads to Magwitch in a foreign language 'he, not comprehending a single word, would stand before the fire surveying me with the air of an Exhibitor' (p. 353).

Thus Pip's essential condition since falling a prey to the social forces embodied in his expectations is that of a dehumanised object, albeit with a high market price. This condition is reflected in his nightmare

visions when in the grip of fever – a description similar to Esther
Summerson's fevered dreams when she lay dangerously ill at
St Albans. In the same way it reflects the essential condition of the
individual caught up in the machinery of the industrial system.

> I confounded impossible existences with my own identity; . . . I
> was a brick in the house wall, and yet entreating to be released from
> the giddy place where the builders had set me; . . . I was a steel
> beam of a vast engine, crashing and whirling over a gulf, and
> yet . . . I implored in my own person to have the engine stopped,
> and my part in it hammered off (pp. 471–2).

The individual is a passive and tormented object within a greater
machine. It is interesting that it is only in the unconscious or semi-
conscious state of a dream or illness that a typical Dickens hero can
grasp the essence of relations within the system with the same degree
of insight his creator achieves artistically, and even then an Esther or
Pip cannot evaluate or understand the full significance of their
nightmare. It is a fatal mistake to limit Dickens's social vision to the
boundaries of his heroes' social awareness.

The dehumanising and alienating characteristics of the system are
also expressed in the experience of the convicts. The convicts who
share Pip's coach-drive from London are fastidiously labelled objects
of general disgust.

> The great numbers on their backs, as if they were street doors; their
> coarse, mangy, ungainly outer surface, as if they were lower
> animals; their iron legs, apologetically garlanded with pocket-
> handkerchiefs; and the way in which all present looked at them and
> kept from them; made them . . . a most disagreeable and degraded
> spectacle (p. 249).

The reference to 'lower animals' reminds us of another degraded
social victim, Jo in *Bleak House*. The representative criminal casebook
in the novel is that of Magwitch – and he is seen not only as a victim,
but like the general case of the convicts on the stagecoach he is
described via the imagery of animals (in particular, a wild dog) and
mechanical life. ('Something clicked in his throat, as if he had works
in him like a clock, and was going to strike' (p. 50).) (Indeed the
world of *Great Expectations* is characterised generally by a proliferation of animal and mechanical imagery.) It is a measure of how

Dickens's views of environment have matured that while Bill Sikes in *Oliver Twist* is 'a bad one' and his murder of Nancy the result of his innate cruelty and depravity, the beast seen fighting on the marshes comes to be recognised by Pip (and the reader) as a man capable of love and loyalty, whose life of crime, starting with an instinctive reaction to poverty and want, is clearly seen as the product of an unjust and indifferent system.

III

As we have seen the theme of the split-man is a major concern in the later novels, and this theme is more fully articulated in *Great Expectations* than in any other novel. One of the chief social concerns in the book is the alienation of a bureaucratised official life as it affects Wemmick and Jaggers.

The opposition between private and official life is both clear to Wemmick and accepted by him. 'No, the office is one thing, and private life is another. When I go into the office, I leave the Castle behind me, and when I come into the Castle, I leave the office behind me' (p. 231). And he later declares, 'Walworth is one place and this office is another. . . . My Walworth sentiments must be taken at Walworth; none but my official sentiments can be taken in this office' (p. 310). Such is his crisis of identity that Pip regards him as if he were two men — the Right and Wrong Twin. Of course the Wrong Twin is the official Wemmick, whose boast, 'my guiding star always is "Get hold of portable property"' (p. 224), is in contrast to the humanistic, qualitative principles with which he organises his private life. On the one hand we have the office in Little Britain and on the other hand the Castle in Walworth, which conforms to the Victorian middle-class ideal of the home as a haven from the business world. (Pip comments on 'all the innocent, cheerful, playful ways with which you refresh your business life' (p. 423).)

In his official existence Wemmick's behaviour is unfeeling and inflexible, merely mechanical — the man is encompassed in a couple of thing-like physical attributes, particularly his post-office mouth which has a 'mechanical appearance of smiling'. This physical likeness softens at Walworth but is accentuated again as he nears his official place of business. 'By degrees, Wemmick got dryer and harder as we went along, and his mouth tightened into a post-office, again' (p. 232). The only time he can assert a human identity is in the private sphere of the Castle.

The Castle represents an attempt by Wemmick to fulfil himself as a whole or complete man in his private life, and shake off the alienating effects of his official role with its division of labour. He boasts, 'I am my own engineer, and my own carpenter, and my own plumber, and my own gardener, and my own Jack of all Trades. . . . Well; it's a good thing, you know. It brushes the Newgate cobwebs away' (p. 230).

Comparison with Pancks is useful. Pancks's official dictum about the 'Whole Duty of man in a commercial country' is similar to Wemmick's official philosophy that 'Everyman's business . . . is portable property' (p. 421). While Pancks labours to give away fortunes to other people in his private life, Wemmick is glad to organise Pip's gift to Herbert in his, thanking Pip for this opportunity to brush away the Newgate cobwebs. Yet the plot offers Wemmick no way out of his double-life as it does for Pancks. There is no artificial deliverance. Wemmick must live with this separation and reconcile himself to the identity problems attendant on his twin existence. Wemmick represents a sober and unsentimental conclusion to the novelistic problems set by Pancks.

How successful is Wemmick's private retreat from the office anyway? As House points out, Wemmick's 'whole private life is a piece of fantastic escapism from work, and is therefore thoroughly controlled by it'.[3] The details of the Castle are described with affectionate comedy which also offers a satire on Gothic imitation. Yet some of these comic details strongly suggest the vulnerability of Wemmick's whole strategy. He fires his cannon 'with a bang that shook the crazy little box of a cottage as if it must fall to pieces, and made every glass and tea cup in it ring' (p. 231). Of course no matter what high jinks Wemmick enjoys at the Castle he is doomed to return the following morning to Little Britain where he plunges into Jaggers's dirty business and continues the pursuit of portable property. Of course, it is the portable property gained in his official sphere that pays for Wemmick's private life. Wemmick's strategy is an ironic parallel to that of Jarndyce. His 'escape' from the system is based on possession of one of the chief corrupting agents within the system. Wemmick doesn't defeat the system, he merely makes his peace with it at considerable human cost and accepts the alienation of his work situation. Though Wemmick's dilemma is well known it is not always realised that Jaggers is an even worse case of alienation by the official nature of the system.

Jaggers's experience is suggestively wedded to the chief social themes of the novel. He is a representative figure for the whole English legal system. His behaviour in court is described by Pip in language which recalls the description of Chancery in *Bleak House* as a man-eating machine. Jaggers 'seemed to me to be grinding the whole place in a mill' (p. 225). Wemmick also testifies to Jaggers's man-hunting legal techniques — 'Always seems to me . . . as if he had set a mantrap and was watching it. Suddenly — click — you're caught!' (p. 221). But the 'dismal atmosphere' of Jaggers's office has wider social implication than its relevance for the legal system. The office is situated in Little Britain and (the name is significant) behaviour within it comments on the moral quality of life within the whole social system. Jaggers 'washed his clients off, as if he were a surgeon or a dentist' (p. 233) and this Pilate-like washing and scenting of his hands prompts Edgar Johnson to ask 'Could there be a clearer symbolic suggestion that much of the business of such a society is dirty business?'.[4]

Jaggers is a totally official man (like Vholes in *Bleak House* who boasted of never taking a holiday). His private residence in Soho is an extension of his office (in marked contrast to Wemmick).

> The furniture was all very solid and good, like his watch-chain. It had an official look, however, and there was nothing merely ornamental to be seen. In a corner, was a little table of papers with a shaded lamp: so that he seemed to bring the office home with him in that respect too, and to wheel it out of an evening and fall to work (p. 234).

For Wemmick dining at Jaggers's private residence is a purely official occasion and though out of office hours no moment for him to reveal the Walworth twin. 'Wemmick drew his wine when it came round, quite as a matter of business — just as he might have drawn his salary when that came round — and with his eyes on his chief, sat in a state of perpetual readiness for cross-examination' (p. 404).

Indeed, Jaggers has extended his official mode of address in court — cross-examination — into private life. His every conversation is an interrogation, in which he bullies and appropriates his listeners, for example 'taking possession of Mr Wopsle, as if he had a right to him' in The Three Jolly Bargemen. Even when dining at Miss Havisham's, Jaggers 'cross-examined his very wine when he had nothing else in hand' (p. 263).

His office chair 'of deadly black horse-hair, with rows of brass nails

round it, like a coffin' obviously suggests the spiritual consequences of
an unrelieved official mentality, while, though Jaggers is not
described (like Pancks or Wemmick) in mechanical terms, we
increasingly identify him with his physical gesture of biting his forefinger before throwing it at his listener so that (as Dorothy Van Ghent
points out) he appears to become 'thinged' into that physical part of
his being (appropriately in an official, bullying attitude).

IV

Pip's 'expectations' touch on all the major themes of the novel, and
are crucial to the theme of class and gentility. *Great Expectations*
comments on the Victorian middle-class value of social aspiration,
and the ideal of the self-made man (see Chapter 3).

Smiles himself saw individualistic aspiration and advancement as
the best means by which the material future of the working class as a
whole could be assured. Yet in *Great Expectations* a general aspiration
for upward social mobility amongst the working class is seen as more
likely to bring wretchedness and frustration to the individual than
either material well-being or spiritual fulfilment. The novel's position
on this question is revealed in the implied positive answers to two
questions. Joe wonders 'Whether common ones as to callings and
earnings . . . mightn't be the better of continuing for to keep
company with common ones, instead of going out to play with
uncommon ones' (p. 100) and in reply to Pip's confidence that 'I have
particular reasons for wanting to be a gentleman', Biddy immediately
asks, 'don't you think you are happier as you are?' (p. 155).

It is important to recognise that Pip's aspirations for gentility and
his dissatisfaction with his prospective life as Joe's apprentice originate
not with Jaggers's announcement of his expectations but years before
as a reaction to Estella's snobbery and scorn for Pip's 'coarse hands and
my common boots'. Pip's reflections that 'They had never troubled
me before, but they troubled me now, as vulgar appendages'
immediately leads to a wish that 'Joe had been rather more genteelly
brought up, and then I should have been so too' (pp. 91−2).

Had Jaggers's unexpected announcement not dramatically
extended the social/economic boundaries of Pip's life he would
almost certainly have spent a lifetime of hopeless, frustrated longing
which would have made his occupation hateful to him. From the

moment of his longings for the socially improbable, Pip describes himself as 'restlessly aspiring discontented me' and admits 'I used to think . . . That I should have been happier and better if I had never seen Miss Havisham's face and had risen to manhood content to be partners with Joe in the honest old forge' (p. 291). Note the significance of 'better'. Thwarted aspiration and consciousness of relative deprivation can corrupt morally and can breed anti-social anger and jealousy. Orlick's anti-social behaviour is not merely the result of 'natural evil' but is also a product of thwarted aspiration. (Orlick accuses Pip of being in his way and keeping him down.) Smiles held it to be every man's duty to aspire to a higher social station, but the whole brunt of *Great Expectations* argues that the working class as a whole would be both happier and better if they accepted the station to which they were born and worked conscientiously within it – in short behaved like Joe and Biddy.

However, if the novel's attack on the myth of the self-made man as a viable ideal for the whole community is unequivocal when the novel explores the vexed contemporary issue of what constitutes gentility, and how a gentleman should be defined and recognised, the development of the theme becomes muddled and problematic. Some critics see the implied recognition that Joe Gargery is a real or true gentleman (or one of nature's gentlemen) as a radical social response by Dickens – a moral (classless) definition of gentility being proposed as an alternative to the traditional (aristocratic) definition in terms of birth, ownership of a landed estate, and a life-style of leisured idleness. In fact Dickens's characteristic use of the concept of natural gentility is little more than a sop to his reading public with conservative (not radical) social/political implications.

Consider Joe Gargery. He represents the 'virtue of industry' and is an 'honest-hearted, duty-doing man' – thus despite his social origins his virtues are located within the framework of traditional middle-class virtues. Indeed he represents a middle-class view of what the ideal worker should be like. His forge represents the necessity of work (to be contrasted not only with Pip's life in London but probably also with the non-functional brewery at Miss Havisham's) while the dirty hands which follow from his honest manual labour stand in opposition to Jaggers's clean and scented hands (which no amount of washing can cleanse of the taint of his dirty business).

However, like all the good workers in Dickens's fiction, Joe's presentation is flawed by elements which prevent Pip's forgetfulness of him from seeming a tragic injustice. First, he is exploited as a figure of fun to a degree incompatible with the dignity he is elsewhere intended to bear. Dickens's original concept of Joe was that of 'a good natured foolish man' and when, for example, Joe breakfasts at Pip's chambers he appears in the role (no doubt intended as entertaining) of being simply foolish. Secondly, throughout the novel Joe's intellectual powers are presented as being those of an adult half-wit, or a not very advanced child. At the opening of the novel Pip, aged about seven, says of Joe, 'I always treated him as a larger species of child, and as no more than my equal' (p. 40).

Of course it is no surprise that Joe is politically conservative. He knows his place (like all good workers from Stephen Blackpool to Betty Higden) and tells Pip, 'You and me is not two figures to be together in London.' Thus he accepts the conventional views of what constitutes gentility in a manner similar to Magwitch (with his hatred of being low). To Magwitch, gentility is merely money and the ostentatious articles of dress, appearance, and display it can buy. On his return, Magwitch approvingly notes Pip's linen, clothes and books, and fingers his watch and ring not merely as signs or symptoms of gentility but as the very thing itself. (We are reminded of the satire on the surfaces of gentility in *Little Dorrit*.) The novel might use Magwitch to make a radical social connection between the criminal underworld and the wealth of respectable society, but Magwitch himself is not a conscious social rebel against conventional class values.

Whenever a social idea is put in the mouth of a working-class character in Dickens's fiction (like Stephen Blackpool's admission of the need for paternalistic, and not representative, democratic government) the political implications are inevitably conservative. Joe is given an important speech to legitimise Pip and himself going their separate ways — and significantly it is an uncanny anticipation of a consensus, functionalist model of society.

'Pip, dear old chap, life is made of ever so many partings welded together, as I may say, and one man's a blacksmith and one's a whitesmith and one's a goldsmith, and one's a coppersmith. Divisions among such must come, and must be met as they come' (p. 246). What is implicitly recognised is not merely a difference of social/economic functions but the organisation of these into a hierarchy of differentiated social statuses. Joe goes on to revealingly define the social image he has of himself.

'I'm wrong in these clothes. I'm wrong out of the forge, the kitchen, or off th' meshes. You won't find half so much fault in me if you think of me in my forge dress, with my hammer in my hand, or even my pipe. You won't find half so much fault in me if, supposing as you should ever wish to see me, you come and put your head in at the forge window and see Joe the blacksmith there, at the old anvil, in the old burnt apron, sticking to the old work. I'm awful dull, but I hope I've beat out something nigh the rights of this at last (p. 246).

Joe wilfully subordinates himself to a social role – 'Joe the blacksmith'. Even his language reflects this – he uses the specialised vocabulary of his job in general conversation (e.g. 'welded together' and 'beat out'). This is true of most of Dickens's lower class characters – e.g. Toodles (in *Dombey and Son*), and Bagnet and Mr George (in *Bleak House*). They express themselves in the specialised vocabulary of their trade or social role, and this works against Dickens's insistence that their humanity transcends their specialised function, often shown in the novels to be a mere question of wages and hire.

Joe has no conscious identity outside his job. In this sense he is an unconscious victim of the division of labour. However, this reduction of man to a social role does not alienate him. While others in the novel try to assert a fulfilling private identity, Joe looks to his skilled and useful job as a means of transcending his lack of a mature adult personality in private life. In his need of a useful official role to give him dignity, Joe is a mirror-opposite of Wemmick. Of course this reduction of man to a function is only liberating for Joe because of his retarded intellectual development. Joe is similar here to Frederick Dorrit in *Little Dorrit*, of whom we're told 'in private life, where there was no part for the clarionet, he had no part at all' (p. 282).

Thus Joe sets problems of interpretation. On the one hand he shrinks his humanity by relegating himself to a social/economic function to be identified in terms of the *objects* associated with it – his forge dress, hammer, anvil – and yet on the other hand by implying that he is one of nature's gentlemen the novel asserts that his general humanity transcends his specialised role. However, if we accept that by implication Joe, 'this gentle Christian man', *is* one of nature's gentlemen then this does not make him Dickens's *ideal* gentleman. This will become clearer if we examine the moral changes experienced by Pip and consider especially the ending of the novel.

V

Pip's moral changes are signposted by his different attitudes to the significance of money and the use it can be put to. When Joe announces his intention to visit Pip at Barnard's Inn Pip admits 'If I could have kept him away by paying money, I certainly would have paid money' (p. 240). That is, he was willing to use money to buy off a friend. Later after his illness Pip realises that money alone is inadequate to repay the debt he owes Joe. Pip is now aware of the existence of authentic values which cannot be translated into equivalent money terms.

Pip's instinctive desire to reject the fortune Magwitch had offered him was indicative not just of the repugnance and disgust excited in him by Magwitch – his imagined crimes as well as his table manners – but also of his belief that Magwitch's money was dirtier and more tainted than Miss Havisham's would have been. The money Pip had received from Magwitch's convict messenger was 'two fat sweltering one pound notes that seemed to have been on terms of the warmest intimacy with all the cattle markets in the country' (p. 107). When the now respectable Pip repays Magwitch for the 'loan' he does so in notes which 'were clean and new'. The novel implies that this distinction between clean and dirty money is spurious. However, Pip doesn't explicitly state this. The plot intervenes to simplify the resolution of this theme. Magwitch's money is confiscated by the crown – 'I had no claim, and I finally resolved, and ever afterwards abided by the resolution, that my heart should never be sickened with the hopeless task of attempting to establish one' (p. 458). The point about Pip's 'refusal' of Magwitch's money is not that he fails to reject the distinction between clean and dirty money but that he also positively refused to accept money from Miss Havisham when he knew whom his patron was. The implication borne out by Pip's business career with Herbert, is that Pip no longer felt that he had a right to accept something for nothing. In the future he must work for his own money.

But he does not work for it back at the forge, despite his original feeling that it would be right for him to return to the village and marry Biddy. The novel sidesteps the implications of Pip's return, i.e. having been educated into appreciating intelligent, urbane, literate society Pip would now be imprisoned by returning to the claustrophobic society of The Three Jolly Bargemen. The plot resolution (Biddy is already married to Joe, leaving Pip free to join Herbert overseas) conveniently avoids this problem. However, the fact that Pip returns to Herbert, not Joe, has important implications for the novel's treatment of the gentility theme.

Herbert Pocket earlier in the novel said of his father, 'it is a principle of his that no man who was not a true gentleman at heart, ever was, since the world began, a true gentleman in manner. He says no varnish can hide the grain of the wood; and that the more varnish you put on, the more the grain will express itself' (p. 204). Compeyson's advantage over Magwitch at their trial was the result of this manner and varnish only. Yet though the novel asserts that gentility at heart (the grain not the varnish) is what really matters – hence Joe is one of nature's gentlemen – the *ideal* gentleman to Dickens (represented in this novel by Herbert Pocket and his father, in *Bleak House* by Jarndyce, 'a gentleman of a humane heart', and in *Little Dorrit* by Clennam) is a gentleman in *both* heart and manner. Thus Joe falls short of the ideal in that he lacks varnish, manner and polish – qualities not sufficient in themselves to confer true gentlemanly status on the bearer but not to be dismissed as unimportant. They have a positive value and are held to be desirable *in addition to* (*though they are no substitute for*) gentility of the heart (i.e. moral gentility).

In its chief themes and social vision *Great Expectations* presents a critical opposition to mid-Victorian society, in particular commenting on the fastidious, ostentatious and complacent nature of bourgeois respectability. However, the interpretive middle-class value index certainly comes into play at the conclusion of the novel, with important consequences for the gentility theme.

It is the frank and open, urbane, socially skilled Herbert (who can give Pip his lesson in table manners with tact and cheerful delicacy) who approaches Dickens's ideal of gentility. And despite his moral equality Joe would be expected to defer socially to Herbert, and have the good sense (as he does) to see this deference as natural and inevitable. Within the moral class of true gentlemen the gentleman of heart would be expected to defer socially to those who were both gentlemen of heart and manner. Of course, moral equality without corresponding social equality is an easy and empty gesture on the novelist's part. Thus the gentility theme is concluded in a manner consistent with many of the conventional assumptions about class current in mid-Victorian society. It is in no way an attack on class as an institution. An unequal distribution of wealth and the material prizes of society is not being criticised in itself.

Indeed *Great Expectations* tacitly accepts the chief assumptions and conventional beliefs about class and the class system in mid-Victorian England. The most common contemporary view of the class system was of a ladder (a social hierarchy) in which the rungs did not move but individuals did. It is clear from the conclusion to Pip's history as well as Lizzie Hexam's marriage in *Our Mutual Friend* that Dickens felt that in certain cases it was right for particular individuals to cross class lines, but that these class divisions should still remain.

Within the later novels generally the implied view of the class system is of a hierarchy of differentiated functions. At certain points in the novels (e.g. Lizzie Hexam's social mobility consequent on her marriage) the element of hierarchy will be emphasised (this is usually so when dealing with the 'natural' social aspiration of middle-class characters), while on other occasions the element of functional divisions will be stressed (e.g. when Joe expresses why it is right that his future path should be kept separate from Pip's). Indeed the functional element is usually stressed when dealing with the experience of working-class characters whose vocabulary often emphasises their functional role. In both cases, however, it is the same social model which is being used, and this is a ladder view of society, described by Raymond Williams as 'a perfect symbol of the bourgeois idea of society'.[5]

It is worth looking more closely at the way in which the middle-class value-index operates in the novel's plot resolution. By associating himself openly with Magwitch at the trial Pip had put himself outside the pale of conventional class values. His business career in the East, however, serves to integrate him back into bourgeois society. Furthermore, the qualified but not inconsiderable material success which Pip gains abroad is won in the best traditions of the middle-class myth of self-help, earlier criticised in its *general* applicability to the *whole* of society.

> Many a year went round, before I was a partner in the House; but, I lived happily with Herbert and his wife, and I lived frugally, and I paid my debts . . . I must not leave it to be supposed that we were ever a great House, or that we made mints of money. We were not in a grand way of business, but we had a good name and worked for our profits, and did very well' (p. 489).

Pip's business career involves a parade of traditional middle-class virtues — thrift, earnestness, duty (he repays his debts), industry, perseverance and patience (his deserved promotion). The profits of the firm (like the firm of Doyce and Clennam a throwback to an earlier stage of entrepreneurial capitalism) are thus a symptom of moral application, consistent with the entrepreneurial ideal.

The effect of this is that Pip no longer appears a problematic person when he meets Estella on revisiting Satis House. His final stance in the novel is not a subversive one — like Arthur Clennam he settles into a life of modest usefulness as a partner in a small, individual business firm. Though Pip's material success is qualified it is comfortable. He may have rejected society (i.e. its false social values) but Pip still remains socially acceptable. However, his final position is given no general or future significance for society as a whole.

Of course, in addition to Biddy's marriage the fact that Herbert was established in a business career within an expanding firm is the crucial plot means by which Pip is provided with an alternative to going back to the forge, and hence a satisfactory closed plot ending is achieved. It is significant that once again the resolution of the hero's experience is made possible by an (albeit indirect) money gift from an individual benefactor — in this case Pip's secret gift to Herbert, completed by Miss Havisham, which creates a situation from which Pip himself is to benefit. Herbert's dreamy, fanciful character leaves an unearned gift as the *only* means by which his promising position in the business world, so necessary to a satisfactory plot close, could be achieved. This emphasises the amount of luck involved in the eventual integration within his society of a characteristic Dickens hero (Esther, Pip or John Harmon) in the mature work, usually due as much to the generosity of others as to individual achievement. Of course, consideration of the plot close leads inevitably to the question of the rewritten ending. The original ending which keeps Pip and Estella apart (they briefly meet by accident years later and continue in their separate paths, Pip as a bachelor and Estella remarried to a country doctor) is a more open and muted one. It is not happy but there is a modicum of comfort in Pip's business success. The ending seems artistically right and strikes a tone similar to the closing paragraphs of *Little Dorrit*.

The rewritten ending closes the romantic relation between Pip and Estella in a conventionally happy fashion, but one inconsistent with the whole tone and mood of Pip's narrative. The change de-monstrates Dickens's continued stake in the literary market (see Chapter 3). The chief reason for following Lytton's advice is clear from a letter to Forster in which Dickens declared that he had 'no doubt that the story will be more acceptable through the alteration'. The reasoning would have been approved by Gowan. The second ending certainly works against the unity and coherence of the text and confirms the general truth that the plot resolutions are the least successful aspects of the mature work. The final novel to be considered, *Our Mutual Friend*, demonstrates this point even more forcefully and it too is seriously flawed by the clash of artistic integrity and market considerations.

8 *Our Mutual Friend* – The Dust-Mounds and The Principle of Speculation

I

Dickens's social vision in this, his last completed novel, encompasses familiar ideas and themes. This is suggested by one of those thematically loaded descriptions of London which characterise his later work.

> A grey dusty withered evening in London city has not a hopeful aspect. The closed warehouses and offices have an air of death about them, and the national dread of colour has an air of mourning. The towers and steeples of the many house-encompassed churches, dark and dingy as the sky that seems descending on them, are no relief to the general gloom; a sun-dial on a church-wall has the look, in its useless black shade, of having failed in its business enterprise and stopped payment forever. . . . The set of humanity outward from the City is as a set of prisoners departing from gaol, and dismal Newgate seems quite as fit a stronghold for the mighty Lord Mayor as his own state-dwelling (p. 450).[1]

Here encapsulated in one passage are most of the themes and relationships which form the artistic capital for Dickens's social vision in his later novels – the suggestive relations of, and thematic connections between, the warehouses and offices and death; the City and prison; the socially respectable (Lord Mayor) and the criminal (Newgate). Equally familiar is the failure of the Church to influence the quality of everyday life, and the pervasive influence of market-place relations and values (even the workings of a sun-dial are described in terms of an unsuccessful money/business relationship). Indeed the market nature of the social relations of everyday life – the most insistent and important idea in the later fiction – plays a characteristically central role in *Our Mutual Friend*, (1864–5).

As we have seen before, the discussion of the use of emblems or repeated images offers a particularly rewarding point of entry into the imaginative world of Dickens's mature novels. However, the two emblems invested with a general social significance in *Our Mutual Friend* – the river and the dust-mounds – both present problems of interpretation.

We will consider the river first. It is a common literary metaphor which takes the movement of a river from source to sea as suggestive of the passage of life, its ebb and flow, its movement and mystery. There is a similar connotation in the image of the waves in *Dombey and Son*. This traditional literary use of the river is relevant to certain passages in *Our Mutual Friend* – as, for example, when old Betty Higden dies beside the river she has heard calling her, 'Come to me, come to me! . . . I am the Relieving Officer appointed by eternal ordinance to do my work' (p. 567), and when Lizzie Hexam stands by the river pondering on her father's future life 'unable to see into the vast blank misery of a life suspected, and fallen away from by good and bad, but knowing that it lay there dim before her, stretching away to the great ocean, Death' (p. 115). However, this is not the river's main significance for the novel's social vision – nor, it seems to me, is the idea of immersion in the river as a form of ritual baptism or cleansing (which will be considered later when discussing Eugene Wrayburn's rebirth) crucial to the river's suggestiveness for society as a whole. Of course the mature novels' characteristic touch with symbols is the open (not mutually exclusive) relation between realistic and figurative interpretations, and we must try to preserve the balance between the river as an emblem and its realistic or topographical identity. To this end, when we consider the river as social fact what was most striking about it to contemporaries (and what is given most emphasis in the novel) is its pollution.

In a letter to Cerjat (July 1858) Dickens declared, 'The Thames in London is most horrible. I have to cross Waterloo or London Bridge to get to the railroad when I come here, and I can certify that the offensive smells, even in that short whiff, have been of a most head-and-stomach distending nature.' It is to be expected that the visual image of the polluted river would be associated with the industrial process which had produced this comparatively recent change in its appearance. To contemporaries the river was one of the most sensuously arresting symbols of the contamination of social life by the industrial process and in *Our Mutual Friend* Dickens artistically exploits this fact. The novel emphasises the pollution of the Thames. Near its source the river is pure. 'In those pleasant little towns on Thames, . . . you may see the young river, dimpled like a young child, playfully gliding away among the trees, unpolluted by the defilements that lie in wait for it on it's course, and as yet out of hearing of the deep summons of the sea' (p. 567). In its contact with the city (and industrial society) the once-pure river becomes defiled and contaminated. It flows through the corrupt and corrupting riverside areas ('where accumulated scum of humanity seemed to be washed from higher grounds, like so much moral sewage, and to be pausing until it's own weight forced it over the bank and sunk it in the river' (p. 63)) and past the wharves and warehouses, visible emblems of the pervasive market ethos and appropriately linked with imagery of death (their lettering 'looked . . . like inscriptions over the graves of dead businesses' (p. 219)) – and the change in the river's character and appearance is so marked 'that the after-consequences of being crushed, sucked under, and drawn down, looked as ugly to the imagination as the main event' (pp. 219–20).

Thus in the novel the river's pollution becomes a concrete physical sign that something is wrong in mid-Victorian society – a visible symptom or emblem of a corrupt society.[2] This corruption is related not just to the industrial process in general but to the stage of capitalist development marked by the mid-Victorian period. It is worth noting that near the source of the river stands the paper mill where Lizzie Hexam finds work after fleeing London. The paper mill is a throwback to an earlier form of entrepreneurial capitalism – a small independent business where relations with employees are personal and kindly. The mill is associated, through its Upper Thames location, with the pure and optimistic beginning of the river's journey. This journey to the city (and an economic climate dominated by shares) can be read as a metaphor for the historical development of Victorian capitalism.

Certainly the relation between the river and the other major emblem of the novel, the dust-mounds, is crucial to the novel's examination of the general quality of social life.

That some sort of equation between the mounds and wealth is intended is clear from a series of verbal associations throughout the novel which forge a suggestive link between wealth and the chief ingredients of the mounds, e.g. wastepaper and ashes. Wastepaper and rubbish blown around the city streets on a windy day is referred

to as 'That mysterious paper currency which circulates in London
when the wind blows' (p. 191), and when Riderhood informs on
Gaffer Hexam in Lightwood's office the silence was 'broken only by
the fall of the ashes in the grate, which attracted the informer's
attention as if it were the clinking of money' (p. 202). The mounds are
described as containing dust, dirt, wastepaper, and rubbish of various
sorts – and yet this amalgam was valuable, fetching a high market
price, and of course the dust-mounds constitute the bulk of Harmon's
fortune on which the plot of the novel centres. Thus in society's
market ownership of dirt and rubbish (the mounds) could be literally
equivalent to the possession of money.

The fact that through the mounds wealth is given a multiple series
of unsavoury connotations (we are reminded of the description of
Tellson's bank in *A Tale of Two Cities*) clearly implies some comment
on society's dominant motive of pursuit of wealth. However, it is too
simplistic to equate the mounds with wealth and assert that the
novel's moral is that money is dirt and rubbish. The novel uses the
emblem of the mounds in a flexible, adaptable fashion. For example,
while describing the slow process of clearing the mounds the
direction of the emblem's relation to the world of the novel is
suddenly changed to incorporate an attack on the political system:

> My Lords and gentlemen and honourable boards, when you in the
> course of your dust-shovelling and cinder-raking have piled up a
> mountain of pretentious failure, you must off with your
> honourable coats for the removal of it, and fall to the work with
> the power of all the queen's horses and all the queen's men, or it
> will come rushing down and bury us alive. . . .
> We must mend it, lords and gentlemen and honourable boards,
> or in it's own evil hour it will mar every one of us (pp. 565–6).

However, the chief objection to claiming that the novel asserts that
money is filth is that it is an attitude to money, a value-system in
which pursuit of wealth and economic well-being is all-important
which is being commented on through the unsavoury association
with the dirt of the dust-mounds. The code of values being attacked in this emblematic fashion is that which we have called the
market mentality. Of course, this market-orientated philosophy of
life when translated into general social behaviour involves at its very
core an attitude to people, but as a way of judging and valuing it is
perhaps most clearly recognised in a degraded attitude to money as

the primary and absolute value in social life. The suggestion implied in Jaggers's repeated washing and scenting of his hands (that the official business of the system is dirty business) is now taken a stage further. The everyday social business of mid-Victorian England — seen in the novel as essentially a form of speculation in people and things; a mode of behaviour dominated by the money values of the market ethos — is now seen as a morally dirty business. The comment on the general condition made through the novel's use of the mounds is linked within the scheme of the novel to the Voice of Society, which as we shall see crystallises this general social condition on the plane of values (as a way of thinking, feeling and judging) just as the mounds give it a visual realisation in the imaginative landscape of the novel.

However, mention of the visual realisation of the dust-mounds takes us to the chief problem in the novel's handling of the emblem. It has been argued that a sensuous particularisation of detail is needed if an emblem or symbol is to satisfactorily sustain its figurative function, but what we know about the mounds is due more to House's research than to Dickens's own descriptions, which do not attempt to detail the sights and the smells of the dust-mounds. As a result in the realistic scenery of the novel the mounds occupy a very shadowy existence indeed. The novel's reticence on just what was contained in the mounds is important. House has argued that one of their chief ingredients was human excrement (which as a fertiliser would be a chief contributor to their overall value) and that Dickens euphemistically referred to human dung through the polite term 'dust'. Certainly contemporary readers would be alive to hints and suggestions that Dickens might delicately refrain from fleshing out in order not 'to offend the young person', and artistic tact need not prevent a novelist from communicating his desired idea or effect. But while House's argument, which draws on documentary sources, that the dust-mounds did contain human excrement is convincing there is no evidence for this within the novel itself. Indeed the amount of detail given about the appearance and make-up of the mounds is in inverse proportion to the weight of suggestive meaning the mounds were clearly intended to carry.

It is a severe handicap to any objective reading of the novel, which takes nothing away from the text and adds nothing to it, that the mounds lack a vividly realised identity, for the weakness of their artistic realisation compromises their thematic importance in the formulation of the novel's social vision — an importance which is

only fully appreciated if we recognise their relation to the Voice of
Society, to the operation of shares, and to Boffin's miserly persona,
which expresses the generalising suggestiveness of the mounds on the
level of individual characterisation. For example, the novel connects
living off rubbish and living off shares. The waste-products of the
mounds offer a handsome living to their owner; the 'melancholy waifs
and strays' who scavenge through the London rubbish 'searching and
stooping and poking for anything to sell' (p. 450) try to eke out a
living through society's waste. Fledgeby fattens off stock-market bills
which he buys in bulk as so much wastepaper. 'Half the lump will be
wastepaper one knows beforehand. . . . Can you get it at wastepaper
price? That's the question' (p. 483). The implication is that the stock-
market speculators are merely more respectable, and more glittering
scavengers.

II

In *Our Mutual Friend* the familiar theme of society as a market-place
has a particular relevance for the economic climate of the 1860s, for
the market-orientated frame of reference for everyday life is
presented in this novel as a form of speculation. Stock-market
speculation had grown throughout the mid-Victorian period to
produce by the mid-1860s a whole class of nouveaux riches,
represented in the novel by Veneering. The novel emphasises the
importance of speculation within the economic life of the country.

> As is well known to the wise in their generation, traffic in Shares is
> the one thing to have to do with in this world. Have no
> antecedents, no established character, no cultivation, no ideas, no
> manners; have Shares. Have Shares enough to be on Boards of
> Direction in capital letters, oscillate on mysterious business
> between London and Paris, and be great. Where does he come
> from? Shares. Where is he going to? Shares. What are his tastes?
> Shares. Has he any principles? Shares. What squeezes him into
> Parliament? Shares. Perhaps he never of himself achieved success in
> anything, never originated anything, never produced anything?
> Sufficient answer to all; Shares. O mighty Shares! To set those
> blaring images so high, and to cause us smaller vermin, as under the
> influence of herbane or opium, to cry out, night and day, 'Relieve
> us of our money, scatter it for us, buy us and sell us, ruin us, only we

beseech ye take rank among the powers of the earth, and fatten on us!' (pp. 159–60)

Like the 'great expectations' of Pip an abstraction has been dramatised as a thing-like force, and like Chancery and the Circumlocution Office it is an external force, related to the humans who created it in a hostile and threatening manner. Shares divide society into two groups – exploiters and exploited. Lammle's friends and fellow speculators 'seemed to divide the world into two classes of people – people who were making enormous fortunes and people who were being enormously ruined' (p. 313). Through the operation of shares, speculators 'fatten' on the 'smaller vermin' of the rest of society. This directs us to the repeated imagery of birds or animals of prey, suggesting a general individualistic and competitive scavenging throughout society. Imagery of this kind was applied to Chancery characters in *Bleak House*, and in this novel it is used of Gaffer Hexam, Rogue Riderhood and his daughter Pleasant, Wegg, the Lammles, and Wrayburn – characters from all social groups.

The novel's chief argument that the market principle of speculation is not confined to the stock-exchange but infiltrates all areas of society as a social frame of reference is reinforced by parallel means. Much of the comedy in the book touches on the concept of speculation. It has always been characteristic of Dickens's method to make serious social comments in a comic playful context, which does not, however, remove their relevance or sting.

For example, of the Boffins' plan to adopt an orphan we are told that:

it was found impossible to complete the philanthropic transaction without buying the orphans. For, the instant it became known that anybody wanted the orphan, up started some affectionate relative of the orphan who put a price upon the orphan's head. The suddenness of an orphan's rise in the market was not to be paralleled by the maddest records of the Stock Exchange. He would be at five thousand per cent discount out at nurse making a mud pie at nine in the morning, and (being inquired for) would go up to five thousand per cent premium before noon. The market was 'rigged' in various artful ways. Counterfeit stock got into circulation. Parents boldly represented themselves as dead, and brought their orphans with them. Genuine orphan stock was surreptitiously withdrawn from the market. It being announced by emissaries posted for the purpose, that Mr and Mrs Milvey were coming down the court, orphan scrip would be instantly concealed, and production refused, save on a condition usually stated by the brokers as 'a gallon of beer'. Likewise, fluctuations of a wild and South-Sea nature were occasioned, by orphan-holders keeping back, and then rushing into the market a dozen together. But, the uniform principle at the root of all these various operations was bargain and sale; and that principle could not be recognised by Mr and Mrs Milvey (p. 244).

The tone is light and humorous but the underlying concept of speculating in people as commodities reflects family ties as unnatural and perverted as those of Mr Dolls and Jenny Wren.

Even the criminal inhabitants of Mr Inspector's police-office are seen as objects in a business transaction. The police station itself, with its 'methodical book-keeping' is described as a business firm. 'The sanctuary was not a permanent abiding-place, but a kind of criminal Pickford's. The lower passions and wills were regularly ticked off in the books, warehoused in the cells, carted away as per accompanying invoice, and left little mark upon it' (p. 833).

The point about the orphan stock-market is reinforced by Veneering's dinners, which have nothing at all to do with generosity, fellowship or true hospitality. Instead they are mere economic investments to a social end in which friendship is cultivated in order to strengthen the foundations of Veneering's uncertain social position. In effect Veneering speculates in his 'friends'. Twemlow being 'cousin to Lord Snigsworth, of Snigsworthy Park' is 'a remunerative article' and hence 'in frequent requisition'. Podsnap is just as useful a social asset:

Perhaps, after all — who knows? — Veneering may find this dining, though expensive, remunerative, in the sense that it makes champions. Mr Podsnap, as a representative man, is not alone in caring very particularly for his own dignity, if not for that of his acquaintances, and therefore in angrily supporting the acquaintances who have taken out his Permit, lest in their being lessened, he should be (pp. 683–4).

It is an appropriate comment on the mercenary principle behind Veneering's 'hospitality' that when he hosts Lammle's wedding reception 'nobody seems to think more of the Veneerings than if they were a tolerable landlord and landlady doing the thing in the way of business at so much a head' (p. 166).

If Veneering's dinners are investments then Bradley Headstone has speculated in education and the social role of the schoolmaster to free himself from a working-class environment and gain the social dividend of respectability. Headstone's method of learning and retention of knowledge is described as a business operation, as if he were a merchant dealing in education.

> From his early childhood up, his mind had been a place of mechanical stowage. The arrangement of his wholesale warehouse, so that it might be always ready to meet the demands of retail dealers – history here, geography there, astronomy to the right, political economy to the left – natural history, the physical sciences, figures, music, the lower mathematics, and what not, all in their several places – this care had imparted to his countenance a look of care. . . . He always seemed to be uneasy lest anything should be missing from his mental warehouse, and taking stock to assure himself (pp. 266–7).

Wegg's thoughts as Boffin approaches his stall neatly summarise a way of thinking and valuing which is general in society – 'Are you in independent circumstances, or is it wasting the motions of a bow on you? Come! I'll speculate! I'll invest a bow in you' (p. 90) – and this way of thinking and valuing is given expression in the Voice of Society. Although it is first heard round the Veneering dinner table, the Voice of Society is more than just the value stance of fashionable or high society (i.e. a class voice), but is a general frame of reference throughout society, as rampant amongst down-and-outs (Wegg, Riderhood, Mr Dolls) and the lower middle class (Charley Hexam, the unreformed Bella) as in 'bran new' fashionable society. It is a voice which values both things and people in the same quantitative money terms, crystallised in the image of Podsnap's plate.

> Hideous solidity was the characteristic of the Podsnap plate. Everything was made to look as heavy as it could, and to take up as much room as possible. Everything said boastfully, 'Here you have as much of me in my ugliness as if I were only lead; but I am so many ounces of precious metal worth so much an ounce; – wouldn't you like to melt me down? (p. 177).

Podsnap values people in the same quantitative terms. At his own party 'The majority of guests were like the plate, and included several heavy articles weighing ever so much' (p. 177) and 'nothing would have astonished him [Podsnap] more than an intimation that Miss Podsnap, or any other young person properly born and bred, could not be exactly put away like the plate, polished like the plate, counted, weighed and valued like the plate' (pp. 189–90).

The Voice of Society proclaims marriage to be (as Mrs Lammle confesses of the intended match between Fledgeby and Georgiana) a 'partnership affair, a money-speculation'. The best example of marriage seen as a nice problem in economic rationale is the view of the Contractor on Eugene's marriage to Lizzie Hexam.

> It appears to this potentate, that what the man in question should have done, would have been, to buy the young woman a boat and a small annuity, and set her up for herself. These things are a question of beefsteaks and porter. You buy the young woman a boat. Very good. You buy her, at the same time a small annuity. You speak of that annuity in pounds sterling, but it is in reality so many pounds of beefsteaks and so many pints of porter. On the one hand, the young woman has the boat. On the other hand, she consumes so many pounds of beefsteaks and so many pints of porter. Those beefsteaks and that porter are the fuel to that young woman's engine. She derives therefrom a certain amount of power to row the boat; that power will produce so much money; You add that to the small annuity; and thus you get at the young woman's income. That (it seems to the Contractor) is the way of looking at it.' (p. 890).

Probably the most articulate and coherent expression of the Voice of Society is provided by Boffin in his miserly persona. Though an act, his cynicism, like Gowan's, is an accurate reflection of the general condition. For example, here is Boffin the miser lecturing Rokesmith:

> 'A man of property, like me, is bound to consider the market-price. . . . I've got acquainted with the duties of property. I mustn't go putting the market-price up, because money may happen not to be an object with me. A sheep is worth so much in the market, and I ought to give it and no more. A secretary is worth so much in the market, and I ought to give it and no more' (p. 523).

His support for the investment principle ('and we have to recollect that money makes money, as well as makes everything else') is appropriate, for the Voice of Society embodies and legitimises as a general frame of reference the speculation principle inherent in the operation of shares as an institution.

Thus the mounds, shares, the Voice of Society, Boffin the miser, and Podsnap's plate are all bound together within the novel's structure to produce a coherent and unified social vision – an indictment of the quality of everyday social relations in all areas of the system. *Our Mutual Friend* offers no hope for the regeneration of society as a whole but there is hope for individual happiness and fulfilment in private life. However, to gain the chance of this it is necessary to 'be dead' to the values of the social world, and to be deaf to the Voice of Society.

III

When, in Book 2, Chapter 5, Fledgeby visits the premises of Pubsey and Co., he finds Riah not in the shop but up on his private roof-garden talking with Lizzie Hexam and Jenny Wren. In the text which follows the opposition between the downstairs shop, where the business is carried on, and the roof garden is given a multiple suggestiveness. The difference between the official sphere and the private, the prison and the garden, the spiritual death of a life governed by the market-ethos and the possibility of happiness and fulfilment outside the influence of the mounds and the Voice of Society – all this is embodied in the text which centres on an ironic reversal of the concepts of life and death.

Fledgeby calls Riah down into the shop and when they return to the roof-garden Jenny Wren exclaims,

'Why it was only just now . . . that I fancied I saw him come out of his grave! He toiled out at that low door so bent and worn, and then he took his breath and stood upright, and looked all round him at the sky, and the wind blew upon him, and his life down in the dark was over! – Till he was called back to life,' she added, looking round at Fledgeby with that lower look of sharpness. 'Why did you call him back?' (p. 334).

Jenny Wren's invitation to Riah ('Come up and be dead!') is

paradoxically an invitation to free himself from the alienation of his official life as Fledgeby's front – to attain fulfilment as a human being. But this can only happen if Riah dies to (i.e. rejects as a proper or viable frame of reference) the values of the world (those social values embodied in the Voice of Society). As elsewhere in the later novels humane and fulfilling social relationships are seen as being possible only in opposition to the dominant moral code of society, and attainable in the private sphere (hence the roof-garden).

Jenny tells Fledgeby what it is like to be dead, ' "Oh, so peaceful and so thankful! And you hear the people who are alive, crying, and working, and calling to one another down in the close dark streets, and you seem to pity them so! And such a chain has fallen from you, and such a strange good sorrowful happiness comes upon you!" ' (p. 334). The quality of 'death to the world' is best understood by comparison with the values of 'life' in 'the close dark streets'. In a later scene Fledgeby tells Jenny Wren, 'Instead of coming up and being dead, let's come out and look alive. It'll pay better, I assure you' (p. 785), and on Jenny's reply that 'it's always well worth my while to make money' Fledgeby approvingly adds 'Now, you're coming out and looking alive!' (p. 786). The values of 'life' as it is lived in mid-Victorian England are those of the market, thus the values of 'death' are authentic values which repudiate the market ethos.

By becoming 'dead' Riah achieves a rebirth which sets a pattern for all the spiritual rebirths in the novel (in all cases involving a death to the dominant social values of money, property, respectability, etc. – the values embodied in the Voice of Society). However, Riah's rebirth, involving his resignation from his official post as Fledgeby's stooge, is problematic in a similar fashion to Pancks's withdrawal of labour from Casby. Like Pancks, Riah 'perceived that the obligation was upon me to leave this service' (p. 796). But Riah's resignation does not involve the economic deprivation which would put pressure on him to come 'alive' again. The existence of the model factory run by his fellow-countrymen beside the 'pure' upper Thames (an idealistic alternative to his occupation under Fledgeby) is as convenient a plot device to have it both ways as the firm of Doyce and Clennam was to Pancks. In both cases the plot resolution enables the problem set by the novelist to disappear. Indeed, following the more realistic acceptance of his condition by Wemmick, the freeing of Riah by artificial plot means appears a sentimental relapse. As we shall see this is typical of the artificially induced optimism of the ending of *Our Mutual Friend*.

Just as Riah's rebirth involves a denial of his old self (the social image of the grasping Jewish moneylender which Fledgeby exploited), so Eugene Wrayburn's conversion involves a rejection of his old social self. He is presented at first as a type of the aristocratic dandy (a more rounded development of Harthouse in *Hard Times*). The badges of his social position are boredom and self-possession.

Indeed the opposition of rival lovers Wrayburn and Headstone is presented as a study in class relations — the problem (central to *Little Dorrit* and *Great Expectations*) of social definition. Eugene's position is unambiguous. His birth, public school education, profession and life-style all proclaim him to be a gentleman. His self-assurance is the product of the ease with which he can define his social position and the certainty that his self-image will be accepted by society. However, Bradley Headstone's social situation is the very reverse. His newly won respectability is vulnerable. Like Gowan he is between two classes. Yet what is interesting is that while Eugene is attacked as a type of aristocratic gentleman from the traditional middle-class stance (he is bored, indifferent, idle), Headstone (who embodies all the reverse qualities of work, perseverance, earnestness, etc.) is himself portrayed unsympathetically. His career comments on the dangers of a general aspiration amongst the working class for upward social mobility. Headstone's violent striving for respectability is to be contrasted to the patience and content of Joe Gargery and Dickens's other good working-class characters.

In the crucial scene when Headstone and Charley Hexam confront Eugene in his chambers the self-assured Wrayburn uses the mannered code viciously to keep Headstone in his place as social inferior. We are reminded of one of the themes of *Little Dorrit*. Headstone's lack of mastery over the required social surfaces of respectable society exposes him to Wrayburn's easy, slighting contempt. Headstone, like most of the characters of *Little Dorrit*, is playing the social game of surfaces (his 'decent' clothes and watch-chain advertise his respectability) but he does not play the game well enough. ('He was never seen in any other dress, and yet there was a certain stiffness in his manner of wearing this, as if there were a want of adaptation between him and it, recalling some mechanics in their holiday clothes' (p. 226)). We are reminded of Joe in his best Sunday suit.

However, his passion for Lizzie shakes Eugene's sense of social identity and forces him to re-examine his unthinking acceptance of society's dominant values. In marrying Lizzie he wilfully violates society's expectations of how a gentleman should act (like Pip's association with Magwitch at the trial). Predictably the Voice of Society condemns him out of hand. His 'death' to the values of the world is seen as absurd and incomprehensible. However, the artistic presentation of his rebirth is unconvincing and relies less on character development than on the shadowy symbolic overtones of baptism or ritual cleansing of sin which accompany his rescue from near drowning in the Thames.

Bella Wilfer's rebirth does not demand rescue from drowning. The chief agent in her conversion is Boffin who, in his guise as miser, reflects what Bella takes to be her own values in a form that appals her. He shows her, in himself, 'the most detestable sides of wealth' (p. 846). Bella reacts by taking up a moral stand in the market with reference to Boffin's treatment of Rokesmith – that is, an unprofitable one which corresponds to the death described by Jenny Wren on Riah's roof-garden.

However, the final evidence of Bella's rebirth – her loyalty to her husband when he is arrested – suffers artistically because of the coyness and sentimentality with which her married life generally is described. It is in keeping with the general sentimentality of the novel's conclusion that Dickens should utilise the middle-class ideal of the pretty, playful, little wife/housekeeper to conclude Bella's moral journey in such a precious fashion.

The other chief conversion or rebirth, that of John Harmon (Rokesmith) is the most problematic of all. As this is bound up with the closed nature of the ending it will be discussed in this later context. But what of those characters who do not need to be reborn; who stand from the beginning in opposition to the mounds and the Voice of Society? The chief of these are Lizzie and the Boffins, but their stand in the market-place for qualitative values involves damaging artistic problems.

IV

Lizzie Hexam represents a fusion of ideas present in Amy Dorrit and Joe Gargery. Like Amy she can be improved but like Joe she knows her place. Like Amy she resists the corrupting effect of her environment (the waterside inhabited by 'accumulated scum of humanity' (p. 63)), but while her moral survival may be acceptable the absence of the riverside influence on her speech, grammar, and accent, is quite implausible. Of course, this works to prevent the social distance from Eugene being felt in its full force when they meet, one of the ways in which the novel cheats in its presentation of the issues involved in their romance.

The other problem with Lizzie is that while her attitude to love and marriage stands in stark opposition to the Voice of Society (she tells Bella, 'Does a woman's heart that — that has the weakness in it which you have spoken of . . . seek to gain anything?' (p. 590)) Lizzie herself accepts society's conventions about class and gentility (like Joe and Magwitch). She knows and accepts her place. She admits to Eugene, 'I am removed from you and your family by being a working girl' (p. 761). Unlike her brother she is not a social aspirer. She achieves upward social mobility only because it is given to her and her role throughout is passive. Her view of the surface requirements of gentility is that of Magwitch and indeed Mrs General. When Jenny Wren asks her if she can imagine herself a lady, Lizzie replies, 'More easily than I can make one of such material as myself, Jenny' (p. 404). Yet Lizzie's surface has been sentimentally softened to bear few traces of her social environment. Lizzie's acceptance of her place can be likened to Betty Higden's staunch independence — both reflect an idealised middle-class view of the good worker.

The Boffins too are described in terms of middle-class virtues — chiefly work (Boffin holds up the model of the bee to Eugene) and 'a religious sense of duty'. Unlike the case of Joe Gargery the Boffins' presentation as natural gentlemen is made explicit. Betty Higden tells Mrs Boffin, 'It seems to me . . . that you were born a lady, and a true one, or there never was a lady born' (p. 252). Not surprisingly natural gentility is accompanied with all that it characteristically implies — childishness (Rokesmith regards the Boffins as 'single-hearted children' (p. 429)) and vulnerability (Rokesmith is needed to protect Boffin from the charity spongers and in particular from Wegg). However, surprisingly it appears at first that the Boffins lack the concomitant virtue of knowing their place, for when they come into their money they aspire to join the fashionable world.

This provides one of the chief problems in the Boffins' role. What is the difference between the Veneerings' indulgence in ostentatious display and luxury and the similar behaviour of the Boffins when they go in for society (and indeed socialise with the Veneering set)? The usual answer is that the Boffins are not spoiled or corrupted by what is no more than innocent, childish revelling in a fairy-tale situation. When Mrs Boffin declares to her husband, 'I want society' she does so 'laughing with the glee of a child' (p. 144). For her plunging into High Society is a form of grown-up play. Unlike Pip's aspirations Mrs Boffin's social ambitions are presented squarely in the context of comedy. This prevents most critics from recognising how disturbing many aspects of the Boffins' behaviour would be without this comic gloss. For example, Boffin (who had lectured Wrayburn against idleness, and whose work stood in opposition to the speculation principle and the world of shares) does after all (under pressure from his wife) exchange his work for an idle life of luxury. 'We have come into a great fortune, and we must do what's right by our fortune; we must act up to it' (p. 144). Acting up to society's expectations about class and money is uncomfortably reminiscent of the Merdles' claim that they owed 'a duty to society' which justified and legitimised behaviour which for them was convenient and self-interested. Another example is Mrs Boffin's ostentatious display of expensive goods in that portion of the Bower given over to her taste. The articles she buys ('garish in taste and colour, but . . . expensive articles of drawing-room furniture' (p. 99)) are valued quantitatively and are ostentatiously displayed in a self-satisfied manner which recalls Veneering's 'bran new' varnish and Podsnap's plate.

Not only does the novel exploit the comic possibilities of the Boffins to paste over the contradictions in their role, but the incongruity of their position in fashionable society helps to justify John Harmon's problematic decision to 'come alive' to claim his fortune. The implication is that if the whole fortune (and the goods and the leisure activities it can buy) is to go to the Boffins it will be wasted on 'two ignorant and unpolished people' who, unlike Harmon, are unequal to the full enjoyment of its aesthetic and cultural possibilities.

Of course, consideration of the Boffins' role involves the difficulty of Boffin's 'false' corruption by wealth and his acting out of the role of miser. That Boffin's corruption should turn out to be an act has direct relevance to the unity and coherence of the text. That Boffin can handle Old Harmon's money and enter the corrupt social environment of fashionable society where the Voice of Society is the universal reference and yet escape contamination would appear to contradict the force and logic of the novel's social vision. Presumably Boffin's childish innocence keeps him immune from corruption by the environment in a manner analogous to Amy Dorrit in the Marshalsea. (Again it is a back-handed tribute to the power of the environment to see defence against its pressures as necessarily involved with the maintenance of childish innocence.) However, it still appears artistically right that Boffin's coming alive to the values of the world should be real and dissatisfaction with the fake nature of Boffin's corruption has led many critics to regard the plot revelation that Boffin was only acting as a late change of plan. While this is an unfair accusation it directs us to the disturbing nature of the plot resolution which has been generally condemned as the least successful ending of the mature novels.

V

Old Harmon's legal will forms an environment which, like the suit of Jarndyce and Jarndyce in *Bleak House*, the all-embracing prison of *Little Dorrit* and Pip's 'expectations' is intended to reflect the essential social condition within the system. The individual resolves of John Harmon and Bella are enclosed and constrained by the stipulations laid down by Old Harmon, whose will makes commodities of people. Bella is left to John Harmon, 'like a dozen of spoons' (p. 81). Both John and Bella are trapped and victimised by the will as if caught up in a machine. But it is possible to escape from this condition. However, this necessitates being dead to the world. We have seen how Bella rejects the patronage of Mr Boffin to fulfil this condition. John Harmon meets it both spiritually and literally. He is literally declared dead when Radfoot's corpse is found by Gaffer Hexam, and his decision to take on a new identity and attempt to win Bella on his own merits (following another escape from drowning given symbolic overtones of rebirth) indicates a death to the mercenary values which would have impelled others to claim the inheritance by compelling Bella to marry him.

However, the whole point of the ending of the novel is that Harmon does come alive again, and in accordance with his private agreement with Boffin claims the fortune he earlier rejected. Does this decision to take on his old identity indicate that he has also 'come alive' in Fledgeby's sense?

The reasons given for Harmon's change of mind are important. One justification is his natural desire to offer his wife as much material comfort as he can. 'I love those pretty feet so dearly, that I feel as if I could not bear the dirt to soil the sole of your shoe. Is it not natural that I wish you could ride in a carriage?' (p. 748).

In another conversation with Bella, Harmon makes two general

points about wealth which in effect amount to his chief justification to
come alive. Both these points would appear to have authorial support
although they contradict the imaginative logic of the novel's social
vision. Asking Bella if she would like to be rich John reassures her as
follows.

> 'But all people are not the worst for riches, my own.'
> 'Most people?' Bella musingly suggested with raised eyebrows.
> 'Nor even most people, it may be hoped. If you were rich, for
> instance, you would have a great power of doing good to others'
> (p. 747).

Harmon's assertion that not even 'most people' are liable to be
corrupted by wealth is breathtaking in its complacency and wilful
self-delusion. Harmon completely puts aside his own life-history
(before he admitted that he knew of 'nothing but wretchedness that
my father's wealth had ever brought about' (p. 423))as well as what
he sees every day in the social world around him. Of course, at this
point the emblematic significance of the mounds has to be completely
ignored (the market mentality has been demonstrated as having a
general relevance for the world of the novel – but now not even
'most people' adhere to the Voice of Society). The failure to integrate
the key image of the mounds with the plot resolution has serious
consequences for the structural unity of the novel.

The other point in Harmon's justification is also problematic.
Money offers the power to do good to others, he assures Bella.
Interestingly it is in this novel that the individual benefactor on the
Pickwick, Cheeryble, and Jarndyce model reappears in Boffin's
attempts to aid Johnny the orphan, Betty Higden, and Sloppy. In all
but the last case Boffin has a very limited success, and some critics see
this aspect of his role as a parody on the earlier benefactors. However,
Harmon's remarks which put before us the whole ethos of private
charity and the individual philanthropist, the good rich man, are
clearly unironic. Yet how does Harmon actually spend his money
when he 'comes alive'? He plans a few surprises for his wife, on a scale
of luxury which seems excessive and self-indulgent. Earlier Bella had
said playfully that she was sure 'that baby noticed birds'. As a result
Harmon plans this surprise. 'Going on a little higher, they came to a
charming aviary, in which a number of tropical birds, more gorgeous
in colour than the flowers, were flying about; and among those birds
were gold and silver fish, and mosses, and water-lilies, and a fountain,

and all manners of wonders' (p. 838). The scale of this reminds us uncomfortably of Veneering's 'bran new' surfaces and golden camels. Similarly, Bella discovers that 'on Bella's exquisite toilette table was an ivory casket, and in the casket were jewels the like of which she had never dreamed of, and aloft on an upper floor was a nursery garnished as with rainbows' (pp. 848–9), and so on.

The good to others which will result from Harmon's wealth will (apart from the rewarding of friends which will be considered in a moment) have to be taken on trust. It would also appear that Harmon has no intention of working and will spend his future time sitting at home planning more surprises for his wife. That Harmon abandons work as readily as Boffin did before him compromises the novel's attack on the speculation principle (the moral/social opposite of work).

It is interesting to note the quality of the language with which the breathtaking luxury of the Harmon household is described. This language ('all manners of wonders' and 'jewels the like of which she had never dreamed of') imposes the mood and tone of a fairy-tale romance on a great novel of social realism. The sentimental tone echoes the language used of Bella's married life. Indeed the distribution of economic aid to those who might have, or did, suffer when John Harmon was regarded as dead (in effect an all-round rewarding of friends) also reinforces the fairy-tale elements in the plot resolution. This 'compensation' is not only a throwback to the characteristic endings of the earlier novels (e.g. *Martin Chuzzlewit*) but is the fitting and expected end to a sentimental romance. 'In tracing out affairs for which John's fictitious death was to be considered in any way responsible, they used a very broad and free construction' (pp. 874–5). Among those rewarded are Jenny Wren, Riah, Mr Inspector (who gained the equivalent of the government reward for actually solving Harmon's 'murder') and Mr Wilfer (appointed Harmon's secretary). Thus the novel's ending supports patronage as well as property.

This wholesale rewarding of the good is problematic. The success of Riah or Jenny Wren in rejecting the dominant market philosophy would make more sense if they were not ultimately rewarded with the very thing which is presented as the chief agent of corruption in society – money. Once again the plot resolution ignores the sug-gestiveness of the mounds which has resonated throughout the social world of the novel. Even accepting that the mounds represent an attitude to money (rather than money in the abstract) it seems strange to give it (with its potential to sully and defile) as a reward to those who have so far kept their hands clean. Furthermore, this type of ending (hand-outs for the good and punishments for the bad (e.g. Silas Wegg)) is alarmingly similar to the message of the moral autobiographies given out to the children at Headstone's school, which had earlier been criticised because they suggested an investment in morality – 'it always appearing from the lessons of those very boastful persons, that you were to do good, not because it was good, but because you were to make a good thing of it' (p. 264). It is yet another contradiction in the ending that the conclusion might be taken as suggesting the advantages of a speculation in morality.

Using a considerable private fortune to help deserving victims of the system recalls Jarndyce – and in a sense Harmon as well as Boffin reflects an artistic return to the individual benefactor. This is a curious reappearance, especially if we give to this showering of money any general significance for the salvation of society as a whole. Will individual philanthropy clear the dust-mounds from the social horizon or purify the river? It would be a very muddled moral indeed which suggests that the mounds could be metaphorically cleared by the operation of money.

It is significant too that while at the end of *Little Dorrit* Clennam and his wife go down into the streets to a life of moderate success, at the conclusion of *Our Mutual Friend* Harmon and Bella retire into a private world and excessive material comfort. The Jarndyce solution of *Bleak House* had been implicitly revalued in *Little Dorrit*. Now it appears to have won back authorial approval. How secure can a private retreat be as a haven from a corrupting environment if the retreat itself is founded on possession of one of the chief agents of corruption? It is the problem of Jarndyce and Wemmick. Yet there is no suggestion at the end of the novel that Harmon's retreat is not completely secure. Comparisons between Clennam and Harmon are interesting. Clennam accepted society for what it was, in order to fight for authentic values. Harmon, on the other hand, 'comes alive' distorting what his experience and history have told him society is like, choosing to idealistically view it as it might or could be. He retreats from the implications of the essence of the system to play at being rich in a home which corresponds to the middle-class ideal (down to the behaviour of his pretty little wife). Harmon appears at the end of the novel not as a tragic man (like Clennam) but as a bourgeois apologist.

By coming 'alive' he has become integrated back into mid-

Victorian society, whose values (and dominant voice or frame of reference) he had earlier rejected. But the means of this integration is luck rather than character — i.e. Boffin's decision to gift him the bulk of what is legally his. Thus once again a money-gift is the means of the contrived plot resolution and the method by which the hero is rendered no longer problematic.

The concessions Dickens makes to the reading public at the end of this novel are absolute. There is even a suggestion of a future romance between Jenny Wren and Sloppy, as ill-advised as if John Chivery were to go sweet on Maggy at the end of *Little Dorrit*, as well as the suggestion that Wrayburn's scars, like Esther's pockmarks, may be fading. *Our Mutual Friend* has the most closed ending of the mature novels and virtually everything is coated in a sentimental gloss. This is especially true of Twemlow's vindication of Eugene's action in marrying Lizzie which shocks the dinner guests at Veneerings' in the closing chapter and sends Mortimer Lightwood back to his chambers in the Temple 'gaily' — indeed, 'gaily' is the closing word of the novel.

Following the opinions of Lady Tippins, the Contractor, the financial Genius, etc., Twemlow asserts an independent point of view.

I am disposed to think . . . that this is a question of the feelings of a gentleman. . . . If this gentleman's feelings of gratitude, of respect, of admiration, and affection, induced him (as I presume they did) to marry this lady . . . I think he is the greater gentleman for the action, and makes her the greater lady. I beg to say, that when I use the word, gentleman, I use it in the sense in which the degree may be obtained by any man. The feelings of a gentleman I hold sacred, and I confess I am not comfortable when they are made the subject of sport or general discussion (pp. 891–2).

Twemlow's words clearly have authorial support. They represent the culmination of Dickens's developing treatment of the gentility theme. More explicitly than in the case of Joe Gargery the category of gentility is defined in moral (not socially exclusive) terms. Gentility becomes an open social category accessible to the Boffins as well as Lizzie Hexam. However, as we have witnessed in other novels, if the implications of Dickens's position are examined, they amount to an empty social gesture — not a radical or subversive opposition to class as an institution. Humphrey House is worth quoting at length on Twemlow's proposition. House questions,

> How can any action of his [Eugene] make a 'greater lady' of a girl whose moral superiority to him has been hammered in with such unremitting emphasis, except on the assumption that she gains in status by becoming his wife?
>
> Two things are interesting in this speech: its obvious sincerity and its obvious sophistry. Twemlow's ingenious phrasing very imperfectly conceals a sort of satisfaction in the fact that Eugene is really doing a very generous thing in marrying Lizzie, and that she is doing very well for herself by marrying him.[3]

The implications of Twemlow's words are in fact consistent with the treatment of class and gentility in *Great Expectations*, which tacitly accepted all the conventional middle-class assumptions about the class system. Within the open moral class of gentlemen qualifying and restricting social factors operate to produce gradations of gentility which are more than just a simple product of moral worth. In fact what determines one's degree of gentility (in addition to the primary factor of moral worth) is possession of the learnt social skills and surfaces of the mannered code. This is why Lizzie achieves a reflected gain in gentility by marrying Eugene, and why the Boffins (though they too are moral gentlemen) defer to the greater gentleman, John Harmon, by standing down from the inheritance in his favour. Within this moral group social deference, status differences, and differential enjoyment of economic privileges characteristic of the wider system are all preserved. What is being offered is merely an idealised form of industrial class society as it existed in mid-Victorian England.

Of course, Twemlow's vindication of Eugene is the final gesture towards an optimistic, hopeful, closed ending. Yet if Twemlow's words bring disharmony to the feast Twemlow is too harmless and innocent a figure to change or silence the Voice of Society. That Dickens's spokesman should be such an ineffectual figure implies the strength of the forces ranged against the few individuals who orientate themselves to qualitative value. Twemlow is not a social prophet for a future moral-change within society. This depressing insight undermines the superficial happiness of the ending. Although Veneering may fall as dramatically as he arrived on the scene (and follow Lammle into exile) the operation of shares will produce new men to take his place. The opposition between the social vision and plot close is the most extreme and unresolved of the later novels.

The social vision itself is a unified and uncompromising social indictment in which the parts — the mounds, shares, Podsnap's plate, the Voice of Society, Boffin the 'miser' — are organically related to reinforce the whole in its stark and depressing condemnation of the market nature of mid-Victorian society. The novel scrupulously details the impoverishment in the quality of everyday life beneath the impressive and sparkling material surfaces of an expanding economy. The pervasive influence of the speculation principle and relations of exchange-value is shown to be the unacceptable face of mid-Victorian economic progress and prosperity. Compromising this social vision we have the complete capitulation to the expectations of the reading public and its demand for a closed 'happy' ending. The lack of coherence in the total structure brought about by the failure to resolve the social vision and the plot close is chiefly due to the mutually reinforcing operation of the middle-class value index and optimistic closed ending (seen in particular in the method of integrating John Harmon back into society), but also partly to a failure of artistic nerve and control. To some extent *Our Mutual Friend* is a weary novel which reworks old material, and in certain respects looks back to Dickens's earlier mode of fiction (e.g. the reappearance of the individual philanthropist, the hand-outs of the ending reminiscent of *Martin Chuzzlewit*). In addition, in the manner of the earlier novels the Betty Higden poor-law satire is not so well integrated into the total structure as Chancery or the Circumlocution Office. We are left with the inescapable judgement that despite the richness and coherence of the novel's social vision, of the three long novels of Dickens's maturity *Our Mutual Friend* is the most damagingly flawed by unresolved contradictions.

9 Conclusion

The readings of the five selected novels all reveal, albeit to different degrees, that what gives Dickens's mature fiction its essential character is the fact that in his role as novelist Dickens was both imaginatively obsessed and artistically inspired by the market nature of everyday social life, and yet at the same time acutely conscious of his own economic stand in the literary market. Critical demonstration of the market-place nature of society was the chief imaginative motor for the mature fiction and yet these novels were themselves valuable commodities, directed at a specific audience with an expert and practised aim.

No writer could judge the temperature of the reading public better than Dickens. Above all he wrote to be read and his commitment to his realistic art never overruled his expert judgement of what his public would accept. He always adhered to middle-class standards of delicacy and propriety in presenting his material; he used an index of middle-class values to structure his novels and offset the pessimism of their social vision; and he never satisfactorily freed himself from the convention of the optimistic closed ending which satisfied the implicit demands of his middle-class reading public. It must be emphasised that the closed ending is not an accidental aspect of the Victorian novel form but is directly related to the expectations and demands of a middle-class reading public, which wished to see the virtues of hero and heroine (defined in terms of the values of the middle-class interpretive code) rewarded, celebrated, and hence legitimised through a happy ending of love, marriage and children (itself part of the middle-class ethos of home and hearth). Only in the sober, subdued endings to *Little Dorrit* and *Hard Times*, and the original ending of *Great Expectations*, did Dickens achieve the relatively qualified and undemonstrative open ending which the novels' social vision implicitly demanded.

As a novelist Dickens was hostile to the contemporary social experience of the mid-Victorian middle classes, and when he used middle-class values as touchstones for moral worth he invariably chose those associated with the earlier, heroic entrepreneurial stage of capitalist development. However, if he remained an outsider, uncommitted to any social, political or pressure group platform he was never an uncommitted participant in the literary market and to the end he felt a deep-rooted need for the reassurance of knowing that his audience was still at his feet.

The readings of the individual novels have emphasised the contradictions which followed from Dickens's ambiguous position in the social market-place — both critic and participant. However, there is something of critical arrogance in demanding that a writer should be willing to divorce himself from the sympathies of his reading public in the service of his art. It must always be remembered that Dickens lived and wrote in an historical situation. One must look past his confusions and omissions, his artistic weaknesses and mistakes of historical foresight (e.g. his fear that a mid-Victorian revolution was imminent) to recognise that Dickens saw more of the tensions and contradictory social realities of industrialism underlying the stable and prosperous surface of mid-Victorian England than any other contemporary writer. He added something new to the English novel. He is the first great English novelist of the industrial city, whose work inaugurates a tradition tapped in different ways by Gissing, Wells, Joyce, and Lawrence; and he is the first great novelist of the alienated man in a modern bureaucratised world.

The inconsistencies in the mature novels may flaw them as total works but they do not invalidate the many insights into the nature of nineteenth-century industrial society (indeed of industrial society as a type) which the novels contain. In particular the crucial analogy between society and the market-place which is central to the vision of the later fiction was a major literary contribution to the understanding of the day-to-day effects on the lives of the population of the new industrial environment. What the novels reveal about the way in which the new industrial economic relations and social institutions permeate the quality of everyday social life, and colour the general experience, makes Dickens the most modern and relevant of the great nineteenth-century English realists.

Notes

NOTES TO CHAPTER 1

1 W. E. Houghton, *The Victorian Frame of Mind, 1830–1870*, p. 366.
2 All page references to the novels will be to the Penguin editions.
3 H. House, *The Dickens World*, p. 217.
4 'The sociologist who neglects this dimension of the unique character of literature and of the technicalities of fiction will be unable to perceive exactly how a novel constitutes an analytic and synthetic mode of social reality.' M. Zeraffa, 'The novel as literary form and as social institution', in E. and T. Burns (eds.), *Sociology of Literature and Drama*, p. 37.
5 Edgar Johnson, *Charles Dickens. His Tragedy and Triumph*, p. 769.
6 Sir W. S. Holdsworth, *Charles Dickens as a Legal Historian*, p. 81.
7 E. Muir, *Essays on Literature and Society*, p. 210.
8 C. Ricks, 'Great Expectations', in J. Gross and G. Pearson (eds.), *Dickens and the Twentieth Century*, p. 200.
9 J. Carey, *The Violent Effigy*, p. 112.

NOTES TO CHAPTER 2

1 'The hallmark of the great realist masterpiece is precisely that its intensive totality of essential social factors does not require a meticulously accurate or pedantically encyclopaedic inclusion of all the threads making up the social tangle.' G. Lukács, 'Tolstoy and the development of realism', in D. Craig (ed.), *Marxists on Literature*, p. 291.
2 E. Johnson, *Charles Dickens: His Tragedy and Triumph*, p. 803.
3 R. Williams, 'Social criticism in Dickens. Some problems of method and approach', in *Critical Quarterly*, VI.
4 R. Williams, *The English Novel from Dickens to Lawrence*, p. 49.
5 L. Goldmann, *Towards a Sociology of the Novel*, p. 13.
6 See his introduction to *The Violent Effigy*.
7 See P. Collins, *Dickens and Crime*.
8 A. Kettle, 'Dickens and the popular tradition', in D. Craig (ed.), *Marxists on Literature*, p. 215.
9 G. Steiner, 'Marxism and the literary critic', in E. and T. Burns (eds.), *The Sociology of Literature and Drama*, p. 175.
10 R. Williams, 'Dickens and social ideas', in M. Slater (ed.), *Dickens 1970*, p. 81.
11 B. Hardy, *The Moral Art of Dickens*, p. 4.
12 F. R. and Q. D. Leavis, *Dickens the Novelist*, p. 301.
13 G. Smith, *Charles Dickens: Bleak House*, p. 47.

14 G. Lukács, *Studies in European Realism*, p. 6.
15 B. Hardy, *The Moral Art of Dickens*, p. 4.
16 E. Muir, *Essays on Literature and Society*, p. 214.
17 Reification refers to the process by which the human world is seen as a world of objects, and society is portrayed as an external 'thing' constraining man, something fundamentally non-human and hostile.
18 L. Goldmann, *Towards a Sociology of the Novel*, p. 6.
19 D. Van Ghent, 'On Great Expectations', in *The English Novel: Form and Fiction* (1953); also included in S. Wall (ed.), *Charles Dickens*, p. 376.
20 S. Wall (ed.), *Charles Dickens*, p. 377.
21 H. House, *The Dickens World*, pp. 134–5.
22 K. Marx, in T. B. Bottomore and M. Rubel (eds.), *Karl Marx, Selected Writings in Sociology and Social Philosophy*, p. 169.
23 L. Goldmann, *Towards a Sociology of the Novel*, pp. 7–8.
24 Also in S. Wall (ed.), *Charles Dickens*, pp. 285–8.
25 Also in *ibid.*, pp. 297–300.
26 *Ibid.*, *loc cit.*
27 R. Barnard, *Imagery and Theme in the Novels of Charles Dickens*, p. 76.
28 G. Lukács, *The Meaning of Contemporary Realism*, p. 56.
29 G. Kitson Clark, *The Making of Victorian England*, p. 86.
30 W. L. Burn, *The Age of Equipoise*, p. 66.
31 A. O. J. Cockshut, *The Imagination of Charles Dickens*, p. 97.
32 'We need not quarrel with the basic fact that, in the still-continuing process of siting population in the cities and towns rather than in towns, villages and hamlets, the fifties were the decisive turning point.' G. Best, *Mid-Victorian Britain, 1851–75*, p. 24.
33 D. Fanger, *Dostoevsky and Romantic Realism*, p. 81.
34 H. M. Daleski, *Dickens and the Art of Analogy*, p. 273.
35 A. O. Cockshut, *op. cit.*, p. 90.

NOTES TO CHAPTER 3

1 Sir Leicester himself declares: 'Mr Rouncewell, our views of duty, and our views of station, and our views of education, and our views of – in short, all our views – are so diametrically opposed that to prolong this discussion must be repellent to your feelings and repellent to my own' (p. 454). There is only one hint of the possibility of a future compromise. By handing his daughter over to the equivalent of a Mrs General who will polish away until the required surface is formed, Rouncewell is trying to make 'ladies' of his daughters according to the received conventions of the fashionable world. It was a familiar strategy for the self-made man to try and achieve gentlemanly status for his children through education. Is the specialised education of Rouncewell's daughters the first step in a general orientation to aristocratic values which would narrow the gulf between the two 'diametrically opposed' sets of class values? Is it too fanciful to acknowledge this as the first link in a chain which might lead to one of Rouncewell's heirs buying or marrying his way into ownership of Chesney Wold itself?
2 This is one of the occasions where there is a general consistency between

Dickens's reported opinions and the evidence of the novels. In a letter to W. C. Macready (October 1855), Dickens remarked that Victorian society had 'no such thing as a middle class (for though we are perpetually bragging of it as our safety, it is nothing but a poor fringe on the mantle of the upper)'.

3 G. Lukács, *Studies in European Realism*, p. 48.

4 See W. L. Burn, *op. cit.*, p. 247.

5 R. Williams, *The English Novel, from Dickens to Lawrence*, p. 49.

6 M. Goldberg, *Dickens and Carlyle*, p. 37.

7 H. Perkin, *The Origins of Modern English Society, 1780–1880*, p. 258.

8 H. House, *The Dickens World*, p. 164.

9 C. P. Snow, 'Dickens and the public service', in M. Slater (ed.), *Dickens 1970*, p. 127.

10 G. Lukács, *Studies in European Realism*, p. 141.

11 W. Myers, 'The radicalism of *Little Dorrit*', in J. Lucas (ed.), *Literature and Politics in the Nineteenth Century*, p. 80.

12 Dickens's relations with the literary market are also bound up in his serial form of publication, which by encouraging episodes to end on notes of sensation, melodrama, and suspense, greatly influenced Dickens's realistic method, accounting for the proliferation of theatrical scenes and exchanges which give to the early novels in particular the character of popular drama. Indeed, Dickens wished his relations to the reading public to be similar to those between the great popular dramatists and their public. This desire to have his public at his feet influenced the nature of his realism. Though the organic unity of his later novels is greatly improved, elements of melodrama and sensationalism are still present, and Dickens still cannot resist the theatrical overtones of scenes such as Bucket's revelation of Tulkinghorn's murderer to Sir Leicester, or Boffin's admission to Bella that his miserly greed was only an act.

NOTES TO CHAPTER 4

1 All page references to the novel are to the Penguin edition (Harmondsworth, 1971), edited by Norman Page, with an introduction by J. Hillis Miller.

2 See Thomas Carlyle, *Past and Present*, Book III, Chapter II in A. Shelston (ed.), *Thomas Carlyle: Selected Writings*, pp. 279–80.

3 M. Goldberg, *Dickens and Carlyle*, p. 73.

4 A. Kettle, 'Dickens and the popular tradition', in D. Craig (ed.), *Marxists on Literature*, p. 237.

5 *Ibid.*

6 R. Barnard, *Imagery and Theme in the Novels of Charles Dickens*, p. 74.

7 Kitson Clark has written of the mid-Victorian period that 'it is important to remember how far in such matters as social reform the effective action was still, and by prevailing theory ought to have been, in private hands, or if public action were needed, localised in scope, the result of the initiative not of a ministry or of a legislature but of those directly concerned.' G. Kitson Clark, *The Making of Victorian England*, p. 45.

8 W. L. Burn, *op. cit.*, p. 117.

9 B. Hardy, *The Moral Art of Dickens*, p. 14.

10 B. Hardy, 'The complexity of Dickens', in M. Slater (ed.), *Dickens 1970*, p. 47.

NOTES TO CHAPTER 5

1 All page references to the novel are to the Penguin edition (Harmondsworth, 1967), edited by John Holloway.
2 B. Hardy, *The Moral Art of Dickens*, p. 18.
3 *Ibid., loc. cit.*
4 G. M. Young, *Victorian England: Portrait of an Age*, p. 87.
5 E. D. H. Johnson, *Charles Dickens: An Introduction to His Novels*, p. 51.
6 J. Wain, '*Little Dorrit*', in J. Gross and G. Pearson (eds.), *Dickens and the Twentieth Century*, p. 176.

NOTES TO CHAPTER 6

1 G. Woodcock, *A Tale of Two Cities* (Penguin edition, Harmondsworth, 1970) — Introduction, p. 9.
2 All references for *A Tale of Two Cities* are to the Penguin edition (Harmondsworth, 1970), edited by George Woodcock.
3 John Gross, 'A Tale of Two Cities' in J. Gross and G. Pearson (eds.), *Dickens and the Twentieth Century*, p. 196.

NOTES TO CHAPTER 7

1 All references to the novel are to the Penguin edition (Harmondsworth, 1965), edited by Angus Calder.
2 R. Dabney, *Love and Property in the Novels of Dickens*, p. 140.
3 H. House, *The Dickens World*, p. 50.
4 E. Johnson, *Charles Dickens: His Tragedy and Triumph*, p. 990.
5 R. Williams, *Culture and Society, 1780–1950*, p. 317.

NOTES TO CHAPTER 8

1 All page references to the novel are to the Penguin edition (Harmondsworth, 1971), edited by Stephen Gill.
2 A similar effect is intended by the description of the pollution of the City atmosphere. Appropriately the London fog becomes increasingly dense and black as one moves from the outskirts towards the City, business centre of the capital and source of society's morally contaminating value code of speculation (see p. 479).
3 H. House, *op. cit.*, p. 163.

Select Bibliography

SOCIAL/HISTORICAL BACKGROUND

G. Best, *Mid-Victorian Britain, 1851–75* (London, 1971).

T. B. Bottomore and M. Rubel (eds.), *Karl Marx, Selected Writings in Sociology and Social Philosophy* (Harmondsworth, 1963).

A. Briggs, *The Age of Improvement* (London, 1959).

——, *Victorian Cities* (London, 1963).

——, *Victorian People* (London, 1954).

A. Briggs and J. Saville (eds.), *Essays in Labour History* (London, 1960).

W. L. Burn, *The Age of Equipoise* (London, 1964).

S. G. Checkland, *The Rise of Industrial Society in England, 1815–1885* (London, 1964).

G. Kitson Clark, *The Making of Victorian England* (London, 1962).

W. E. Houghton, *The Victorian Frame of Mind, 1830–1870* (Yale, 1957).

H. Mayhew, in P. Quennell (ed.), *London Labour and the London Poor (1851)*, (London, 1949).

H. Perkin, *The Origins of Modern English Society, 1780–1880* (London, 1969).

E. Royston Pike, *Human documents of the Industrial Revolution* (London, 1966).

A. Shelston (ed.), *Thomas Carlyle: Selected Writings* (Harmondsworth, 1971).

F. M. L. Thompson, *The English Landed Classes in the Nineteenth Century* (London, 1963).

D. Thomson, *England in the Nineteenth Century* (London, 1950).

E. L. Woodward, *The Age of Reform, 1815–1870* (Oxford, 1936).

B. Willey, *Nineteenth Century Studies: Coleridge to Matthew Arnold* (London, 1949).

G. M. Young, *Victorian England: Portrait of an Age* (2nd edition, Oxford, 1960).

LITERATURE AND SOCIETY

Z. Barbu, 'Sociological perspectives in art and literature,' in J. Creedy (ed.), *The Social Context of Art* (London, 1970).

L. Baxandall (ed.), *Radical Perspectives in the Arts* (Harmondsworth, 1972).

E. and T. Burns (eds.), *Sociology of Literature and Drama* (Harmondsworth, 1973).

L. Coser, *Sociology through Literature* (New Jersey, 1963).

D. Craig (ed.), *Marxists on Literature* (Harmondsworth, 1975).

D. Daiches, *The novel and the modern world* (Chicago, 1960).

——, Chapter 18, 'Criticism and sociology', and Chapter 19, 'Criticism and the cultural context', in *Critical Approaches to Literature* (London, 1956).

M. Eagleton and D. Pierce, *Attitudes to Class in the English Novel: from Walter Scott to David Storey* (London, 1979).

T. Eagleton, *Marxism and Literary Criticism* (London, 1976).

——, *Criticism and Ideology* (London, 1978).

R. Escarpit, *Sociology of Literature*, translated by E. Pick (2nd edition, with new introduction by M. Bradbury and B. Wilson, London, 1971).

R. Fox, *The Novel and the People* (new edition, London, 1979).

R. Girard, *Desire, Deceit and the Novel* (Baltimore, 1965).

L. Goldmann, *Towards a Sociology of the Novel*, translated by A. Sheridan, (London, 1975).

——, *The Hidden God* (1956), translated by P. Thody (London, 1964).

J. Hall, *The Sociology of Literature* (London, 1979).

R. Hoggart, 'Literature and society' in N. Mackenzie (ed.), *A Guide to the Social Sciences* (London, 1966).

I. Howe, *Politics and the Novel* (New York, 1957).

P. J. Keating, *The Working Classes in Victorian Fiction* (London, 1971).

E. Knight, *A Theory of the Classical Novel* (London, 1969).

D. Laurenson and A. Swingewood, *The Sociology of Literature* (London, 1972).

F. R. Leavis, 'Literature and society' and 'Sociology and literature', in *The Common Pursuit* (London, 1952).

Q. D. Leavis, *Fiction and the Reading Public* (London, 1932).

H. Levin, 'Towards the sociology of the novel', in *Refractions* (New York, 1966).

L. Lowenthal, *Literature and the Image of Man* (Boston, 1957).

G. Lukács, *The Historical Novel* (London, 1962).

——, *Studies in European Realism* (New York, 1964).

——, *The Theory of the Novel* (1920) (London, 1972).

——, *The Meaning of Contemporary Realism* (London, 1972).

P. Macherey, *A Theory of Literary Production* (London, 1978).

E. Muir, *Essays on Literature and Society* (London, 1949).

H. V. Routh, *Money, Morals, and Manners, as Revealed in Modern Literature* (London, 1935).

J. Ruhle, *Literature and Revolution* (London, 1969).

D. Spearman, *The Novel and Society* (London, 1966).

A. Swingewood, *The Novel and Revolution* (London, 1975).

L. Trilling, *The Liberal Imagination: Essays on Literature and Society* (London, 1964).

I. Watt, *The Rise of the Novel* (London, 1957).

——, 'Literature and society' in R. N. Wilson (ed.), *The Arts in Society* (New Jersey, 1964).

R. Wellek and A. Warren, 'Literature and society', in *Theory of Literature* (Harmondsworth, 1963).

R. Williams, *Culture and Society, 1780 – 1950* (Harmondsworth, 1963).

M. Zeraffa, *Fictions: The Novel and Social Reality* (Harmondsworth, 1976).

THE ENGLISH VICTORIAN NOVEL

W. Allen, *The English Novel: a Short Critical History* (London, 1954).

A. Kettle, *An Introduction to the English Novel*, vol. 1(London, 1951).

J. Lucas (ed.), *Literature and Politics in the Nineteenth Century* (London, 1971).

M. Praz, *The Hero in Eclipse in Victorian Fiction*, translated by A. Davidson (Oxford, 1956).

K. Tillotson, *Novels of the Eighteen-forties* (Oxford, 1954; revised 1956).

D. Van Ghent, *The English Novel: Form and Function* (New York, 1953).

R. Williams, *The English Novel, from Dickens to Lawrence* (London, 1970).

——, *The Country and the City* (London, 1973).

All the above have useful chapters on Dickens.

DICKENS CRITICISM

M. Andrews, *Dickens on England and the English* (Sussex, 1979).

R. Barnard, *Imagery and Theme in the Novels of Charles Dickens* (Oslo and New York, 1974).

J. Butt and K. Tillotson, *Dickens at Work* (London, 1957).

J. Carey, *The Violent Effigy: A Study of Dickens's Imagination* (London, 1973).

A. O. J. Cockshut, *The Imagination of Charles Dickens* (London, 1961).

P. Collins, *Dickens and Crime* (London, 1962).

——, *Dickens and Education* (London, 1963).

R. J. Cruikshank, *Dickens and Early Victorian England* (London, 1949).

R. Dabney, *Love and Property in the Novels of Dickens* (London, 1967).

H. M. Daleski, *Dickens and the Art of Analogy* (London, 1970).

A. E. Dyson, *The Inimitable Dickens* (London, 1970).

M. Engel, *The Maturity of Dickens* (Oxford, 1959).

D. Fanger, *Dostoevsky and Romantic Realism: a study of Dostoevsky in relation to Balzac, Dickens and Gogol* (Cambridge, Mass., 1967). (This contains a chapter on Dickens.)

G. H. Ford, *Dickens and his Readers: Aspects of Novel Criticism since 1836* (Princeton, 1955).

G. H. Ford and L. Lane (eds.), *The Dickens Critics* (Oxford, 1965).

R. Garis, *The Dickens Theatre* (Oxford, 1965).

J. Gold, *Charles Dickens: Radical Moralist* (Minnesota, 1972).

M. Goldberg, *Dickens and Carlyle* (Athens, Ga., 1972).

J. Gross and G. Pearson (eds.), *Dickens and the Twentieth Century* (London, 1962).

B. Hardy, *The Moral Art of Dickens* (London, 1970).

——, *Charles Dickens: The Later Novels* (London, 1968).

P. Hobsbaum, *A Reader's Guide to Charles Dickens* (London, 1972).

H. House, *The Dickens World* (Oxford, 1941).

Sir W. S. Holdsworth, *Charles Dickens as a Legal Historian* (New Haven, 1928).

T. A. Jackson, *Charles Dickens: The Progress of a Radical* (London, 1937).

E. Johnson, *Charles Dickens: His Tragedy and Triumph*, 2 vols. (London, 1953).

E. D. H. Johnson, *Charles Dickens: An Introduction to his Novels* (New York, 1969).

N. M. Lary, *Dostoevsky and Dickens* (London, 1973).

F. R. and Q. D. Leavis, *Dickens the Novelist* (London, 1970).

J. Lindsay, *Charles Dickens: a Biographical and Critical Study* (London, 1950).

J. Lucas, *The Melancholy Man* (Sussex, 1980).

J. Hillis Miller, *Charles Dickens: The World of his Novels* (London, 1958).

G. Orwell, 'Charles Dickens', in *Inside the Whale* (London, 1940); most recently reprinted in *Decline of the English Murder and Other Essays* (Harmondsworth, 1965).

R. L. Patten, *Charles Dickens and his Publishers* (Oxford, 1978).

F. S. Schwarzbach, *Dickens and the City* (London, 1979).

M. Slater (ed.), *Dickens 1970* (London, 1970).

——, (ed.), *Dickens on America and the Americans* (Sussex, 1979).

G. Smith, *Dickens, Money and Society* (Berkeley and Los Angeles, 1968).

——, *Charles Dickens: Bleak House* (*Studies in English Literature*, 54) (London, 1974).

C. P. Snow, *The Realists: Portraits of Eight Novelists* (London, 1978). (This contains a chapter on Dickens.)

S. Wall (ed.), *Charles Dickens: a Critical Anthology* (Harmondsworth, 1970).

A. Welsh, *The City of Dickens* (London, 1971).

E. Wilson, 'Dickens, the two scrooges', in *The Wound and the Bow* (Boston, 1941).

Index

References to characters in the novels are limited to where there is some discussion of their roles. Bold figures indicate a chapter devoted to the relevant book.